WANDERING HOME

Books by Paul Stutzman

The Wandering Home Series
Book One: The Wanderers
Book Two: Wandering Home
Book Three: Wander No More

Adventure Memoir
Hiking Through
  One Man's Journey to Peace and Freedom on the Appalachian Trail
Biking Across America
  My Coast-to-Coast Adventure and the People I Met Along the Way
Stuck in the Weeds
  A Pilgrim on the Mississippi River and the Camino de Santiago

With Author Serena Miller
More Than Happy: The Wisdom of Amish Parenting

Contact
www.paulstutzman.com
www.facebook.com/pvstutzman
pstutzman@roadrunner.com

Wandering Home

Paul Stutzman

Wandering Home Books
Berlin, Ohio

DEDICATION

To my parents
Paul D. and Sovilla S. Stutzman

I dedicate this book to my parents, with love and appreciation for
their commitment to Jesus and their dedication to their family.
They have instilled character and faith
in each of my four sisters and me.
I am able to write about love and acceptance and going home
because I have lived it.

AUTHOR'S NOTE

The characters you will meet in this book are imaginary. You may see traits and qualities that feel familiar and that make you think you know the people of this story. I hope so. Perhaps you have met similar characters on your own journey. You may even recognize a bit of yourself in these pages. We all seek a place of safety, of comfort, a place where we are accepted, a place called home.

Although Johnny's story is fiction, it is built on the most trustworthy reality, spiritual truths.

Thank you to all those who continue to read my writings, those who kept prodding me to resume Johnny's journey, and Elaine Starner, for her assistance in putting this book together.

1

Johnny Miller was twenty-three when he died the first time.

On a Texas highway, his bicycle veered into the path of a truck, and both Johnny and the bike suffered devastating injuries. The bicycle was never ridden again; it ended up in the Hebbronville landfill. Johnny died in the ambulance as it raced toward Corpus Christi on a sunny spring morning in 1973.

The voices of those who worked to save him faded away, and he felt no sensation at all as he floated through a corridor of some kind, drifting along and turning from side to side with no effort but a thought. At the end of the corridor, a brilliant white light appeared; it grew larger and larger, until he suddenly burst out into an area shimmering and pulsing with light.

From out of the light came a being that stopped his heart—if it were still beating, which he was beginning to suspect it was not.

"Annie! Is it really you?"

"Yes. I came as soon as they told me you were on the way."

"What happened? Did I really die?"

She smiled at him, that same tender smile that he remembered and missed so much.

"That's one way to look at it, dearest. Up here, we see it as really coming to life."

"I was riding my bicycle … I must have had an accident. Oh, I've missed you so much; it's been such a long time that you've been gone."

"A long time? I just arrived in Heaven this morning! Let's hurry and go inside, so I can show you around before the rest of the family arrives later today."

"I can't believe this is really happening. Pinch me; make sure I'm dead."

"Oh, Johnny, you're so funny."

She giggled and reached over to give his arm a gentle pinch, then grabbed his hand and said, "Come. We're going home."

Annie suddenly stopped, as though listening to someone.

"What?" Johnny said.

She looked at him with a clear, strong look in those lovely dark blue eyes, a look that held no sorrow or pain, and she said, "Not yet."

"What do you mean?"

"Not yet, Johnny. It's not yet time for you to be here. I've just heard: You will need to go back."

"No! I'm here with you now. We're together, and I don't want to lose you again. I don't want to go back! I won't go back!"

***

Maureen caught a slight movement in the strong, tanned arm as the needle eased into the vein. She glanced at the face covered with bandages and swelling bruises. The lips that had been torn open were moving; she was certain of that. She was also certain God could still save this boy. She had seen His miracles. *Father, help this poor child. We can't do much, but You can do everything.*

At the desk, two nurses chatted quietly and looked up as a big man in a dark gray Stetson hurried through the door. With a few long strides, he stood in front of them.

"Johnny Miller. I understand he's here."

2

Naomi was young and in love, but she sometimes wondered if the sounds of joy would ever return to her home. Although the weeks of rain were finally over and the spring days had turned warm and sunny, the cloud of sadness over the Miller farm lingered on.

For a short time, life had seemed perfect. Naomi and her parents were the only people living in the six-bedroom farmhouse, but the solid white home remained the hub of a cheerful and steady swirl of family life. Her older, married sisters and their families stopped in often and sometimes stayed for the day. Nieces and nephews ran underfoot. Brother Johnny had just married; he and his new wife lived in the smaller house a few steps away. Annie's voice joined the milking chorus, and her vibrancy and zest brought a new joy to life on the Miller homestead.

Then, in the span of a few hours, Annie had been snatched away from them. Now things were oh, so different.

Naomi had heard the Biblical warnings preached often in her Amish church: Life is a vapor, disappearing quickly. However, Annie's vapor had vanished far too soon.

Their Amish tradition also taught that all events that transpired were God-ordained, and they must accept all that happened as

God's will for their lives. Naomi wanted to fully believe that; she wanted to be obedient, but doubts nagged at the edges of her belief. So many questions still troubled her.

Annie's influence had pulled Naomi's wayward and restless brother back onto a proper pathway. He had joined the church and settled into farming life. But after his wife's death, Johnny seemed to have lost his anchor. His family saw all the old disquiet again surface in his life, and although the Millers were heartsick when Johnny chose to leave the farm and embark on a pilgrimage to wrestle with his sadness and grief, Naomi was not surprised at his choice. He had centered his life on Annie, and now he would need to somehow reconstruct a new one.

Johnny had left at the end of a bleak winter. The weeks that followed should have been bursting with springtime, hope, and new life, but continuous rain had soaked and then flooded fields, and the farmhouse had seen far too little sunshine. Johnny was somewhere out there in America on an old bicycle that he had purchased as a boy. That thought hung as heavy as the rain clouds. How that bicycle could even get him out of town was beyond Naomi's imagination. Where was he? What was he seeing? What was he doing? Was he safe? She prayed daily that her brother's path would eventually lead home.

Her father, John, said little about his son's departure, but Naomi understood that he carried twin sorrows. He grieved Annie's death and he was deeply disappointed that his youngest son's life had followed this detour. He had hoped that Johnny would eventually take over the family farm. Johnny was the fourth generation to tend these 120 acres, and he had shown such promise as he worked under his father's guidance. Now it seemed as though Johnny had lost all interest in life, as well as the farm. Naomi knew her father, the bishop of their church, to be a man of prayer. She suspected he spent much time interceding for his son.

The Miller family gleaned some small encouragements from

the letters Johnny sent home. His messages were short, but each held a story or two of adventures and discoveries. Almost every one spoke of farming or ranches and cattle. Perhaps this focus meant he would eventually return to their life. But Naomi, who likely understood her brother better than anyone else in the family understood him, acknowledged to herself that she had no idea where Johnny might find a home—or what "home" would look like if he ever did discover it.

Naomi found it difficult enough to accept the possibility that Johnny might never return to the farm, but even more distressing was a thought that she kept pushing back into the furthest recesses of her mind, denying it any space in the scenarios she prayed and wondered about. That thought was that her brother might not even wish to return to an Amish world. The ramifications of such a choice pained her considerably. If Johnny's choices were such that a shunning was required …

No, she would not even think of it. She would trust God to hold Johnny securely. The sorrow of losing Annie and the sadness of being helpless to assuage Johnny's grief had driven her to seek God's healing hand. She and her boyfriend, Paul, had many conversations about God's hand in their lives, His sovereignty, and His promises. Paul reminded her constantly that sometimes it just took Johnny a while to find the right path, and he, too, trusted God to bring Johnny home. Paul knew her brother well; they had been close friends since childhood.

One undercurrent of joy ran through these unusually dark spring months, and that was the very private joy that she took in the love she and Paul had found. Instead of bubbling over in giddy exuberance, her joy ran quiet, serene, and steady—waiting for these clouds to pass.

***

As her mother, Mandy, put the finishing touches on the noon meal one day, Naomi ran up the sidewalk and into the big kitchen. She waved a letter.

"It's from Johnny. The postmark is from a town in Texas."

"He's making good time, then." Naomi heard the hopefulness in her mother's comment.

They had tried to piece together Johnny's journey by following postmarks, marking towns on the pages of their atlas. Texas had looked enormous, and no one ventured a guess as to how long it would take Johnny to pedal across that state. But only three states stood between Texas and Johnny's goal of Florida. Was he still intent on Florida?

"Wait until your father comes in for lunch, and then you can read it to us."

John soon came through the back door, along with Naomi's older brother, Jonas, who in Johnny's absence had taken a few days from his own lumber business down the road to help his father with spring planting. The moment their prayer was finished, Naomi tore open the letter.

> *Dear Mom, Dad, and Naomi,*
>
> *It is the middle of the night and I cannot sleep. I am in Laredo, Texas, at a house owned by the McCollum Equipment Company. Dad you will certainly recognize that name. I actually met the owner, Bill McCollum, and spoke with him for a long time. He really does give away 90 percent of the company's profit, just like his newsletter says.*

Johnny wrote about his encounter with Bill McCollum, the man behind the Laredo plow. McCollum's newsletters were something of an institution in the Miller household; Naomi could not remember a time when the latest issue of the newsletter had not held its place on her father's reading stand. John read every word from the successful businessman who had influenced so many folks with his passion for missions. Naomi glanced at her father as she read Johnny's words. Her brother had actually met the man!

"Does he say anything about coming home?" asked Mandy. Naomi's voice rose with excitement.

> *I came to a realization last night; well, I suppose it's been gradually brewing in the back of my mind and emerged clearly just last night. My ride is almost over, and I'm coming home. I can't wait to smell newly plowed sod and cut hay and hear the rustling of those tender corn shoots. I discovered who I am, who I have been all along. I'm a farmer. I want to farm, Dad, if you'll still have me. See you soon.*
> *Love, Johnny.*

Naomi looked up, her face glowing. Johnny was coming home. Mandy blinked away tears; John gave a deep sigh of relief.

Johnny had said nothing about whether or not he wanted to remain in the Amish church, but he wanted to come home and farm, and to Naomi that meant he was also coming back to the life he knew. He was not going on to Florida. Mandy had confided to Naomi that Florida seemed a place so far removed from their Amish world that Johnny would have surely been swallowed up and lost to them. But now he was coming home instead!

The cloud that had hung over the farm for weeks broke and drifted away. Lunch became a feast of joy and thanksgiving and even merriment. Johnny would soon be home.

The crunch of car tires on the gravel driveway drew Mandy to the kitchen window.

"It's a sheriff's car. Why would he be coming here?" The merriment at the table ceased instantly. The sheriff only appeared in their quiet community when there was trouble of some kind. John rose and opened the door before the man in uniform had a chance to knock.

"Are you the parents of Johnny Miller?"

"We are," replied John. "What's wrong?"

"I'm sorry, but your son has been in an accident."

"Is he hurt?" cried Mandy.

"Yes, he was hurt badly. The hospital called our office, and they say it's very serious."

3

Naomi leaned her head against the window, trying to pillow her face on her hand. Constant rain had made the long trip even more tedious. For hours now, their driver had been creeping along under the speed limit, straining to see through the sheets of rain, and wary of streams of water rushing over the highway. They had started out soon after lunch, driving all day and all night, with two drivers changing off at intervals. Mandy had packed food so that they did not have to stop for meals.

It seemed they would never arrive. Through the dark night, Naomi kept hearing the ringing of the brass bell that hung on the side of their barn. She had been the one to pull the rope and send out the call for help yesterday as Mandy hurried to make preparations for travel and John went down the road to the pay phone to call their driver. The clanging rang out over the countryside, telling the entire valley that the Millers needed their neighbors. She could not forget that she had also rung that bell on the day Annie died.

Finally they were here, finding their way through the streets of Corpus Christi. They had stopped twice to ask for directions.

Tired, Naomi watched the city slide by and wondered yet one more time what they would find at the hospital. The three of them had spoken little on the long trip and had slept even less, each sitting with their own thoughts and prayers. She had wished many times that Paul were here with her. She and Paul had just decided to tell their parents of their plans to marry. But yesterday afternoon the two had said hurried goodbyes and Paul had stayed behind to help other neighbors with the Millers' chores and milking.

In the hospital parking lot, John handed cash to their drivers. The two would find hotel rooms for themselves and the Millers. They were not only hired transportation but also trusted friends, and the Miller family wanted no delay in seeing Johnny.

Several receptionists sat behind a long desk in the main lobby. One of them greeted the family, and in response to John's questions told them Johnny Miller was in Room 3404. The green elevators would take them to the third floor.

The three looked around the large lobby, looking for green elevators. One of the receptionists rose and offered to escort them, and Naomi caught the woman's discreet glances at their clothes and the caps on her and Mandy's heads.

The elevator doors slid open to the third floor, and they were faced with a labyrinth of hallways. Off to the right was a large area where nurses sat behind a horseshoe desk. John took the lead and asked where they might find Room 3404.

Down one hallway, around a corner, first door on the right. The door to Room 3404 stood half open. Naomi was the first to enter, but she stopped so abruptly that Mandy, following closely, bumped into her.

"Oh, I'm sorry, we must have the wrong room." The number beside the door was 3404, but an auburn-haired woman sat beside the bed, holding the hand of the patient, whose face was a patchwork of bandages. Dozens of stitches tracked between the bandages, and what little skin was exposed bore bruises in shades of green, yellow, and blue. A big man stood at the foot of the bed, and another man in a blue suit and red tie read a newspaper in a chair by the window.

Naomi quickly began to back both herself and her mother out of the room, but the young woman looked up and spoke quickly.

"Wait! Are you Johnny's family?"

"We are looking for Johnny Miller, yes. But we must have the wrong room number," Naomi answered, gazing at the body lying on the bed. This could not be her brother. The puffy face was clean-shaven and the hair on his head almost gone, although the few patches of hair still there were the same color as Johnny's. But if this was her brother, who were these people?

"Oh, I'm so glad you're here!" the young woman said. She rose, took a few steps, and put out a hand to gently motion them toward the bed. "Please, come in. This is your Johnny. Really."

Naomi glanced back at her parents. Her mother's face was tired and pale, and her eyes brimmed with tears. John said nothing but went to the other side of Johnny's bed. He looked down at his son, at the tubes running into his arms and into his skull, and he bowed his head and tugged at his beard. Neither of the other two strangers spoke as they watched the family reunion, but the woman who had been holding Johnny's hand spoke again.

"It's so good that you're here."

"Well, we have quite a party here, don't we? How's he doing, Audrey, dear?"

A nurse, short, round, and all brisk energy came through the door. This woman had red hair unlike any red that Naomi had ever seen growing naturally on someone's head.

"Johnny's family is here," Audrey offered.

"I'm so *glad* to meet you. I'm Maureen, and I've been praying for your boy. He's making progress. I'm sorry to ask you now, since you just arrived, but could you step out for a few minutes? If you'd like, you can all wait in the family lounge. Audrey, can you show them where it is? I'll only be a few minutes here."

"But can you tell us how he is?" Now that they were finally here, Naomi knew her mother would not be budged until she had a report on Johnny's condition.

"The doctor was here this morning, and he'll be stopping in again soon. You can talk with him then, dear," the nurse said, her voice slowing and softening a bit.

"I'll need to make a few phone calls," said the big man as he picked up the dark gray Stetson lying on the table. "Mr. Miller, good to meet you. I'm Bill McCollum. Met your son a few days ago and we had a good, heart-to-heart talk. I was the first one the hospital called—I think because they were looking for contact information and found my business card in Johnny's wallet. They weren't sure how to find you. I've instructed them to do everything they can to save him. I assured them I'd take responsibility until you arrived. I hope that all meets your approval." He shook John's hand, and nodded to Mandy and Naomi.

"Well—thank—thank you," John was not usually at a loss for words. He was a preacher, after all. Now, though, Naomi saw that he was completely out of his familiar world and taken aback by the man's words. Was this *the* Bill McCollum? And how strange that he had taken all the responsibility for Johnny.

McCollum was already out the door, and no more questions could be asked or answered. Maureen waved her hands, as though she were sweeping them all out. "Don't worry, dear. We'll take good care of him," she assured Mandy.

"Come, I'll show you where we can wait." Audrey led the group down the hallway, falling into step beside Naomi. She was at least six inches taller than Johnny's sister, but the two young women were about the same age.

"Did you fly in this morning?" Audrey asked.

"No. We drove. That is, we hired drivers to bring us here. We do not fly."

Audrey obviously had not expected such an answer; for a moment, she had no reply. Naomi wondered if this woman had ever met an Amish person before. The man in the blue suit with the newspaper tucked under his arm spoke for the first time.

"You've had a long drive, then. Have you eaten?"

"Yes, we packed food for the trip."

No one else sat in the lounge, but the television screen played soap opera drama to the empty room. The blue-suited man walked over to the set and snapped it off as the others sank into soft chairs.

"I'm Samuel Cohraine and this is my daughter, Audrey. We met Johnny when he was traveling through Los Angeles. Let me give you a card, in case you need to contact me later." He handed John a small white card. "The hospital apparently called McCollum and my office, too. We flew in from California, and Mr. McCollum was already here with Johnny."

Naomi, sitting on one side of John, glanced at the card as he read it. *Samuel Cohraine, Attorney at Law.*

"We certainly appreciate everything you've done for our son," John began, and Naomi heard his voice falter.

"We *wanted* to be here." Audrey's quick reply was emphatic.

"But how is he? What do the doctors say?" Mandy needed to know her son was out of danger.

"The first twenty-four hours were touch and go, they told us. When we first arrived, the doctors really didn't give us much hope that he would survive. The medics had already resuscitated him once on the ambulance ride into the city. He's still in critical condition, and we haven't seen any sign of consciousness. The doctors aren't telling us much more. It's just a waiting game, I suppose. I would think they'll give you more details since you're his family." Samuel seemed to have taken charge now, as he answered Mandy's questions.

Mandy slumped back against the chair and closed her eyes. Naomi wondered if her mother was praying ... or was she close to collapsing from fatigue and worry? They had driven nineteen hours without rest.

"Do you know what happened?" asked John.

"They said he was hit by a truck. It probably is a miracle he survived. He was on a bicycle, you know."

"Yes, we know."

"I assure you, Mr. Miller, this is an excellent hospital. Your son's in good hands. And that nurse Maureen has become his fierce protector. She's like a lioness guarding her cub. I know she's been praying over him, too. I don't think that's part of the normal nursing routine, but she's determined that boy is going to live and be healed and walk out of here," Samuel said.

"I think I know why, Dad," Audrey spoke up quietly, with a small catch in her voice. "I overheard two of the orderlies talking about it. Her own son has been missing in action in Vietnam for over two years."

There was silence. Naomi saw her mother's eyes fly open.

"She has no idea where her son is?" Mandy asked Audrey.

"No," answered Audrey. "But it's almost certain he is in the hands of the enemy—if he's still alive. I can't imagine how difficult that would be for a mother."

Bill McCollum walked through the door, and his presence instantly seemed to fill up the room.

"The doctor's here," he said.

They hurried back to Room 3404, but the still form lying in the bed was the only person there. The bleeps and whooshing of the mysterious machines and devices attached to Johnny seemed all the louder in the stillness of the room. Naomi had never seen her brother so motionless and silent, so lifeless. No, she would not use that word.

The doctor came through the door.

"Dr. Schmidt, this is Johnny's family, the Millers."

"Your son is lucky to be alive," began the doctor. "His body has suffered quite a trauma. He has three broken ribs which will just have to heal on their own, although they'll give him quite a bit of pain in the meantime. His right hip is broken; we'll do surgery to pin that in a few days. Our greatest concern right now is cerebral edema, which is swelling of the brain. That causes a buildup of pressure which in turn can cause damage to the brain cells. Right now, we've got to stop that swelling and relieve the pressure. We've done surgery and inserted a ventric that will drain the fluid, and we've got him on medication to reduce swelling."

"And is that having any effect, Doctor?" Samuel Cohraine went straight to the bottom line.

The doctor hesitated just long enough for Naomi to catch the extreme danger gripping her brother.

"No, he is not progressing as I'd hoped. Even if we save his life, we do not know how much brain damage there has been. We've done everything we can, and now we wait. I'll be honest with you. We need a miracle."

4

Bill McCollum stood at the edge of the room, holding his hat and listening to the doctor's grim words. When Dr. Schmidt walked out the door, the big man again stepped forward and took command.

"Folks, let's get the boy healed. If all our Johnny needs is a miracle, I know the Person in charge of that," McCollum said. "It's time for Him to step in. If anyone here does not have absolute faith that God can heal this boy, then please take your doubt outside, shut the door, and let the Holy Spirit do His work."

An almost imperceptible frown wrinkled Samuel Cohraine's forehead. He drew a deep breath and looked toward his daughter. Their eyes met, but she did not move. The attorney turned and left the room, closing the door behind him.

Naomi saw her father's hesitation. He was an Amish preacher and the bishop of their church district. For all of his life, he had claimed and preached the belief that God was unlimited in what He could do. John would have to test his belief now.

Mandy looked at her husband. "You believe, John. I know you do. We must believe. Yes," her words came out strong and certain, and she nodded to Bill McCollum, "we both believe."

Audrey remained motionless. Unconsciously, Naomi's mind

took in the outward differences between the auburn-haired woman and herself, and she wondered if Audrey had faith in God. Samuel Cohraine had left the room. What was his daughter's belief, if any?

Naomi's heart automatically affirmed belief—conversations and prayers with Paul had built her faith through these long months. She believed and she would pray, but at the same time her mind sifted through the doctor's words. Johnny might not live? Or might never be the same brother she had tagged after, teased, admired, and prayed for during the dark times? She had trusted that God would bring Johnny home again. But now the doctor was telling them it might all end here? Or that her brother might never have his old life back? No, it was unthinkable.

She wished again for Paul. He was Johnny's best friend. He should be here, with her and with Johnny. The machines bleeped and blipped, reaching their tentacles down to the bed to clutch her brother's body. Red and green lights flickered and flashed. Surely this was all a dream. Perhaps she could force herself to wake up.

Bill McCollum planted himself at the foot of the bed and raised his hands heavenward. Mandy took her son's hand, and on the other side of the bed, John placed a work-worn hand on the bandages covering his son's forehead. His head dropped onto his chest, and he drew a deep breath. Tears slipped down his cheeks. Audrey stood outside the family circle, yet somehow a part of it.

The door had closed behind Samuel Cohraine, creating their private sanctuary of faith. Bill's booming voice seemed to rock the walls as his prayer brought the power of God into the room.

"Great God of everything we see, do, and are, we thank You today for the many blessings you give us. We humble our hearts before You, knowing we are nothing without You. You alone are the giver and sustainer of life. Here is Your child Johnny. He's in a bad way, and they tell us he needs a miracle. We know and believe that nothing is impossible for You. Just as You raised Lazarus from the dead, we now ask for the return of Johnny to the land of the living. We ask for a full and complete recovery, and we ask it in the name of Jesus who came to rescue us all and whose suffering healed us all."

Naomi did not close her eyes during the prayer. The day and night of traveling, the lack of rest, the uncertainty, these strangers around Johnny's bed, and the doctor's stern prediction of the unimaginable had all left her in a daze. She was listening to Bill's prayer and her mind was assenting to every word, but her eyes stared at the green lines on a screen behind the bed. What did those lines mean? What was happening to Johnny and to all their lives?

Her soft gasp came in unison with Bill's amen. Something had changed on the screen. One line had altered in the pattern that had mesmerized her. Was that a good sign or a bad sign? She suddenly came back to what was happening around her. She looked at her brother, but saw no sign of change.

Bill had laid his hat on the table when he raised his hands in prayer. He picked it up now.

"Well, folks, I'll leave you with your son. I'm sure he'll be happy to see you when he wakes up. Tell him I'll be back in a few days to visit. Sure will be good to see him back to himself once again." And he left the room.

"Maybe I imagined it," began Mandy in a low voice, "but I think … yes, I'm certain. I felt him squeeze my hand."

***

Nurse Maureen stepped into the room to tell John that their driver was waiting downstairs to talk with him. John thanked her and left the room, and Maureen explained that she would be leaving for the day. She would be back in the morning. Her plump hands fussed with the sheet covering Johnny and then one stopped tenderly on his brow as her lips moved in a silent prayer.

John came back to the third floor to report that their drivers had found them lodging, but he had sent them back to the motel.

The Millers would not be leaving the hospital tonight. They would be permitted to stay with Johnny or in the waiting area—and no one could have persuaded them to leave, in any case.

Audrey convinced the family to go with her to the cafeteria. Samuel assured them he would stay with Johnny and find them if there was any change. They had not eaten since breakfast, and Naomi wanted to learn more about these strangers who now seemed to be part of Johnny's life. She suspected her mother also had many questions. However, John was the one who began the conversation with Audrey.

"How did you and your father meet Johnny?" he asked. He was remembering Samuel Cohraine's card, proclaiming the man an *Attorney at Law.* Why had Johnny met with an attorney? That was not the way of their people; they did not engage in the world's court systems or put their faith in lawyers and judges.

"He found my father's wallet lying in the street, and he came to Dad's office to return it. Dad was so impressed with his honesty that he invited him home for dinner and offered him a room in our guest house for the night. I think Dad did it just because he liked Johnny so much. We all liked him. But once we got to know Johnny a little better, Dad even offered him a job."

"Your father offered my son a job? Did he accept?" John asked. Johnny had not mentioned this in his letters.

"No. Dad can be quite persuasive, and most people can't resist his logic and arguments, but Johnny's on a mission and felt he could not stay in California. My dad owns racehorses, you see. And your son seems to have a way with horses. In just a few minutes, he bonded with a colt that will be running in the Kentucky Derby. I don't know all the details, but I'm sure Dad made the job offer as tempting as possible. Johnny turned him down, though."

So Johnny had already been offered a job in the outside world. Other doors had surely opened to him, offering him life far removed from their life on the farm.

"My brother does love horses. At one time, he had dreams of moving west and being a cowboy," Naomi said.

Audrey smiled, "Hmm. That sounds like Johnny." She spoke as though she had known him a long time. What did this woman know of their Johnny? The Millers knew nothing of her or of the two men who had also been in the room.

On their return to Johnny's room, Samuel Cohraine explained that he would have to leave. Now that the Miller family was here, he said, he felt he could get back to his business and his family.

"I'll stay, Dad," said Audrey. "I'll help the Millers navigate around the hospital and the city, and maybe Johnny will wake up before I have to be back home."

The four spent the long night taking turns sleeping on the couch in the family room or dozing in the chair by Johnny's bed. He never moved, never uttered a sound, as they kept watch and the machines went on blinking and beeping.

5

The gray light of morning brought relief. At least, the night was over. A new day was coming.

As the light began to change, it showed the weariness shrouding each face in the room. Naomi wished for a shower and a sumptuous breakfast at their table back home. She would even happily go to the barn and milk, if only Johnny would wake up and life could go back to normal. Watching Audrey pull back her hair into a ponytail and splash water on her face at the sink, she wondered how long it had been since Audrey had slept in a bed or enjoyed a shower. Her instincts told her there was more to know about this girl and her brother.

Maureen came in as soon as her shift started.

"How's he doing, dear?" she asked Mandy.

"No change … yet," replied Mandy.

"Oh, honey, God's holding him. And He's holding you, too."

"Yes, I know that. I believe that," Mandy said, nodding.

Naomi thought about Maureen's missing son, and wondered if that was how the nurse was able to get through each day—believing that God held him in His hands, even though she did not know whether he was dead or alive.

"There is no rock like our God," said Maureen softly as she went to Johnny's bed. "Good morning, sweet boy. Going to come back to us today?" She looked as though she was going to plant a kiss on the bandaged forehead, but then her professional decorum must have ruled; she checked the chart hanging on the bed and turned and left the room.

Naomi walked to the window and watched the dark sky fade into soft grays and pinks above the city skyline.

"How do people live here?" she asked. They had only been absent from home for two days, but she was hungry for scenes of green, for the smell of freshly-plowed ground, and the reassuring sounds of morning in their own farming valley. "I can't imagine living in a place so crowded. Even at this hour! It's already busy down there in the streets. Look! Do you think that's the ocean we can see from here?" John had just come in from a walk down the hallway. He stood beside his daughter at the window and Mandy rose to join them.

"It will be a beautiful day," John said quietly. "Spring. Planting time. New life."

"Are we plowing today, Dad?"

The voice was rough, but the words were clear.

Mandy gasped, and all three swung around. In the chair by the bedside, Audrey leaned forward, her arms hugging her chest and her eyes blurry with tears.

Johnny's eyes were open. They rushed to his side as he struggled to move his body as though to get out of bed, but the effort gave him so much pain that he gave a groan, closed his eyes, and again slipped away into unconsciousness.

The Millers fussed and fluttered over their son who had been lost to them but now was found. They called Maureen back into the room. Johnny lay unresponsive once again, but he had seen them and he had spoken to them. And they had all heard it.

The long night was over. It was a beautiful spring morning.

***

Johnny did not open his eyes again that morning. He spoke, though. Or mumbled. Just words and phrases, but the family understood enough to know that he was talking about things that had happened years ago. The chicken house and the tree house. His little blue car and his horse, Joyce. Plowing and milking and haying. School in Milford and butterflies in autumn.

The doctor came later in the morning. He shook his head—not in despair but in incredulity. The swelling was rapidly subsiding. The patient was recovering faster than he had thought possible, even with the miracle that he had suggested was the only hope. Maureen stopped in whenever she could and rejoiced with the family. She hummed as she changed sheets and IVs.

No one left the room for a meal. No one wanted to miss anything Johnny might say or risk being absent when he finally opened his eyes again. Audrey went to the cafeteria and brought back sandwiches for everyone. They waited. And believed.

In the afternoon, they heard the word *Annie*. And then the longest string of words they had heard all day poured out. No one could understand exactly what Johnny said about his wife, but a few tears slid over the bandages and the stitches, and his distress was clear. Something was wrong. Whatever he was saying about Annie brought him a great deal of anguish. Anger touched part of his tirade. The emotion exhausted him. Mandy wept with her son.

The fresh spring day was fading when he opened his eyes. John had stepped out to the nurses' station to ask a question.

"Hi, Mom, Naomi. Where did Dad go?" he asked. "And if you're all here, who's doing the milking?"

6

Maureen did not mean to eavesdrop. She never meant to, but sometimes nurses become invisible to families of patients. There were times she heard too much, heard things that she would lie awake at night thinking and wondering about. Then she would pray for the hearts whose words she had heard and try to leave things in the Father's hands.

The teakettle whistled and pulled her from her thoughts. She lifted it off the burner, poured the hot water over a teabag, chose the largest lemon tart from the refrigerator shelf, and settled into the dark red recliner that had been her husband's favorite. This was now her usual after-work resting spot. She was home, but her mind was still back at the hospital.

She would never think of meddling, either. But this boy Johnny tempted her to push those limits. He had lain there for four days with nary a word or sign of consciousness, yet he had reached out and grabbed her heart. He was about Doug's age. In the first days, he had hung there between life and death, alone; she was almost certain that Doug was somewhere, also alone and hanging between life and death. She could not find Doug or help him; but this young man had been put under her care, and she would do everything she could for him—and for the sake of his mother.

It had been interesting to watch the mix of people who gathered at the bedside of the unconscious boy. First came the big man with a voice that rolled down the hallway. He had arrived while they were still treating Johnny in the emergency room, and he sat alone and steadfast through the first surgery. Maureen didn't know his relationship to Johnny, but he took charge. He was accustomed to issuing orders and having things happen, that was clear. Yet there was humility, too. He knew how to take orders himself when necessary, and he submitted respectfully to requests of the doctors and staff.

Then the high-powered attorney had arrived. Anyone could tell that this man's skills at manipulation and turning things his own way had made him successful and powerful. Still, Maureen liked him. There was more depth to him than his expensive suit and newspaper, she was sure.

The puzzle was the attorney's daughter. She had none of her father's commanding airs, but she knew her way around, all right. Spunky, that one. And lovely. But she carried her natural beauty lightly. No makeup, hair pulled back into a ponytail. Of course, that all might have been due to their hasty trip from California to Corpus Christi, but Maureen had seen other young women take out makeup bags and apply mascara and lipstick in the ladies' room while a family member lay on his deathbed. Audrey understood there were more important things than makeup and miniskirts. Maureen had even seen her sitting in the family lounge holding the hand of a young wife whose husband was in surgery. She was a gem, that one. Maureen had known that the very first day the girl arrived, and she had wondered then if Johnny would hold on to her—if he had ahold of her at all.

In the first few days, Maureen started piecing together the story. Johnny didn't have ahold of Audrey, it turned out. He was mourning a young wife, killed in a tragic farm accident. He'd been on a bicycle ride from the west coast to the east, taking a break from life, trying to figure out how to go on without his wife. He had swerved into the path of a truck, and now here he lay.

When the Millers arrived, Maureen's first thought was, "At least, his mother can be with him. At least, she knows now where he is." She had been on duty when Mandy first walked into Johnny's room and saw a boy that was almost unrecognizable. Wanting to rush in and wrap Mandy in a comforting hug, she had instead remained at her station, trying to concentrate on her charts.

It was an interesting group, indeed, and Maureen felt drawn to them. She was a nurse because she loved people, loved helping them in their times of need, loved being just a small part of God's gift of healing. She hoped to pass on God's love to all her patients (even though some tried her patience) and prayed over each one; but even before she knew their names, she had felt a connection to this young man and the people who had gathered around him. The Millers' strange dress received some open stares and became the subject of curious conversations in the break room, but their obviously different lifestyle was no barrier for Maureen. She had known others from different cultures and countries, and in her sight there were no dividing walls between God's children who merely looked different on the outside.

Earlier that day she had stopped in Johnny's room after her shift was over for one last check on his progress and to say goodbye to the little group that had been drawn together. Johnny was still "coming and going," Mandy had reported, and she had wondered if her son heard what they said and understood that his family was with him. Maureen had wanted to say, "I'm certain of it," but that was only her own belief. No one could prove such a thing, but Maureen had seen plenty in her many years of nursing. She believed that even with all its science and technology, modern medicine understood only a tiny slice of all that went on in God's complex creation.

What God chose to do in that hospital room, God would do, no matter what medicine said was possible. She leaned back and closed her eyes. The rosary beads draped through her fingers, and with all her heart she desired that her words were sincere as she prayed, "Thy will be done ..."

7

Johnny's few moments of clarity slipped away. He drifted back to sleep, but Naomi had caught just a hint of the old teasing in his voice when she had explained that his friend Paul was at home helping with the milking.

"That poor guy. You've got him wrapped around your little finger, don't you?" Johnny's voice was rough and gravelly, but the edges of his mouth moved a little as though he were trying to grin through the swelling and stitches.

He drifted off to sleep after they had exchanged only a few sentences with him, but his sleep now seemed so calm and peaceful that Naomi was certain her brother would bounce back to his old self again, and soon.

From under all those bandages and bruises, Johnny had emerged briefly, the old Johnny they loved. Mandy wiped her cheeks with a handkerchief, but more tears kept sliding downward. Audrey's smile lit up her entire face as she straightened and stretched, then stood up and left without a word. It was as if the entire room—even the walls—drew a collective sigh of relief and relaxed and rested with Johnny.

***

Suddenly there was more room in Naomi's head to think about other things. The questions about Audrey, for example. How did Audrey know Johnny, and how well did she know him?

Everyone agreed that they wanted to sleep in beds that night instead of the couches and chairs at the hospital. The drivers were summoned, and the Millers walked out of the hospital into a spring evening. Audrey was with them. Mandy had been horrified that Audrey would even consider staying alone at some hotel in this city, and she had insisted that the young woman come with them. Audrey could share Naomi's room, declared Mandy.

That was fine with Naomi. She wanted to get to know Audrey. Before agreeing to Mandy's proposal, Audrey had looked first to Naomi. Naomi grinned and nodded her head, and then the California girl graciously accepted the invitation to become part of the Miller family circle.

She's more alone here than I am, Naomi thought. At least Naomi had family with her. Audrey was on her own in this city.

Yet Audrey seemed curiously detached from her own home and family. She repeatedly brought the conversation back to the Millers and their farm as the girls compared notes about their families and their lives back home. One lived in the beach town of Malibu, California, the other in the farming countryside of Milford, Ohio. Their conversation drifted through the usual, get-acquainted dialogue, but Naomi thought, *We're just dancing around the big question.* Finally, she could wait no longer.

"Tell me how you met Johnny. What was he doing? How was he? Did he seem happy? Did he talk about his plans? How long have you known him?"

Naomi had already heard the abbreviated story of Johnny finding Samuel Cohraine's wallet lying in the street and returning it to its owner. The attorney had invited Johnny to dinner and to stay the night in their guesthouse. Now Audrey elaborated. Johnny had gone with her to their horse farm to see their Derby hopeful, and he had forged a quick relationship with the temperamental horse. Audrey's awed description of how Johnny had handled the horse was so vivid that Naomi could see the scene. She also heard the admiration in Audrey's voice. Samuel Cohraine had liked what he had seen in Johnny, and he made a very attractive offer of employment. The farm needed help with the horses, Samuel said. But Johnny had refused. He left the next day after breakfast.

Naomi listened without interrupting. She listened, waiting for an answer to her question. She watched Audrey's face, and the longer Audrey talked, the more certain Naomi was of the answer. It was not offered in words, but Audrey's voice and face told Naomi this woman was definitely interested in her brother. Audrey's connection with Johnny already seemed more than a casual friendship.

For a moment, fierce loyalty to Annie flared up and began to turn Naomi's heart away from this stranger. Johnny was Annie's husband. He was not available to this woman, no matter how likable she might be. Naomi could not deny the probability that Johnny would marry again. After all, her sister-in-law was dead. Naomi admitted that she had already looked around her circle of friends, wondering if one of them might be a possibility as a future wife for her brother. But it could not be this woman. Johnny was Amish, and this girl was English. Naomi could not imagine how such a relationship could ever be resolved in their world.

But she could tell, too, that Audrey would not push into places where she was not invited. Naomi felt certain that would also include a relationship with a grieving widower. Audrey would respect boundaries Johnny set. But what was Johnny thinking or feeling? Had anything happened that day in California that Audrey was not telling her? Surely Johnny did not return Audrey's interest. Of course Audrey would be attracted to him. He was good-looking and a charmer—how many times had that label been stuck on him even in early childhood? Was it Audrey's fault if she had been caught in the spell? And Johnny might very well have been attracted to her; Audrey was beautiful and, from what Naomi had already seen, a kind and gracious person.

In the end, Naomi could only concede that she liked Audrey tremendously. It could all turn out to be a tangled web, but it was not Naomi's nature to shut out anyone she could claim as a friend.

"I can't imagine what it's like to lose your husband or wife before your first anniversary," Audrey was saying softly. "Johnny told me about Annie, and he spoke of trying to put his life back together. I do know, though, that you can't go back. You can only go forward." She smiled and leaned forward. "He talked so much about you all at home and your farm. He does love that land and that life. I could tell that from the way he lit up when he described it all to me and talked about his family."

"I'm glad to hear that. We were wondering if he would ever come back. I tried to have faith that he would return; but when he left, I know he was questioning whether he wanted to farm or even if he wanted to stay in the Amish church," said Naomi.

"I think Annie's death sent him into a black hole; he couldn't see things clearly and didn't realize what he still had and what he cherished. He needs to sort all that out before he can go forward," offered Audrey.

"I hope he does that soon. We want him back home. He belongs there on the farm."

Audrey was thoughtful for a moment.

"What is Amish, Naomi? What makes your life different than mine? Oh, I know—you drive buggies, and I drive a sports car. You don't have electricity; I fly across the country in airplanes. I dress differently than you do. But tonight, here you sit in your nightgown, brushing your hair, and here I sit in my pajamas, brushing my hair, and we're talking about family and living and dying—experiences we all share. But what is really the difference between us? Is it only in how we dress and what we drive?"

Naomi was taken aback. She had answered questions about being Amish before: what their people did and did not *do*. But when it came right down to it—what *was* the difference between her and Audrey, other than outward choices? Audrey had looked right past their outward differences and connected their hearts.

"I'll have to think about my answer to that," Naomi said. "But I do know I can't imagine what it's like to live your life. And it would probably be quite an adjustment for you to go to town in a buggy instead of that sports car."

"Or wear a dress all the time," Audrey added.

They both giggled.

"Do you even know what freshly-spread manure smells like?" Naomi teased.

"I'll bet it's better than the smog in L.A. What's your least favorite chore? Mine is vacuuming."

"We don't have vacuums, remember? Umm … cleaning up after cooking. I love to cook, but I don't like the cleaning up afterward. I'm a very messy cook."

"How about shopping? How—where do you shop?"

"My only options are a little general store in Milford or driving fourteen miles in a buggy to the county seat—and even in Stevenson we have only two or three stores to choose from."

"We have too many choices in the city. Some people can spend an entire day shopping, but me—I just have a few favorite stores and I get what I need and I'm done. What about fun? What do you do for fun?"

Naomi's eyes stung, and she blinked several times. She missed Paul.

"I wish I could describe what it's like to ride down a country road in a buggy on a spring evening, with your boyfriend …"

Audrey grinned.

"Oh, yes! The boyfriend! Tell me about him."

8

Naomi began to see things through Audrey's eyes. As they climbed back into the van the next morning, she asked Audrey, "Have you ever traveled in a taxi like this?"

Audrey smiled. "No. But I have traveled in ox carts on dirt roads in Mexico."

Mandy turned toward the young woman in astonishment. "Mexico? You've been to Mexico?"

"Yes, my mother works with several orphanages there, and I often travel with her. I hope to teach there someday. Or at least, in a place like that."

"I wonder if visiting Milford would feel like visiting a different country?" Naomi mused.

At breakfast, Naomi felt the stares of others in the diner. This was a frequent occurrence when the Millers were outside their Amish community. Their clothes, their hair, even their demeanor announced that they did not belong to the world around them. Enduring curious scrutiny was probably a new experience for Audrey, thought Naomi, unless, of course, she was accustomed to people staring at her because she was beautiful.

Naomi leaned over and whispered to her new friend, "I think they're trying to figure out how you fit into this family. Do you feel like the black sheep here?"

Audrey gave her a mischievous smile. There was no doubt in Naomi's mind that this young woman enjoyed being taken into the Miller family circle, and Naomi was happy to bring her in.

***

As the four exited the elevator on the third-floor, they could hear Bill McCollum's deep voice. He was raising a prayer of thanksgiving, and the *Amen* seemed to bounce off the walls and roll away toward the nurses' station as they entered the room.

"It's a great morning!" Bill greeted them.

"Yes, it is," said John. Johnny's blue eyes were open and alert, and his voice seemed stronger when he said, "Hi, Dad."

Each of the Millers greeted Johnny. John said little, but his strong hand rested on his son's shoulder in great tenderness. Mandy held her son's hand, and could not let go; Naomi slipped into the usual bantering with her brother that had been so common at home at the breakfast table. Johnny seemed to enter into the optimistic spirit of the new day, even though he still looked exhausted and an occasional twinge of pain crossed his face.

Naomi noticed that Audrey was standing just inside the door with her back against the wall, watching the reunion. "And here's Audrey," said Naomi, as she pulled the young woman toward Johnny's bedside.

"Audrey?" said Johnny.

Naomi heard the confusion in his voice. She knew Audrey did, too, and she felt sadness for her new friend. Audrey had been here before the Millers and had sat by Johnny's bed for days. And he did not remember her.

"Good morning, Johnny. I'm glad you're back," said Audrey.

"Uh, thank you," replied Johnny. A nurse—apparently it was Maureen's day off—and an orderly came in and began pulling the curtain around the bed.

"Let's go to the lounge, folks," Bill suggested and herded them out the door.

"I think I'll go after coffee. Anyone else want a cup?" offered Audrey. Bill and John both accepted her offer, and she stepped into the elevator as they walked on down the hallway.

"He doesn't remember me," said Bill, as they settled into chairs in the lounge. "Doesn't seem to remember anything at all about his bicycle ride. He knows you, though. That's the first thing he said to me when I walked through the door this morning. 'My family's here,' he said."

"I think he looks so much better," said Mandy.

Bill grinned at her. "God always goes far beyond what we expect or imagine. I heard the word miracle floating around among the staff here. Some of them even appear stunned that our Johnny's still alive."

"I know one nurse that isn't surprised. I think she was praying even before you did," replied Mandy.

"We give you our heartfelt thanks for your prayer for healing," said John.

"God's in the business of healing, Mr. Miller. Not just our bodies, but our hearts and minds and souls. That was His whole purpose in coming to this earth and in coming into our lives."

"Yes. His amazing grace."

Naomi heard her dad's thoughtful reference to the title of the old hymn. That hymn always brought tears to his eyes when they sang it at their family singings. Her father had never told her why that song touched him so deeply. Maybe her mother knew, or her brother; but it was a mystery to Naomi.

"I have been wondering," John continued, "if you are the Bill McCollum of McCollum Equipment Company?"

"Yes, sir, I'm that McCollum," the big man answered.

"I've read your newsletters for years and have used your equipment all my life. How did you and Johnny meet? "

"Your boy was seeking hope. I think he found it that day. It's a long story, and I'll let him tell you about it when he remembers everything."

"You took care of everything here when they first brought him in. We are so grateful for that, but we will repay you, of course."

Big Bill waved a hand as though waving away a mosquito. "Don't think about that now. Someday we'll talk about that. What I'd really like to talk about is your farm. I understand you still use our Laredo one-bottom plow."

John laughed.

"Yes, and I hope it outlasts me. I never want to have to switch to using another plow."

It was good to hear her father laughing again, Naomi thought, and comforting to hear talk of things other than brain damage and accidents and surgeries. Even this room looked different in the daylight of knowing that Johnny was finally coming back from wherever he had been.

The men's conversation soon bored her. Big Bill wanted to know everything about the community, the number and size of the farms, the price of property, the work force, and businesses in the area. She did hear him say that his company had begun a search for the perfect community in which to build a new factory. But their conversation held little interest for her. Men talk.

Where was Audrey? Naomi flipped through the stack of magazines on the end table but could not concentrate on reading. The men were talking about spring planting and the work waiting for the Millers once they returned home; most farmers were very late planting this year, delayed by weeks of constant rain. She stood up, thinking she would go and meet Audrey. Maybe she needed help carrying all the coffee back to the third floor.

Bill's next words stopped her and she sat down again.

"Johnny may have a long recuperation period. We have a company jet that I would like to put at your disposal. You would be able to fly back and forth from Ohio to Texas any time you wish to visit your son. And when Johnny is ready to come home, I'll fly him back."

John shook his head.

"We appreciate your generosity, but our people do not use airplanes for travel."

"Even when it is more practical than driving, or more efficient, or the situation is urgent?"

"It may be more practical in the world's eyes, but to us it is living too much according to the world's thinking and standards. We live by a different set of guidelines, although we do appreciate your kindness in offering."

"But, Dad, I can fly! I'm not a member of the church!" In her excitement, Naomi had blurted out the words before she realized she was interrupting the men's conversation and, in effect, arguing with her father, the church bishop.

All eyes turned toward her. She wished she would have thought before speaking, but then she saw her mother's face. Was it actually a smile that Mandy was trying to suppress?

Her father, too, surprised her when he spoke. There was no rebuke in his voice.

"She is right," he said thoughtfully. "She is not yet a member. This would not be the path I would have chosen, but in this case, it may solve our dilemma. We will stay here until we are certain Johnny will live, of course. But I must get back to the farm. Our neighbors are helping out, but they have their own chores and planting to do. Our drivers are just sitting here, waiting on us. While we would like to stay with Johnny as long as we can, we must at some point leave him in God's hands and take care of our responsibilities back home. But Naomi could stay ..."

Audrey came in with coffee at that point, and the discussion was dropped because she reported that the doctor was in Johnny's room and wanted to speak with his parents.

***

They were going to take Johnny off to surgery to insert a pin in his right hip.

"Already?" Mandy worried aloud. "Is he strong enough?"

The nurses assured her that Johnny was in good hands. So it was back to the family lounge to wait yet again.

The long hours of not knowing whether Johnny would live or die had now passed, and Naomi's thoughts no longer dwelt on the possibility of losing her brother. Her thoughts wandered to other things. Would her parents pursue the conversation about her staying in Texas when they went home?

But not a word more was spoken about Bill McCollum's offer until the big man picked up his Stetson and took his leave that afternoon. Surgery was over. Everything went well, the doctor reported. Johnny was in recovery and they could see him soon.

Bill said he must get back to Crystal City. He took John's outstretched hand and promised again, "Just let me know if I can be of assistance to you. My resources are yours. I'd be honored to help out in any way I can."

"Thank you, again, Bill," said John. "I look forward to seeing you again."

"Oh, you will," Bill boomed. "You will."

9

"Johnny, surely you remember Bill McCollum? His company makes the Laredo plow. You met him before your accident. You wrote to us about it. Remember?"

Naomi's prompting was pushing up against badgering. Johnny must remember. Surely with enough prompting and cues, his memory would come back. She would help him, if necessary.

Her brother closed his eyes.

"No, I can't remember how I met him. If he says we met, then I guess we did, but I can't remember it. I can't remember anything about a bike ride, Naomi. I told you that!"

Naomi recognized his tone of voice. The little sister had pushed her big brother a bit too far.

Still, the doctor had said Johnny's memory would most likely come back. He remembered everything about the farm and his life in Ohio. But his bike ride and the people he had met along the way had been erased. He could describe his old childhood bike in detail; but when, in response to his question about how he came to be lying in this hospital bed, his family told him about his trek across the country, he scoffed. "That old bike would never have taken me fifty miles." He shook his head—as much the bandages and tubes allowed—and muttered, "Are you sure I did that? I don't understand ... I can't remember any of it ..."

Several times in the last two days, when pushed to search his memories, Johnny would either flare up in uncharacteristic anger and frustration or would withdraw from conversation and sink into a black mood. The Millers finally decided to refrain from questioning him, but they found this self-restraint difficult. They wanted assurance that nothing of the Johnny they knew had been lost, and they could not help but feel that they themselves, the people closest to him, held keys that might unlock whatever was blocking the young man's thoughts.

The one person Naomi did not quiz Johnny about was Audrey. Johnny treated Audrey with respect and politeness—as he would any guest who came to visit. Yet it was evident that he could not fit her into the puzzle of his past. Naomi caught him watching Audrey sometimes as the family included her in their circle of joking and conversation, but she was certain that Johnny was questioning who Audrey was and what her presence here meant. He was too polite to voice those questions, though.

Audrey kept the same tone in her conversations with Johnny. She greeted him and talked with him as a friend who cared about his well-being, but she never dropped a certain veil of decorum that she had drawn that first day after Johnny had not recognized her. In Johnny's presence, she stepped back from the intimacy of the family circle; but every day she found thoughtful ways to make herself useful, bringing coffee or a newspaper, making calls, helping the Millers' drivers find a neighborhood grocery store, a diner, and a laundromat.

With Naomi, Audrey dropped her reserve completely. The two young women continued to share a motel room, both looking forward to the time they had in the evenings to talk over the events of the day in private. Their conversations roamed to their lives back home. In answer to Audrey's curiosity, Naomi painted a picture of their farm and the Amish way of life; she described everything from butchering to singings. Naomi, in turn, tried to comprehend her new friend's portrayal of California beach life and the wonders and woes of city living. Audrey talked about her life at college and her mother's work with the orphanages, and Naomi wondered what it would be like to hop back and forth from one country to another much as she traveled back and forth to the neighbors'. Naomi confided her dreams of her future life with Paul, and Audrey declared she would be at their wedding. Audrey's dreams were built on her vision to change the world one small life at a time; her heart was with hungry and illiterate children caught in poverty. She saw no reason why the entire world could not change if enough people worked together to give those children a chance at a different life.

They giggled together and shed a few tears together. Their friendship grew and affirmed what Naomi had suspected that first night: they had each found a kindred spirit, and it made no difference to them that in the morning one slipped into slacks and a shirt and the other donned a long dress, pinned up her hair, and covered it with a cap.

***

If Audrey would not have been standing next to her with an arm linked through hers, Naomi could not have borne the sight of the van disappearing down the street—her parents leaving for home, without her. As it was, one tear slid down as she waved goodbye, and for a moment she could not speak.

"I'll miss them," Audrey said.

"Me, too." Naomi's agreement came out in a squeak.

Audrey hugged her.

"Come on, let's get back up to our post," she said, turning Naomi around and shepherding her back into the hospital. "We still have Maureen to watch over us. She's like a mother hen. I'm sure if we need anything, we can depend on her. And I'll be here as long as you need me."

That was what Naomi did not want to think about. How long would Audrey be here? What would she do if Audrey had to leave? Naomi had spoken up so bravely when this plan had first been proposed, but that was prompted by the romantic allure of the idea of being on her own away from home. Now the reality looked lonely and frightening. She was not a city girl. She did not belong here. And although she had come to know the east wing of the hospital like her own house back home, she understood nothing about life in the city outside the world of the hospital. They were in a bubble here, a bubble built around Johnny's hospital bed. But if she had to step outside that bubble, she knew she would be lost.

As it turned out, she remained secure in the bubble.

10

One more surgery rearranged Johnny's nose. The doctor thought this would prevent future problems with his breathing. Johnny's physical therapy started, and Naomi was more than happy to let the therapist wheel Johnny away for a time each day. On the very first day that the therapist helped her brother out of bed and into a chair, Johnny's pain was so great that Naomi thought he might faint. She didn't want to watch him suffer as they pushed his body to extreme limits. He returned from physical therapy exhausted, and usually in a mood that said, *Leave me alone*.

At those times, she and Audrey would sometimes leave the hospital and go back to the motel or to a new diner they had discovered. Naomi found she liked Mexican dishes; and, knowing Naomi would never have such food back home, Audrey took her shopping one day and bought her a cookbook teaching the basics of Mexican cooking. Under Audrey's tutelage, Naomi learned the ins and outs of riding the city buses. And the two shared a great deal of hilarity on the day when, after watching Audrey hail a cab, Naomi stepped up to the curb and mimicked her friend. To her amazement, a cab immediately pulled up in front of her. It was, she told Johnny later, as though she'd waved her magic wand and her pumpkin coach had immediately appeared.

"And I'm sure you made quite picture, in your Amish clothes, waving down a taxi," Johnny said. He was in a good mood that day. They had enjoyed an hour together that was almost like old times. Audrey had gone for a walk, just to get some fresh air, and Naomi felt the temptation once again to attempt to pry open the vault of Johnny's memory.

"Audrey has helped us so much. I depend on her. What would we have done without her? Mom and Dad liked her a lot, too. Mom even invited her to come visit us sometime." Naomi watched her brother's face. She didn't want to push him too much to remember; he dipped easily into those black moods when he was frustrated with either his physical or his mental limitations.

"Who is she? How did you meet her?" Johnny asked, and his voice and eyes told Naomi the truth—any memories of Audrey were still locked up tight. She shrugged as though the details Johnny was seeking were not important. She wanted to keep their conversation light and easy. "She was here when we came. You were unconscious. Probably don't remember it."

"No, no, I don't remember." His voice was beginning to take on that troubled tone. Naomi backed away from the subject of Audrey as quickly as she could.

"I'm just glad she is here. She's been a good friend. Has the doctor said anything about when you can come home?"

"They say I've still got a long way to go in physical therapy." Johnny sighed. "How are things at home? I feel as if I've been gone for years."

"We had weeks of rain, and it was too wet to get into the fields, so planting was very late. But other than that, nothing much has changed. A few new babies in church. Two weddings coming up. Paul's been really busy with new building starts, and Mom and I have been doing the spring housecleaning at your house."

As soon as the words were out, Naomi wished them back. Johnny's house. Johnny and Annie's house, just yards away from the big farm house. But Annie was no longer there. She and Mandy had worked in the smaller house, opening windows and scrubbing until everything shone and smelled like springtime, but the sadness could not be scrubbed away or carried off by spring breezes.

"I want to go home, Naomi. I'm ready to go home. But I don't know if I'm ready to *be* home. That house is so empty without Annie. It's just a shell; all the life is gone and nothing's left inside. If I go back, I'm not sure where I belong."

"You belong with us. But don't worry about that now. Just concentrate on getting well. When you come home, we'll figure all that out together."

Johnny turned his head to gaze out the window. Naomi guessed that all he could see from his bed was the cloudless blue sky, but he stared as though he were seeing something far off in the distance. He looked as though he were going to a place far away.

Maureen came in then, in a flurry of cheerfulness and efficiency. As she went through the routine of administering pills and checking her patient's blood pressure and temperature, she scolded Johnny in a good-natured way and warned him that he had better behave himself and obey his physical therapist. She wanted him walking out of that hospital. Her patient gave no response. His eyes were still on the sky. Naomi was thinking that Maureen's hair was a new shade of red.

"We'll have you up soon. You don't want to miss all of these beautiful spring days. Naomi can even take you for a stroll out in the courtyard."

"Really? We could do that? Oh, Johnny, wouldn't it be great to get outside again?"

Her brother finally looked at her, and she saw that he was back in the room with them.

"Yes. I suppose so. Maureen? Do I have something to wear

other than this … this … sheet you tie around me?"

Naomi opened the door to a small closet. "Some of your things are here."

"Most of your clothes are gone, honey" said Maureen gently. "You made a pretty good mess of them when you went scooting along that roadway."

"Is this your blanket, Johnny?" Naomi held out a bright blanket patterned with orange and yellow stripes. Rather than a full size blanket, it was more like the patchwork lap robes the Miller women sewed at home. It wasn't as heavy, but as she wrapped it around her shoulders she thought that it somehow carried an unusual warmth. Maybe it was the bright colors that created such a cozy feel. She could still smell fresh air and hot sunshine in the threads. Naomi would have liked to keep it around her own shoulders, but she saw Johnny again fighting to remember, and so she unwrapped herself and draped the coverlet across his torso.

He touched the bright blanket thoughtfully.

"Yes. This is mine," he said. Gathering a fistful of the yellow and orange stripes, he pulled the memories up to his neck and under his chin. "What else is there?"

Naomi went back to the closet.

"Your wallet. And your—Annie's—notebook."

"Is there money in my wallet?"

"Dad left cash for both of us. And here's a twenty dollar bill, folded up and tucked in this little slot. Looks like you were saving that for something special. Your driver's license is here. And some business cards." She did not mention that Bill McCollum's name was on one card and Audrey's father's name on the other.

"Wait just a minute, dear," Maureen jumped into the conversation. "Explain that one to me. Your driver's license? I thought Amish didn't drive?"

Just as quickly as the black moods came, the old teasing Johnny could also surface. "You're thinking of Old Order Amish,

Maureen. But I'm Out of Order Amish," he shot back.

For just a moment, Maureen looked truly puzzled. Then she saw the small grin, still hampered by stitches, but her boy was grinning, nevertheless.

"You're right—you are out of order, young man. Never seen one like you, that's for sure," she grumbled and rolled her eyes in pretended dismay as she went out the door.

***

Not many days later, Audrey and Naomi again stood on the sidewalk in front of the hospital and exchanged goodbyes. This time, they were the ones breaking out of the bubble of the hospital world. They were going home to two different parts of the country and two vastly different lives. Audrey's father had called and advised his daughter that it was time to rejoin her family; they were all traveling to Kentucky for the Derby and Audrey would be expected to take part in all the festivities.

On the same day that Samuel Cohraine requested his daughter's return to California, the Millers had called their daughter and, after hearing her report on Johnny's progress, made arrangements with Bill McCollum to fly Naomi home to Ohio.

Naomi was relieved that she would not be left to navigate her days without Audrey. She knew the hospital and its routines well, but she did not want to be alone in the city without her new friend. Audrey admitted she was also happy that their departures coincided because she would have felt decidedly uncomfortable staying at the hospital any longer if all the Millers had returned home. Johnny still had no memory of meeting her or of the day of camaraderie they had shared. Audrey had promised the Millers— and herself—that she would soon be back to check on Johnny and would give them a full report on his progress.

Maureen stood on the sidewalk with them. They were leaving the hospital after saying goodbye to Johnny. Maureen had the day off, but she had appeared to say her goodbyes to the young women. She wrapped her arms around them and they hugged her back.

"Maureen, what would we have done without you?" Audrey asked, with tears brimming in her eyes.

"We're so thankful you'll still be here to care for Johnny," chimed in Naomi. "Thank you, thank you, thank you, for everything you've done."

As the taxi started toward the airport, Naomi looked back at the round figure still waving from the hospital sidewalk. "I hope they find her son."

***

Maureen settled into her chair that night, hands wrapped around the warm mug of tea, lemon tart on the stand beside her. She carefully tucked the small slip of paper on which Audrey and Naomi had both written their addresses into the front of her Bible. She recognized a fresh sense of bereavement. A wise nurse could not be too emotionally tied to her patients, but her mother's heart had embraced these three young people.

"Lord, what's going to happen with that boy? Do you have good plans for him? I sure hope so, Lord, because you know he needs some hope, something to look forward to. And wherever Dougie is tonight, Lord, give him hope, too."

11

Johnny told himself that if one more person said to him, "You're lucky to be alive," he would haul off and punch them. That would stop such idiotic comments.

Lucky to be alive? Anyone who said that did not know the agony of being unable to control his legs and command his body as he had always done before this strange twist in his life. They did not know how he punished his body with excruciating pain, trying to force it to do as he wished. The therapist reported that he was improving more rapidly than expected, but after every session Johnny returned to his bed and brooded in tense anger and frustration at his muscles' resistance to his will.

Lucky to be alive? That's what they said, sometimes joking that it was better than the alternative. Little did they know the alternative he had been cheated of when he was returned to this world. At times, he felt that this now was the death; he had been denied the life.

He could not remember the accident they described. He remembered very little about the bike ride they tried to reconstruct for him. Sometimes there were flashes of memory, as though he were recalling a dream. Snatches of conversations or colors or scenes or aromas sometimes flashed through his senses, but when he reached out to grab hold of and study the images more closely, they evaporated. The blanket, for instance. He knew the smell. The orange and yellow stripes smelled of desert sunshine. He knew that, but *how* did he know that? He did not remember the desert.

He did know that he had seen Annie. She had been waiting for him. She had taken his hand and said, "Come with me" and promised that he was going to truly live.

And then he had somehow lost her again.

What had happened? Was Annie still alive somewhere beyond this sphere within which he was now trapped? Was she still waiting for him to join her and go home with her?

He could not remember the last few months and so he could not sort out what was real and what was only a wishful dream. Sometimes he thought he caught a firm memory; but was it a true memory, or was he only "remembering" a thing because these people around him had told him about it?

Or maybe this was the dream, instead—this nightmarish torture here in this hospital bed, with the pain, the frustration and the anger.

Once, when Maureen remarked to him how much she had enjoyed meeting his family, he squinted at her, trying to read the truth on her face.

"Were they really here, Maureen? I thought maybe I dreamed about it, and it never really happened. Who was here?"

"Your mother. Your father. Your sweet sister Naomi," said Maureen firmly. "Honey, it was real, I can tell you that. They were here. And your friends, too. Bill and Samuel and Audrey. They were all here."

Bill and Samuel and Audrey. Johnny could recall no part of his life, no stories or scenes, where these three had appeared. Audrey stood with the ranks of nurses and doctors and aides in the hospital—someone who belonged to this present scene but nowhere else in his life. He had met her here and had been puzzled about the friendship between her and Naomi, but he had no other setting or story into which to place Audrey, only the story of these endless days while he lay in a hospital bed.

He was positive, though, he had seen Annie. She was alive somewhere. Or was she? Had he dreamed everything? Was he dreaming all of this? Would he wake up soon to hear the sounds of awakening farm life all around him and find his wife still sleeping beside him?

Finally, unable to corral the truth of all the fragmented thoughts pounding through his head, he gave up and admitted he could no longer discern the real from the unreal. That was why he could not make sense of things. That was why his family had left him here—if they had really been here at all. They realized he was going crazy and they could not bear to be with him. Maybe that was why Annie left, too.

This nightmare was what it must be like, he decided, to lose your mind.

12

A tentative knock preceded the appearance of a bearded face peering around the door.

"Johnny? May I come in? I have a package for you."

"Sure," Johnny mumbled.

Every heartbeat sent a tremor of pain through his head; the pressure of blood coursing through his brain would split open his skull and every breath was tearing open his chest, he had declared to Maureen. She had given him two white tablets, but relief had not yet come. When would this pain end?

The man who entered his room was dressed in the blue scrubs of the hospital. Johnny thought he had never seen him before, but he could not be certain. The visitor was about Johnny's age, and the cut of his hair and beard reminded Johnny of someone from back home.

"Hi. I'm Robert. Most people call me Bobby. I suppose one of these days I'll have to grow up enough to be a Robert."

"Do I know you? Or do you know me? I'm not sure what I do and don't know."

The young man grinned. "No, we've never met. I'm an orderly over on the west wing of the hospital, in the psychiatric ward, and I haven't seen you there yet, my friend. I was just coming by the front desk when this package came in, and they asked me to deliver it to you. Sorry if I caused you confusion. But I've been wanting to meet you. You and your bike ride are the talk of the hospital. Besides, there are not many Amish in this part of the country. I'm Mennonite, from Tennessee. So I thought I'd just stop in and see if we have any mutual friends or family."

"Tennessee? And you work here? In Texas?"

"I was assigned to this place. I'm doing my 1-W service. Three more months, then I'll be going home."

Johnny did know something about 1-W service. He had a neighbor back home who had gone—or was it a cousin? Stories and details were incomplete in his head, and people he felt he should be able to identify were still only vague shapes in his file of memories.

"You're pretty far from home, too," he said. Even ordinary words, when they came out of his mouth, felt blurry.

"Yes, but I'm grateful that I'm here and not being forced to kill people in Viet Nam. I registered as a conscientious objector because that is our church's belief; but while I'm here, I've been reading some of the history and have come to realize that COs went to jail and suffered plenty of ridicule and unfair treatment until the government worked out this plan for us to serve the country in other ways."

Johnny heard most of what Bobby said, but his eyes would not stay open. His eyelids drooped, but his ears had picked up the words *Viet Nam.* He saw a young man sitting at the counter in a diner. His right sleeve hung empty. He was telling a story about a little girl in the jungle, a waif in a white dress, throwing a hand grenade into a truck filled with men.

His eyes closed completely, but his heart beat even faster and pain shot through his chest as he took a few deep breaths. Bobby glanced at the monitor above the bed.

"I' m sorry if I've disturbed you. I'll just put this package on the table and come back some other time when we can talk."

He slipped out the door and left Johnny to sink into a deep sleep that brought images of people he recognized and yet could not name.

***

The package was from Ohio. Johnny knew it would be the clothes he had asked his parents to send, but for a moment he held the bundle in his lap, staring at his mother's handwriting on the brown paper. Just a few words in a well-known handwriting evoked emotions from another place and time.

When he untied the package and the brown wrapping fell away, the aromas of home hit him with the force of someone jumping on his chest. He sucked in a choking breath and carefully picked up the blue shirt, holding it to his nose, then burying his face in the plain cloth and taking in deep gulps of his past, of the farm, and of Annie. She had made this shirt for him, and the blue cloth was saturated with all the aromas of home, aromas of love and security and the life they had shared. With his face still buried in the plain shirt, he squeezed his eyes shut and prayed desperately that when he opened them again he would wake from this horrible nightmare and be once again back in that life.

***

Maureen found him asleep later that day, one fist clutching the blue shirt to his face.

Oh, Lord, he looks like a baby sleeping with his favorite blanket, she thought. She was not going to wake him, but he sensed her presence, opened his eyes, and smiled at her. She saw at once that this was the young man Naomi called "the old Johnny."

"Maureen, I need to ask a favor," he said, with that endearing look in his eyes that meant she would probably not be able to deny him. "Do you have a map of the United States that I could use?"

"Whatever for? You aren't going to hop back on a bike just yet, darling."

"But I've got to start planning. I need to get home, Maureen. And when the day does come that I can walk out of here, I want to have my route planned and be able to make a beeline for home."

The image of him hopping on a bike and skedaddling for Ohio made her laugh. But this planning would give him something to think about and work toward. He spent too many hours just lying there and staring at the sky beyond his window. Sometimes when he was in such a gloomy mood, he would not even respond to her teasing or questions. He was somewhere far away.

But on this day, he was very much here. And she was happy to see him full of energy and optimism.

"Please, Maureen? Any maps you have that would help me. I want to get it all fixed in my mind. No more dawdling or detours. I've got to get home."

"I suppose I could find something for you," she replied.

The next day she brought him an old atlas she had pulled from a drawer in her husband's desk.

She had not really known where to look for maps in their house. She had never learned how to read a map, and never drove anywhere beyond her own small town just outside the city. But her husband had been the kind of person who wanted to learn everything he could. He had three dictionaries on the bookshelf, and he'd look up any word he read that he did not know. He had watched the news every night and would pull out the atlas to see exactly where in the country or in the world each news story took place. He had bought a set of encyclopedias when Doug was five, but he was the one who loved to sit in his recliner and spend an entire Sunday afternoon browsing through the pages. Maureen knew his atlas was still in the house somewhere, and she had searched until she found it.

Johnny's delight tumbled out in extravagant thanks. Before she even left the room, he was engrossed in tracing routes through Texas toward Mississippi.

Maureen was happy that he was happy. This was the brightest she had seen him, and she breathed a prayer of gratitude.

13

Johnny recognized a familiar memory—a twinge of guilt. Bobby was turning the knobs on the television, searching through the channels. The orderly had come into Room 3404 to find the patient bored and restless.

"You're looking better," Bobby had said.

"I am better ... I think. Except that I can't do *a thing*. I want to be doing something to speed up this get-well process. I'm tired of this bed and this room."

Bobby laughed. "What's that old saying? *The spirit is willing, but the flesh is weak.* No, I guess that's not a proverb; it's a Scripture. Does seem to apply to you, though."

He walked over to the television. "Want to watch something to take your mind off your frustration?"

Johnny remembered the guilt of toying with the forbidden. His mind brought forth a picture of a tree house, high on a hill. He saw himself reaching up to a shelf and drawing a transistor radio from behind a stack of books. Television was not part of the Amish life, and the television in his hospital room had not been turned on during all the weeks of his stay. Bobby was right, though—it would be a diversion.

He said nothing as Bobby turned knobs and watched the screen as it blinked from one scene to another.

"Not much on, I'm afraid. At least, not much worth watching. News—too much bad news, most of it about the war. We'll skip that. Baseball. Racing."

"Wait!" Johnny tried to sit upright but was forced back into the pillow by the pain that shot through his hip. "Go back. To those horses." He had heard another memory.

An announcer was saying, "Many here are anxious to see the big chestnut colt from California. Sun Dancer struggled a bit in his last race, but he's still the favorite. Could this be the year we see a colt break the two-minute barrier in the world's most important horse race?"

Sun Dancer. He knew that name. Then he saw the horse, a tall chestnut colt, dancing in anticipation and held in his place in the parade of entries only by the mysterious power of a diminutive figure dressed in green and white. Johnny knew that he knew that horse. His hand remembered the feel of powerful muscles rippling across the red neck.

"Ah. It's the Kentucky Derby," said Bobby. "This might be interesting. You like horse races?"

Johnny said nothing, but his eyes strained to see every detail, and his ears tuned into the announcer's voice to catch every nuance, hoping for more clues. This was an important race. Very important. *Sun Dancer. Sun Dancer could win this race.* How did he know that horse? Why was this Kentucky Derby more important than any other?

He watched as the gates flew open and the field stretched out within seconds. He lost sight of the chestnut colt; but according to the announcer, Sun Dancer was holding his own in the middle of the pack. Then Johnny saw him again, at the half-mile marker. The green and white silks were drifting to the outside.

As the horses rounded the far turn and entered the long

homestretch, the announcer's voice rose with excitement; he was shouting into the microphone. Even so, the cheering of the crowd almost drowned out his words. Sun Dancer was on the move, picking up speed as though he never tired, passing horses one by one as they dropped away behind him. He was going to finish all alone, in a blaze of red and green and white.

Then another horse came out of nowhere. He was red, too, but the silks atop his saddle were blue and white. He pulled even with Sun Dancer, and for a moment they ran neck and neck, red flanks gleaming in the evening rays of May sunlight, every muscle straining forward toward the finish line. At the last moment, the second horse, Secretariat, pulled away. The finish line flashed by and Secretariat had set a new Derby record.

But Sun Dancer had also set a record—the second fastest time in Kentucky Derby history. Johnny sagged into his pillow. Given another day, another race, Sun Dancer could still beat Secretariat. Johnny was sure of it. *How did he know this?*

Someone held a microphone in front of Sun Dancer's owner. Johnny's eyes never left the screen. He knew this man, too. He did not listen to the words, but he recognized Samuel Cohraine's voice. And he knew the young woman standing next to the man. He recognized Audrey's shoulder-length, auburn hair. The curtain that had dropped over his memories parted briefly, and a bright collage of partial images rose up: the sun shining on the Pacific Ocean, red hair pulled back into a ponytail, a bright red convertible that was going incredibly fast around sharp curves, and the red horse. None of these pictures were part of his world, he was certain. Yet his mind saw them all in sharp detail.

"Wow. What a race," said Bobby, who had been standing, transfixed, to one side of the television. Then he turned back to Johnny. "Hey, man, are you all right?"

"Yes. No. I ... I'm not sure. I can't sort out what I know. Can't put all the pieces together and make them all fit."

"I understand that's common with head injuries."

"That's what the doctor said. He thinks I will regain my full memory eventually, and he tells me to be patient and be grateful that I'm even alive."

"Yeah, I've heard your story. They say it's a miracle. They say you were dead, but you were lucky … they were able to bring you back again."

No, thought Johnny, *I was not lucky. That was the most unlucky day of my life. They should have left me dead.*

14

"What's going on in here? You getting into some mischief again?" Maureen affected her stern-mother voice but her eyes danced with joy because she had heard Johnny laughing aloud when she stopped in to see him before leaving for the day.

His grin was almost back to its normal width. The cuts were healing and most of the stiches were gone and, today at least, it seemed his spirit was also on the mend.

"This," he said merrily, waving a letter at her. "This crazy friend-soon-to-be-brother-in-law of mine. He wrote to tell me what a commotion Naomi caused in our little community when she flew home." He shook his head and chuckled. "I still can't believe my parents consented to that."

"And I still don't understand why you folks won't fly. But that's your choice, I guess."

Johnny ignored Maureen's comment.

"Apparently Naomi's homecoming caused quite a commotion at the airport."

"Oh? What happened?"

"It's a tiny airport. We probably don't have more than three or four planes going in and out of there a week, and most of those are small planes owned by locals. Bill McCollum sent a jet to take my sister home. A jet! Somehow the grapevine had spread the word that oil tycoons from Texas were expected and they'd be flying in, so of course a small crowd had collected in the café at the airport, just waiting to see what or who might be coming. Paul says that some of the people were convinced no one could land a jet on that short runway. That airstrip has probably never seen such an aircraft descending on it."

"And did it land? Or did Naomi parachute in?"

"Oh, they landed, all right. Let's see," Johnny scanned the pages of the letter, "Paul describes it like this: *That pilot set the huge plane down as gently as a basket of eggs.* Everyone was in awe of the plane and the expert handling, but here's the scene I'm trying to imagine, Maureen—I wish I would have been there!

"The plane stopped, and the stairs dropped. Then the pilot appeared. Paul says there was stunned silence. The pilot was very young and a black man."

Maureen frowned slightly, trying to interpret this.

"What was so surprising? How young was he?"

Johnny shook his head.

"No. You have to understand our community, Maureen. We aren't isolated, but we are ... well ... insulated. Not many outsiders visit. Hardly anyone moves into the community from away. Not that we would not welcome them. It's just that ... I guess people see no reason to visit us or move there. So we rarely meet anyone of another race. And, I'm sorry to say, even with all our churches in the community and "religious" upbringing, there is a lot of ignorant prejudice—even in our Amish church."

"So they couldn't believe someone so young *and black* could be an expert pilot?"

"Right. Paul reports that he heard some pretty crude remarks.

"But here's what I would have liked to see. Naomi then appeared at the door, and they descended the steps side by side, chatting and laughing. Some old guy sitting in the café said, 'Now I've seen it all. A black pilot and an Amish stewardess.'"

Maureen had lived all her life within a multiplicity of races, cultures, and religions. And the idea of folks gathering to watch a jet descend on a runway sounded odd to her. But although the Millers' world seemed strange and foreign, she was beginning to grasp the spirit of the scene Paul had described.

"Paul was there to meet them, and Paul is just as quiet as Naomi is outgoing. So he was not eager to put himself in the spotlight. But he stepped up and Naomi introduced them and Paul shook the pilot's hand. That would have started some buzzing—an Amish man and a black pilot! And then the pilot climbed into the van and drove off with them! I'm sure all kinds of rumors exploded in our community that day."

"The pilot went with Paul and Naomi?"

"Yes. Mom had insisted that he come to supper and stay with them until he flew back the next day. Paul writes that everyone liked him and they had a great time."

Maureen saw the look that entered Johnny's eyes, and she saw him drifting away from the hospital room.

"What I wouldn't give, Maureen, for some of Mom's fried chicken and dressing." The melancholy look passed and his blue eyes turned fierce as he looked at her. "I've got to get home."

"You will, sugar. You just need a little more time before you get on a bike to pedal thousands of miles." Maureen said this with no idea how far Milford, Ohio, was from Corpus Christi.

"No, I can't wait. I'm sick of lying in this bed and waiting. They've put me in a walker in therapy. Why drag myself around here? Why not drag myself toward home? My bike is gone, but I can walk. And although I want to be home, I know I'm not ready yet to be there. But if I walk, by the time I'm home, I'll have done more therapy than any doctor would ever prescribe and by *then* I'll be ready to be home, too."

"Now that's a crazy idea, if I've ever heard one. You're not well enough for such a physical undertaking. I doubt you could get yourself a block from this hospital. And even if you were in perfect condition, walking that far is just plain crazy. Why would anyone want to do that? You be patient, you hear?"

"I can't, Maureen." She heard the despair creeping back into his voice. He could turn in a moment from clarity and energy to gloom and depression. "I can't wait. I've got to be doing something. God's not doing anything. So I'm going to do it."

"What do you mean, God's not doing anything? Seems to me, He's done plenty for you."

"I've prayed. And prayed. This is all some nightmare, and I want to wake up. God has not answered any of my prayers. Maybe He's punishing me. I tell you, He's not even listening. Maybe He's decided I'm not worthy of His attention or answers."

"None of us are worthy, honey," Maureen said gently. "None of us. It's only His grace that lets us in."

"But that's just it, Maureen!" He was ready to explode. "He didn't let me in! He turned me away! He wouldn't let me in."

Johnny was drifting away to that other place again, a place beyond Maureen's reach. She tried to hold on to him, to keep him there in the hospital room.

"God never turns anyone away, Johnny. It may *feel* that way to you, but you can believe that He will never turn you away."

"He did, Maureen," A weariness had settled on Johnny. "I'm here. And Annie's in Heaven. I couldn't go in. I was there. I was there, right at the gates, and I was turned away."

"You were at Heaven's gates? And you saw Annie?"

"Yes. Annie was waiting for me. I've been wondering if I just imagined it all, but now, telling you, saying it aloud—I *know* it was real. I was there. I saw her. She was more beautiful than ever; she was well and happy. I held her hand. She told me that now, finally, I could begin to live. But instead, I'm here." The frustration had ripened into bitterness. "Don't tell me God won't turn anyone away. I was turned away. He must hate me for things I've done. And now He's punishing me by keeping me from Annie and Heaven. Maybe this is hell, knowing Annie is alive and I can't be with her. Maybe God has decided I deserve hell.

"And what has God done for you, Maureen? How can you go on trusting God when He hasn't brought your son home? How can you go through every day not knowing if he is dead or alive? At least, I know Annie is dead. But you don't know. You don't know whether to hope or whether to mourn. It sounds to me like God is tormenting you, Maureen. Why won't He give you an answer?"

Maureen did not respond immediately. Hadn't she asked all those questions herself? She felt doubt, stirred again by Johnny's angry words, begin to creep around the edges of her own faith. She lifted her chin, pressed her lips together for one moment as though gathering force for her answer. Her green eyes met Johnny's blue ones, almost in a challenge.

"I don't know the answers to all your questions, but I know I have to trust God. I can't give up on that. He's my only hope."

15

Bobby began to drop in on a regular basis, either during his breaks or after his shift was finished. Johnny and he did not discover familial connections, but they both spoke Pennsylvania Dutch and sometimes slipped into that dialect. Speaking the language of home gave Johnny a warm, comfortable feeling.

Maureen challenged them to teach her a few phrases, and they all laughed together as her Texas drawl tried to mimic their words. Every now and then, when Johnny felt like his old self, he would tease Maureen by speaking to her in Dutch. She was quickly catching on to his ornery moods, though, and she sometimes turned the joke on him. It was good, Johnny thought, to have someone to match wits with again. He missed her on her days off.

The pain had not abated, though, and he never had more than a few pain-free hours a day. Trying to put his body back together seemed to Johnny to be more tortuous than lying broken in bed. The therapy pushed him to the limit. He wanted to rebuff the physical therapist's insistent demands. He wanted only to sleep and sink into the blackness where his body would not feel pain and his mind would not agonize over losing his memory and losing his wife and losing Heaven.

Annie. Heaven. All lost to him. No, he would not even allow himself to think about it. He would push the call button and beg Maureen for more pain medication so that he could drift off to mindless sleep. She was always adamant. He could have no more medication than prescribed and only at certain times.

Johnny argued with her, coaxed her, and played on her affection for him. He knew he was more than a patient to Maureen. She mothered him and prayed over him. Still, she would not be swayed when it came to his therapy, medication, or treatment.

"Listen, honey, no more of this whining. We're going to get you out of here. You know I'll miss you like the dickens, but you're going to walk out, straight and tall and handsome. To do that, you have to follow our orders, young man. You've got to work with us. You can do it, I know you can. You're strong, Johnny. You're stronger than you know."

"Is the patient acting rebellious again, Maureen?" Bobby came through the door to hear her scolding Johnny. "Want me to straighten him out for you?"

Johnny ceased his campaign for more medication. Maureen was immovable. Besides, Bobby's visits had become a distraction from the pain. The two young men talked about their homes and laughed and joked together. Bobby would get him through another hour, and *then* Maureen would have to relent.

Bobby had a surprise for Johnny on that afternoon.

"We're going to take a little trip," he announced. "I've got permission to take you out and about. Well, out of your room, at least. Thought you might be tired of these four walls. Let's get you into this wheelchair, and we'll take a tour of the hospital."

It *was* good to have something different to look at and think about, Johnny decided, as Bobby wheeled him around corners and down long hallways and they rode up and down elevators. As they rolled along, Bobby kept up a commentary like a true tour guide. In less than twenty minutes, Johnny was completely lost; he could not have found his way back to his room without guidance.

Bobby seemed to know everyone from janitors to surgeons. He stopped to chat with many. In those brief conversations, Bobby somehow managed to give the impression that he was simply transporting a patient from one area to another. Bobby did not lie outright, but Johnny soon surmised that this extensive tour would never have been authorized.

They did not go near the psychiatric ward where Bobby worked. Johnny asked his tour guide about it. Bobby shrugged.

"I don't think I can smuggle you in there. Unless, of course, you requested to be transferred to one of those beds for good." He grinned. "Better stop giving Maureen such a hard time, or she'll threaten you with that."

"What are your responsibilities there?" Johnny asked.

"Oh, this and that. Whatever no one else wants to do. It's okay, really. I've learned to know the staff and the patients, so it's easier now than at first. Hey, here's someone who wants to meet you." He abruptly turned into a room where cigarette smoke hung like a cloud along the ceiling. "Hey, Jim, you're going to burn this place down, smoking in bed."

The patient, Jim, was sitting up in bed with his eyes closed and a cigarette held carefully above the sheets covering his body. Johnny estimated him to be in his fifties, even though his hair showed no signs of silver. His body looked strong and healthy, but his face was a pale gray. Johnny had never heard anything like the harsh grating sound that came with every rise and fall of his chest.

He opened his eyes.

"Bobby, don't deny a dying man a few last pleasures," he said. Between every word or two he gasped for breath, sounding as though he were climbing a long, steep hill.

"Jim, this is Johnny Miller, friend of mine. We're out for a stroll this afternoon."

"Hello, Johnny Miller. What are you in for?"

Johnny was confused for a moment. Bobby filled in the details for Jim, explaining that Johnny had been killed in a bicycle accident, but the marvels of modern medicine had brought him back from the dead. Johnny let him do the talking.

Something like a cackle came from Jim. That was followed by a fit of coughing.

"Well ... good luck ... boy. You've ... got a ... second chance. Don't ... blow it ... Me, ... I know I'm not ... getting another ... chance. I'm done ... I'm just ... waiting for the book to close."

The speech seemed to exhaust Jim. Bobby leaned closer to Johnny's ear and said quietly, "See those letters above the bed? DNR. That means *Do not resuscitate*."

"Just fancy words ... for *Let the sucker die*," interrupted Jim. "Lived through two code blues already. Electrocuted me ... back to life. To a few more days of this." The hand with the cigarette waved in a small arc. "Why would I want to come back ... to living ... like ... this?"

Every word came with a small gasp for breath. Yet Jim seemed intent on talking.

"Here's some advice for you, young man," he wheezed. "I thought I had all the time in the world and spent all my good years pursuing success. Put my family in the back seat ... too often. Missed my daughter's school plays and my boy's little league games." He stopped to catch his breath. "And for what? A large pension—which I will now never use—and regrets. A big fat pile of money and an even bigger pile of regrets."

Johnny wondered where Jim found the strength to talk as much as he did. But the man kept on, struggling with every word. His sadness was evident as he told of the long hours spent building his career and every free hour wasted as he dashed after excitement. Whether it was sky diving or traveling the world, his life had been one big race to the finish line. Now that the finish line was in sight, he realized that his extreme attempts to "really live" had actually resulted in his missing life.

"Johnny, it's the little things that count ... those mundane activities of daily family life. Taking walks with your wife. Answering your kids' questions as they grow up. Being a family. That's ... the real excitement in life. Me, I couldn't see that—until it was too late and I realized I'd missed it all."

His wife had eventually left him. He had no idea where she was now. His children were grown and seldom called. Neither of them had bothered to visit the hospital to see their father.

"This heart of mine is giving out. Just going to quit, any day now. I've heard some doctors are trying ... to do heart transplants, but ... it's too late for me. It's too late for my family. I never ... I never ... tended the family I had. And it withered and died.

"Pay attention, Johnny. Pay attention ... to what really counts in this life."

***

By the time Bobby had wheeled Johnny back to his room, Maureen had left for the day. Johnny's head throbbed, but he was more troubled by Jim's words than by the headache. What really did matter in this life? What was his life now? He had built a life, once, and then it had been ripped away from him. He had nothing left to tend and nourish.

He did not sleep well that night, but it was not the physical pain that kept him awake.

16

Maureen leaned back in the recliner and closed her eyes. The lemon tart on the plate beside her remained untouched. Her hands cradled the hot cup, but she held it only for its comforting warmth. If she would have taken a sip, she would have realized she'd forgotten the usual sugar.

She cared too much, her husband had always said. He had tried to convince her to leave her concern for her patients at the hospital. She should shed her worries about those people's lives just like she took off her uniform each day, he had said. She couldn't carry everyone else's burden; she had to learn to protect her heart, he had said.

Yes, Wayne. And you're the one who died of a broken heart because you cared, she thought.

On this night, she could not shrug off her concern about Johnny's anger toward God. She thought often about his insistence that he had stood before Heaven's gates with his dear Annie. The possibility of such an experience intrigued her. But even more, she ached for his feeling that God had rejected him.

And today, a new worry had popped up.

Johnny had been bright and cheerful. He was poring over that old atlas, marking lines along roadways and making notes in the margins. He had turned on the charm and asked her to name and describe some of the streets that led out of Corpus Christi. The atlas, he explained, did not show city streets, only towns and highways. He wanted to know what types of neighborhoods surrounded the hospital, what streets led north, and what the surrounding countryside was like.

She knew immediately what he was plotting. She was not going to be an accomplice to this lunacy. He wheedled and charmed. And finally, she reluctantly gave in. If left to himself, he could die out there, she thought. If he was going to do something crazy, at least she could arm him with information.

He had used the word *escape*. "I've got to escape, Maureen," he had said. Surely, surely, he would not slip away without the doctor's release? Surely he was only planning, as he had first assured her, possible routes to take when he was finally deemed ready to leave the hospital? He wouldn't be so foolish as to walk off on his own, before his body was ready?

Surely not.

He wouldn't … Would he?

***

Johnny shuffled along behind the walker. *I walk like an old man,* he thought. During this time, when simply moving down the hallway was so painful and slow, his thoughts often went back to Joyce. Strange—back in those days his greatest desire had been to drive a speedy and flashy car, but the horse, Joyce, and the black buggy had been the only approved choice; yet now the memories that kept pushing back into his sight were not of the little blue car he eventually owned but of the rhythmic rise and fall of Joyce's rump, the feel of the leather in his hands, and the smell of crisp autumn evenings as he and Annie drove the gravel roads of home.

Annie.

He had dressed that morning, pulling on his plain pants and shirt from home. Maureen had the day off, and he thought it would be the perfect time to test his body's limits. He had heard Naomi and Audrey talk about the cafeteria, and he decided to have a cup of coffee there. Would the nurses stop him? He rolled his walker down the hallway and saw only one person at the nurses' station. Coincidence presented opportunity; the nurse's back was turned when the elevator doors opened; a man and a woman exited, and he slipped into the elevator before the doors again closed.

Exiting on the first floor, he stood for a moment against the wall. The exhilaration of success at this small outing coursed through his spirit, but the short walk from his room to the elevator had exhausted his body and that final spurt of energy to sneak through the elevator doors had sapped the last of his strength. His legs were trembling; he leaned more heavily on the walker and looked around for a place to sit and rest. On the opposite side of the hall, a door stood ajar. Under its small window hung a sign in block letters said CHAPEL.

His boyhood tree house had been a kind of chapel; he had spent hours up there, and during especially hard times he had written notes to God, pouring out his heart as he wandered his way toward the Almighty. He remembered his notes to God.

He was no longer certain he wanted to move toward God. His anger simmered constantly. For some reason, God was ignoring him. Maybe he was being punished. Annie had been a gift he did not deserve. Perhaps God was punishing him now for his stubbornness and his drinking in the restless years before Annie.

He did not know what God was thinking. But he did know he felt every bit as lost as he had when he wrote those notes to God as a teenager. He had kept the notes and stuffed them into his empty beer bottles. Were those beer bottles still in the tree house?

He forced his feet to move across the hall and pushed open the door. Six short pews filled the tiny room. Johnny's eye for woodcraft gave brief admiration to the lines of a simple pulpit carved from a dark, rich wood. A white cross hung against a blue wall behind the pulpit. On the wall to his left, several figurines (of saints? he wondered) stood in recesses that reminded him of caves. Candles flickered. On the opposite and outside wall, three tall and narrow windows, made up of tiny pieces of colored glass, filtered the sunlight through their prisms.

Johnny felt like a stranger trespassing on private property. This place of worship was foreign to him. Yet he was not here for worship. He only wanted to sit for a moment and rest. He pushed aside the walker and fell heavily onto a pew. Admitting he had pushed too far, he decided he would go back to his room as soon as his legs stopped trembling.

The late afternoon sunlight shifted slightly, and light filtering through the stained glass windows broke into many pieces and showered patches of deep-hued color all around him. He stared up at the center window. The dance of color and light reminded him of those moments in the tree house when sunlight had transformed broken beer bottles into conveyors of beauty. The light had been transforming. Another explosion of light in his life had also occurred the night he had met Annie.

Annie. She would have liked the colors of the picture in the window, especially the purples and blues. Her tender heart might have shed a tear at the sorrow on the faces of the people at the foot of the cross and at the agony in the lines of the body stretched out above them. The gold of the halos seemed to vibrate in the sunlight. Annie would have deserved a halo. Did people wear halos in Heaven? Johnny had never heard any preacher talk about halos, but he knew their significance in paintings. Thinking back, he decided he had seen no halo when Annie had met him at the gates of the eternal city. She had been radiant, but she had no halo.

"That's an amazing story, isn't it? Do you know what that cross represents?"

The unexpected voice startled Johnny. He was still at the gates of Heaven with Annie.

"Cross?"

"Yes, in that window. The man dying there on the cross."

"I'm sorry. I was thinking about my wife, Annie. She died, too. A while back ..." His eyes went again to the golden halos.

"I'm sorry to hear that."

Johnny finally looked at the voice. It belonged to a man, a long stringbean of a man, as Mandy would say, standing toward the right front corner of the chapel. Johnny had not noticed him there; he must have been standing in the shadows just beyond the windows. The man moved toward him.

"Are you a patient here?" he asked.

"Yes. I was riding a bicycle and was hit by a truck. They say I died. I was on my way to Heaven. But now I'm back here. I'd rather be dead, I think."

"You know of Heaven, then. And you also know that that man on the cross died so you can be there someday."

"I've known that for a long time. I grew up Amish, and heard it preached since I was a child, but my wife was the one who showed me how God can forgive the messes we've made of things and can give us new lives. I needed a new life and God gave me one, but now ... there's nothing left. God gave me everything. And then He took away everything. And now I have nothing."

"Because of that cross, you do have life. That's the whole reason Jesus suffered ... so we all could live. And heal. All of his wounds meant healing for us."

"But there was no healing for Annie! And she, of all people, *deserved* to be healed and to live. Why did God let her die?"

"I cannot answer that, my friend. But I can tell you, if you're looking for healing, this is the place to be—at the cross. It's the reason Jesus came to the earth in the first place—He wants to heal all that keeps us from truly living."

Truly living. Annie had said something like that. As she had met him on his way to Heaven, she had said he could *truly live.*

"That picture is the turning point for the history of this world. But it's not the final picture. Jesus is not on the cross anymore. He's alive now, and he's still in the business of healing. Did you know the name of this city refers to that scene right there?" The tall man nodded at the center window.

"I thought I was in Corpus Christi."

"You are. *Corpus Christi* is a Latin phrase meaning *the body of Christ.* How about that?" the stranger grinned. "Here you are in a hospital in Corpus Christi, hoping to heal, and it is just that body of Christ, broken on the cross, that makes your healing—all healing—possible."

The man's voice was strong with conviction and obvious excitement. Johnny looked at him fully and for the first time noticed the white circle of cloth around his neck. Was he a priest or a preacher?

"I've always thought that Christ's death on the cross brought our *salvation.*"

"Oh, it did! Think about it—what is salvation? It is *rescue.* Jesus came to earth back then and comes into people's lives now to rescue us, in all kinds of ways."

"I didn't want to be rescued from dying." Johnny did not try to keep the anger from his voice, but he felt uncomfortable when the stranger did not reply immediately.

The man only gazed at him thoughtfully, so he plunged ahead.

"You probably won't believe me, but I glimpsed what life after death could be like. I would rather have stayed there."

"You saw Annie, too, didn't you?"

Who was this man? How did he guess that he had seen Annie?

"Yes. And then I was pulled back here. They were 'saving' me, they said. Or else God sent me back. I don't know which. I just know that I'm here, and I don't want to be and don't know why I

have to be here or why I couldn't enter Heaven. I don't know …
and I don't understand …"

He shook his head and closed his eyes against the heavy
confusion closing in on his mind once again. What would his dad
say about all this talk of being rejected at Heaven's gates? Had he
really seen Annie? He must sound crazy, to say that he'd been in
Heaven with his dead wife. Was he losing his mind?

"We can seldom see things as God sees them. But Jesus says
to you, 'Just trust me, Johnny.' Because His purpose is to heal you.
It's why God came to this earth. And He can be trusted. He always
keeps His promises."

Johnny said nothing. He sat motionless in the short pew, his
eyes still closed. He didn't care if he was rude. He did not want to
have this conversation—because what could he say? The stranger
was feeding him words he had heard dozens of times. He knew the
words, but he was no longer certain he had any confidence in them.

Finally, the courtesy John and Mandy had built into Johnny's
character prodded him gently and he felt compelled to at least
acknowledge that he had heard the man. He opened his eyes.

He was alone in the chapel.

17

"I'd like to visit Jim again," Johnny told the orderly one day. Bobby agreed to take him to Jim's room; it would be too far for Johnny to walk.

They had no sooner arrived than Bobby was paged. He would be back soon, he said. That was fine with Johnny. He wanted to talk with Jim alone.

"I've been thinking about what you said about tending the things that matter," he began.

"You have family?" Jim asked.

"No ... Yes. I have sisters and a brother. And my parents. But my wife died almost a year ago. I'm trying to figure out exactly what it is I need to tend. What's left of life now? Annie and I were building a life. Now she's gone ..."

"You have family, son." Jim's voice was gentle, though still gasping and grating. "Get back to your family and you'll see things more clearly."

"That's what I've been thinking. I think that's the only way I'm ever going to figure this out—back home, with my family."

"How much longer will you be here?"

"Uh ... well ..." Johnny dropped his voice. "I'm thinking of leaving soon. Walking out of here. I can't endure too many more days of lying in a hospital bed, just thinking and *waiting*. I've got to be doing something. They say I need more therapy, but I can do my therapy walking home. I've got to get home."

Jim seemed delighted.

"Oh ho! Breaking out, are we? A rebel and an adventurer! Good for you! Good luck, boy!"

"I'm not certain exactly how I'll get back home—I don't really know where I am or how far I have to go—but I will do it. I know I can."

"Listen, boy, I hear purpose! Did you hear the purpose in what you just said? That's a sign you're on the road back."

Johnny felt excitement rising within. He would go home. That would be the first step. He was remembering the aroma of the clothes sent from home, the smell of love and safety and security. Surely once he was safely home he could figure out the answers to all the questions that still tormented him.

"I wish you well, Johnny. You've got a second chance. Don't make the mistakes I did. Look for life at home, son. Pretty much of everything that matters in life is right there, at home."

Jim stopped for a moment, his rough breathing sounding more painful than usual. Then a slow grin began around the cigarette clenched between his teeth, and he squinted at Johnny as though measuring the young man's determination. "Tell you what. You take me along. I know the South like the back of my hand. Been all over. Spent way too much time playing around instead of being at home. Take me along. One last adventure for the old heart."

Johnny's astonishment left him speechless for a moment. This man had said himself that his heart would give out at any time. He could barely move from the bed to a chair without assistance. How could he even walk out of the hospital?

"How would that be possible?"

"Oh, we can dream up some escape plan. The more daring and

outrageous, the better. Steal a wheelchair. Dress as orderlies. You could wheel me out on a gurney. I might slow you down a little, but we'll make up for lost time because I know this city and this state. I'll get you where you need to go. No wandering around like a lost orphan. Whaddya say, kid?"

Johnny was shaking his head. The man was pleading.

"I don't want you to die trying to help me," Johnny said.

"I'm not doing it only to help you. I'm doing it to have one last adventure. I don't care if it kills me. Yes, it probably will. But I'd rather die in the quest of your second chance at life than just fade away while I lie here waiting and thinking about how I've wasted my own life. This life is enough to kill a person, too. Or haven't you noticed that?" he asked wryly.

Johnny couldn't argue with that point. He too had been feeling as though these last weeks had been wasted. He shook his head again, but promised Jim he'd think about it.

Bobby was standing in the doorway, and Johnny wondered how much of their conversation he had overheard. As Johnny turned his wheelchair to go, Jim spoke once more.

"Hey, Bobby. Open that closet door. There's a cane in there. Bring it out."

Bobby withdrew a carved cane—actually more of a walking stick than a cane. The wood bore nicks and scratches, but there were carvings along its length. Rough lines created the shape of a mountain with a date scratched beneath it. A more skilled depiction of an owl showed the intricacies of feathers and eyes. Letters spelled out *David, Robert, James;* and on the opposite side of the stick was a single word, *Shiloh,* and a geometric design that had no meaning to Johnny. The end showed evidence of what must have been many miles of use.

"My grandfather whittled that himself," Jim said. "Those three names are my father and his two brothers. I'm not sure what everything else represents. I did not know my grandfather well; he died the summer I was eight. This was passed to my father and then to me. I've actually used it for the last five years myself. Johnny, I want you to have it. To remind you of what I've told you as you live your second chance. And if I never leave this place, at least part of me will go with you. Bobby, you're a witness here. Once I'm gone, my friend Johnny gets this walking stick."

"Sure thing, Jim. I'll see to it."

18

As much as Johnny wanted to forget the conversation with the stranger in the chapel, he could not sweep some of the man's words out of his mind. The stranger had said that Jesus came into people's lives to rescue them.

Well, I admit it, he thought. *I need rescue. What kind, I'm not sure. But I need help, that's for certain.* That was it, he admitted. That was why he was feeling so angry and frustrated. He felt helpless. And hopeless. He could not make his body obey him. His mind seemed to go off on its own, too, sliding down too many gloomy and unproductive paths.

"Jesus says to you, 'Just trust me, Johnny.'" That's what the man had said. *Just trust Jesus? Sounds so simple. But it's really so complicated.*

Wait a minute! I've never seen that man before. How did he know my name?

Because the puzzle of this question seemed easier to solve than the puzzle of exactly how he could trust Jesus, Johnny went in search of information.

"Maureen, I was in the chapel the other day, and I met a man there. Tall. Skinny. He looked like he might have been a priest. Is he the chaplain here? How would I find him to talk with him?"

"We do have a chaplain, but he's certainly not tall and skinny, and he's been on some kind of leave—family illness called him to Mississippi. So whoever you met was not our chaplain." She looked at him closely. "How did you get down to the chapel?"

He ignored her question.

"I wonder who this fellow was."

"I can't say, honey. Maybe just someone visiting a patient?"

"But he knew my name, Maureen. How could that happen?"

"Hmm. That is strange. But you know, Johnny, you are a celebrity around here. Coming back from the dead, and all that. And as far as I know, you're the only Amish person most of these people have ever seen. He may have just heard your story and figured out who you were."

"But I don't look Amish, do I?" Johnny had cut his hair short and shaved his beard when he left home. His hair had not yet grown to its previous long length; some of it, in fact, had been shaved before surgery. And although he had let his beard grow again since his face had begun to heal, in his mind he did not yet look like an Amish man. Especially in these hospital gowns. Oh— he remembered that he had worn his Amish clothes that day.

"I don't know, honey. I'm sure he just heard about you from the hospital grapevine."

But Maureen's nonchalant theory did not satisfy Johnny. The man had known his name. And come to think of it, the stranger was the one who first mentioned seeing Annie in Heaven. Johnny had not told him that; he had guessed.

Johnny quizzed Bobby about the stranger. Bobby, too, shook his head. No one he knew, he said. Johnny wondered if he had imagined the entire conversation in the chapel.

In the end, with no answer to his questions about the man's identity, Johnny was left to ponder only his words: *Jesus says to you, "Just trust me, Johnny."*

19

He was done waiting. The time had come to go home.

Johnny had reached the end of his patience. Or maybe it was that he had finally gained enough strength that he was convinced he could actually walk home. After voicing the argument to Maureen that such an expedition would be even better therapy than shuffling along the hospital hallways, he felt his conviction and determination growing every day. What seemed a bizarre and foolhardy idea to Maureen became Johnny's one focus. He would take charge of his life again. He would not wait for others to give permission, and he could not wait for God to send a miracle. He would decide himself what was best; and this therapy of his own devising seemed best to his restless and stubborn mind. He had determined to walk home, and he would do it.

Once he had made the promise to himself, this new purpose gave him more energy and … could it be *hope* that began to rise within him? If so, it was the first flutter of hope he had felt in a long time. He studied Maureen's atlas daily. He would need some sense of routes that led north.

His pain was still constant, but he began taking only half of his medication. He complimented himself on his skillful sleight of hand, pretending to take two tablets even while Maureen was standing by his bed, but secreting one of them away to a hoard he would take with him when he left the hospital. He had come to depend on the pain killers; without them, the agony kept him awake at night. Now, though, he was willing to lie awake and suffer if it meant he would have drugs with him on the road.

He pushed harder in therapy. Nurses and therapist approved his more positive attitude. They believed he had finally turned a corner. As far as he knew, no one suspected that his increased discipline was meant to reach one goal.

This one goal, after all, was all he had to live for right now. What else was there? Annie and his life with her had disappeared. He did not know what situation he would find at home—would the farm still be offered to him? Would he be able to farm, or would lingering disability make that impossible? The only thing he could be sure of was that he was going to walk out of this hospital when *he* was ready, not when someone else gave him permission.

He watched the routines and schedules of the nurses and aides. He noted the times for report, when one shift ended and another began and nearly all the staff were meeting to be updated on patients' conditions. His plans considered Maureen's schedule, especially. She was learning to read him accurately, and he did not want to give her any inkling of what he was about to do. He did not want a confrontation with her if she caught him in his escape.

An escape it would be. Simply convincing the doctor to release him was too pale an adventure for Johnny Miller. He wanted to do things his way. He craved the challenge. Besides, he knew neither the doctor nor the therapist would consider letting him go at this point. Finding a way around the obstacles gave him something to work toward, a reason to start each new day.

He had not forgotten Jim's plea. The man wanted to go on one last adventure, and Johnny had decided to take him along. Jim could navigate this city and, he had said, most of the South. Johnny was relying on that. But what if Jim's dying heart could not survive the ordeal of walking? Perhaps they would not walk all the time. Maybe they would hitchhike or take a bus. Jim would know the best way to travel through each leg of the trip.

What if Jim died along the way? And if he did not, what would he do once they reached home in Ohio? Those questions kept popping up, punching holes in Johnny's planning, but he refused to let them detour his determination. He would cross those bridges when he came to them. He would help Jim, and Jim could help him.

This gave him another goal to push toward. He would need to talk with Jim privately about their plans, but Jim's room was on another floor and far enough away that Bobby had always wheeled Johnny up to that floor for any visit. Now, Johnny was determined to walk the distance himself.

He donned his clothes from home every morning. He pushed himself up and down the hallways. Nurses and other patients greeted him; everyone seemed happy to see him finally come alive. He pushed farther and farther on his outings, still leaning on his walker but relying on it less and less.

One day he finally entered an elevator and punched the number for Jim's floor. The nurses were in report when he had left his room. They'd find out soon enough that he wasn't there; it was almost time for breakfast to be delivered. But the exhilaration of this preliminary short escape fueled Johnny's resolve. He would see Jim, and they would set the day and time to leave the hospital. Johnny found himself grinning as he shuffled down the hallway toward Jim's room.

The usual drift of smoke just outside Jim's door was absent. Maybe Jim had not yet lit his first cigarette. The door stood ajar. Johnny knocked gently, pushed it open ahead of his walker, and entered the room.

The bed was empty, neatly made up.

A nurse appeared at Johnny's side. He recognized her. He thought her name was Sandy.

"Jim died last night, Johnny," she said quietly.

***

Frustration gave way to fury. He needed Jim. Once again, God had taken away something—someone—he needed. He met Maureen on his way back to his room. She opened her mouth to say something, but the dark look on his face stopped her. She simply stepped aside and let him pass.

He was short and rude to the aide who brought his breakfast. He was not hungry, he said. "Don't bother leaving it. I won't eat anything." Maureen said nothing to him that morning, letting him sulk like a bad-tempered child. He could tell no one the reason for his anger. Seething, he railed against God.

Bobby appeared in his doorway later in the morning. He held Jim's carved walking stick.

"Sandy said you were up there this morning. So you already know," Bobby said.

Johnny nodded and could not meet Bobby's eyes. He looked out the window at the summer sky.

"You know, he wanted you to have this." Bobby laid the walking stick on Johnny's bed, within his reach. "I promised him I'd deliver it to you."

"Thanks," Johnny managed to say.

"I'll stop in later," Bobby said, and he disappeared.

The walking stick lay across Johnny's legs. He stared at it for a moment and imagined its light pressure sent a burning sensation through his limbs. Then he reached out, picked it up with both hands, and held it out from his chest. Energy flowed into his arms and down through his torso, as though the carved rod of wood was electrified. He could hear Jim's voice and remembered his advice.

"Pay attention, Johnny. Pay attention to what matters in life."

Johnny could think of only one thing that mattered right now: going home.

Jim, I needed you. But now I'll have to do it myself, he thought. *You've sent me this, and it's my sign. Now is the time.*

***

Escape must happen during the one half hour of shift change and report. Nearly all his jailors would be occupied. Johnny knew this because he had discovered it was almost impossible to summon help or get any drugs during that time, so he soon understood the routine of "report." That thirty minutes—even less—was his only window of opportunity.

He dressed the next morning in his Amish clothes. No one would think this unusual. He had been doing so for some time, more comfortable in the garments of home than those hospital gowns. For one moment, he held the blue shirt to his face, breathing in the memories of Annie and home. He would soon be there, and then the world would start to set itself straight again.

Today he also put the new black hat on his head, looked at himself in the mirror, and smiled at the visage he saw there. His hair and beard were both growing longer, and the hat on his head brought an amazing change. He was no longer Johnny the patient. He was an Amish man, visiting someone in the hospital.

He nodded to the image in the mirror and wished the Amish man a successful journey. *This is probably not the best idea you've ever had, now is it?* warned one part of his brain, still practical in spite of his desperation.

But the desperate side of Johnny ignored the practical. *Are you going to stand there talking to yourself or are you going to get moving?*

20

Ready? He patted a pocket. Felt the comforting shape of treasured pain killers he had wrapped in a tissue. His wallet in another pocket. The orange and yellow blanket draped over the same arm that carried Annie's notebook. One last thing. Reaching into the closet, his hand closed around Jim's walking stick.

At the doorway, he gave one glance backward in a silent farewell to the life he had known there, then stepped into the hallway. Should he stop at the psych ward to say goodbye to Bobby? No, Bobby would probably be obligated to report the escape. He could not risk that.

Silently, he thanked Bobby. On their excursions, the orderly had been an entertaining tour guide, showing Johnny alleys and ells where most of the public never traveled. At first, Johnny had plotted his escape through some of those less-traveled byways and doors, but he soon realized any unusual presence there would attract attention and possibly questions. The safest way out would be a brazen walk right through the large front lobby. Simply blend into the crowd. He would be just one more person coming or going in this busy place.

The key to slipping out undetected would be to avoid looking anyone in the eye. He had been here too long and, in one sense, his walks with Bobby had been a disadvantage; too many people who worked here had come to know him, at least by sight. *Just look down, pretend you know what you're doing.* He'd learned that trick to extricate himself from numerous scrapes in his teenage years.

He reminded himself to straighten up as much as the pain in his body allowed. Walk firmly. His face still bore faint shadows of bruises and the tracks of stitches. A bent, shuffling gait coupled with that face would be a giveaway. He did not want to invite any second glances or concerned questions.

His mind flew through all these cautionary points in the short time it took to reach the elevator.

A few yards from the elevator, he stopped and leaned against a drinking fountain, taking a moment to steady himself. These few seconds would either open his prison door or slam it shut. The elevator slid open and shut in clear view of the nurses' station; anyone at the station could spot him—had they been vigilant. But, as he had hoped, only one nurse sat behind the desk. Her head was bent over a stack of charts, and she missed the oddly dressed man balancing himself precariously with the help of a walking stick.

The elevator doors opened and the front end of a cart loaded with breakfast meals emerged. Johnny pulled his black hat down over his forehead and bent to the drinking fountain. He saw the wheels of the cart roll by, saw tennis shoes following the cart wheels and passing him. No one called out or offered a good morning. It was as though he was invisible.

Johnny's confidence soared as he walked out of the elevator on the main floor. The most dangerous part was already behind him. He was a few steps from freedom. It was a great day.

Across from the elevator, he saw the doorway to the chapel. A swift glance around told him he was alone in the hallway. Johnny crossed to the door and pushed it open. He did not know why, but he felt drawn to stop there one more time.

A young woman with a small child dressed entirely in yellow stood in the front corner, lighting a candle. Johnny took off his hat and slid into the back pew, not wishing to disturb the two or draw their attention. The light did not fall through the windows in the same way it had on the afternoon of his previous visit. He stared at the stained glass depicting the suffering Jesus. *The cross is the place to come for healing.*

Turning to leave, the young woman and her daughter walked back the short aisle. The child stared at Johnny.

"Mommy, that man looks funny. Why does he wear clothes like that?" she asked in a young voice that nevertheless carried throughout the chapel.

The woman looked apologetically at Johnny and he gave her an understanding smile.

"Shhh. I believe he might be a man of God, Annie," the mother answered in a low voice as she hurried her daughter past the last pew and out the door.

Johnny felt himself wobbling at the edge of dizziness. Was he still imagining things? *Annie? Did she say, Annie?* And equally as shocking, the woman had thought him a man of God, a priest or preacher. *Me, a man of God?*

He would not sit here and let these thoughts assault him. Why had he stopped in the first place? Rising so quickly that sharp pain shot through his hip and almost doubled him over, he gritted his teeth over a quiet groan. After the wave of pain had subsided, he straightened and walked out the chapel door.

At the edge of the lobby, he paused and surveyed the scene, taking in the short distance to the front doors and freedom. This was the central hub of the building, a channel where the constant tide of activity mixed visitors and staff. Dieticians, pharmacy workers, and maintenance people streamed through this central lobby, some leaving from their night shift and chatting with their replacements on the day shift, some going from one wing to another. Johnny recognized one technician who had stuck his arm too many times and a short and grumpy man who worked in x-ray.

Would they recognize him? Even if someone did know him, perhaps they would think he had been officially released; his hat and walking stick might send that message. He tried to straighten his body and walk as confidently as possible. He felt happy and triumphant; and forgetting his own advice to avoid looking anyone in the eye, he even wished a few people good morning. He smiled with satisfaction when a petite candy striper who frequently worked on the third floor passed him without a glance.

He wondered how many of these folks had been instrumental in saving his life. For one brief moment, he contemplated yelling for their attention and waving his stick like a symphony conductor as he broadcast thanks to all of them for what they had done.

Just as quickly, his mood changed. He was not thankful. Maybe instead of shouting thanks he would bellow curses on those who had brought him back to the land of the living dead.

The urge to curse these people came with an intensity that chilled him. What was wrong with him? He dropped his head, kept his eyes on the floor, and made no commotion at all.

Outside on the sidewalk, in almost the same spot Audrey and Naomi had said goodbye to Maureen, he paused and turned his face upward to the hot sun. A rush of freedom washed the strange comments of the woman in the chapel from his consciousness.

He was out! No one had stopped him.

Now what?

21

On the street, traffic moved briskly. Johnny looked around and realized he had no idea how to find his way through this city. He had asked Maureen about streets and neighborhoods, but everything she had told him suddenly fled from memory. The outside world looked nothing like he had imagined it from his limited view at the window of the third floor. And from his spot on the sidewalk of a busy city, he could not recapture the perspective he had had as he looked down at lines on a flat map.

He did remember Naomi laughing about her first attempt at hailing a taxi. Stepping to the curb, he planted his feet carefully to stabilize himself and then raised his walking stick in the direction of a waiting cab. To his amazement, the driver waved and pulled up right beside him.

"Where to, buddy?"

Johnny tried to recall streets Maureen had named or roads he had traced in the atlas while plotting his route out of the city.

"Do you know where Route 77 is?"

"I drive a taxi, buddy. I know every street and road in Corpus Christi. Where do you want to go?"

"I'm headed to Milford, Ohio."

"Ohio!" exclaimed the taxi driver. "That's at least a thousand miles away." He gave a short laugh, but Johnny noticed the shrewd scrutiny in the black eyes watching him in the rear view mirror.

"Actually, I just want to be taken to the edge of town. And doesn't Route 77 then lead up toward Houston?"

"Route 77 will get you to Houston, yup. But up at that end of town, 77 runs with Interstate 37 for a while, and you don't want to be hitchhiking on that highway. Those semis will blow you over."

"Is there another route?"

"If you were driving the whole way, I'd say go back down to the causeway over Neuces Bay, but walking along there is not a good idea, either. Say," the black eyes in the mirror stared hard at Johnny, "are you sure you want to be walking? None of my business, but you don't look real healthy."

The sensible part of Johnny's brain had been telling him the same thing. The driver was probably thinking by now that this was some sort of joke or that his fare had just walked out of the psych ward at the hospital. Maybe he even suspected the truth that Johnny had left without the doctor's official release. Escaping the hospital and hailing the cab had taken far more effort than he had expected. At the moment, he could not imagine walking even one mile today. But that stubborn, desperate part of him refused to give up on the plan. He would walk home. Even if it took a year, he would hobble home.

"Just drive. Take 77. I'll tell you when to stop," he said, resting his head against the seat behind him.

He must have dozed. His body simply surrendered and refused to exert itself any further or stay alert. The cab driver's voice woke him and he saw that they had turned off the interstate.

"There's a little place just up ahead, if you're hungry," the driver offered. "They've got good breakfasts."

Johnny remembered then that he had not yet eaten.

"That's good; I am hungry," he replied. "Stop here. I'll walk."

"You sure, buddy?" The black eyes in the mirror looked doubtful. But Johnny thought they were also kind eyes.

"Yes. I rested. I'm ready."

The taxi driver pulled off the highway into a semicircle of bare dirt. Johnny had no idea what the purpose of this cleared area might be; it was devoid of all grass and trees, and there was nothing else here. Just dirt. The driver stopped the taxi and turned around to face Johnny.

"What do I owe you?" asked Johnny, pulling out his wallet.

"Look, son, whatever's happened to you ... well, it's none of my business. But you look like you've had a real good pummeling. I wonder how the other fellow looks. Take some advice. That diner is about a mile up the highway. Stop there. Eat. Get some local knowledge from the regulars. The little town of Odem is just a few miles farther. Not a whole lot there, but you will find a motel and a small general store. Take some time to rest. Think about what you need for this trip. If you're really headed for Ohio, you'll need more than that blanket and a notebook."

Johnny lifted the walking stick.

"And I've got an extra leg."

"A blanket and a stick. What more could any person need?" The driver shook his head. He opened his glove compartment, rummaged around, and withdrew a pen and a crumpled napkin from McDonald's. "Here," he said, scribbling on the napkin. "Here's my home phone number. Call me when you realize that Ohio is nonsense—even with three legs. I'll be off work and home by 4 this afternoon. Or call me any time."

Johnny paid the driver and with a few stifled gasps slowly extricated himself from the taxi. The driver shook his head again, but compassion shone in the black eyes. "Good luck, buddy."

As the taxi swung back out into the highway, Johnny raised his walking stick and called after the driver, "I'll be out of Texas by the time you're home. And I am the other guy."

22

The first time Maureen made her rounds, she found Johnny's room empty. No alarm bells went off then; Johnny had been hobbling about for over a week now. The exercise was good for him. His breakfast tray waited; he would be back soon.

Not much later, though, she realized Johnny had not returned from his wanderings. The breakfast still waited, untouched. A thin whisper of alarm rose in her. She yanked open the door to his closet. Empty.

That scoundrel. He's actually done it. And he knew the best time to pull it off would be during shift change and report.

"Couldn't even leave me a note," she muttered in disgust. Of course he would not. She had warned him such a stunt would not only be crazy but also downright dangerous. He knew she would try to stop him. That boy was so hard-headed. Creative, yes. But so foolish! How could he imagine this plan would be successful? He wouldn't last two blocks.

At least, he wasn't a thief. Wayne's old atlas lay on the stand. But its presence there meant that Johnny didn't even have a map.

Should she make some excuse to leave and go after him now? He had at least a two-hour head start. But two hours would not count for much when he could only hobble along—and when he didn't know where he was going. He wouldn't get far.

All she could do now was to report him gone; when her shift ended this afternoon, she would look for him. She remembered her reluctance when he had begged her for information on routes leading out of town. Now she was thankful for that conversation. At least, she knew what was on his mind. He could not walk far, and she would find him.

***

The first step on the shoulder of the highway sent the freedom of the open road coursing through his body. He had known this feeling before, although he could not remember why or where he had felt this way. Although his family and the people who had gathered around his hospital bed had tried to help him reconstruct his bicycle ride, he could not call up names of cities or recollections of scenes, but he knew the memory of this freedom.

With the second step, every feeling except pain abandoned him. Perhaps he would not be out of Texas by that night. Perhaps the taxi driver's pronouncement that "Ohio is nonsense" was more realistic than his eager and optimistic plans. After only two steps, he paused to lean heavily on his new friend, Jim's carved walking stick, and murmured a prayer. He was not certain exactly what he prayed for—safety, healing, hope? He knew only that he needed help.

He took a deep breath and looked around. Route 77 was a divided, four-lane highway, but only an occasional car passed. The wide expanse of blue sky overhead felt familiar, too, although he knew that home was hills and valleys. Never, at home, could he see this much sky at one time. Low, shrubby trees dotted flat pastures and tilled fields stretched away to the horizon. He wondered how long it would take to plow such a field with a horse.

A train track ran parallel to the highway; the rails ran along the bottom of an incline on his right. If he could not walk, could he take a train? He had read about hoboes, but he had no idea if people really did hop on and off trains undetected or if such stories were glamorized myths. His own sense of humor presented a grim image: a young Amish man trying to jump on a moving train car when he could barely lift a foot to step forward. The young man tumbled forward, face down on the track as the train rumbled away. No, hopping on a train would not work.

One step at a time, Johnny. That's the only way you'll get to Ohio, one part of his brain urged. *Start walking.*

Another familiar voice uttering one word also pushed him forward. He heard Maureen's voice forming the word, and he was not sure if this was a word of alarm or a word of comfort: Odem.

The taxi driver said Odem was just a short distance up the road. Maureen had mentioned she lived just north of Odem. Part of Johnny would have welcomed her friendly face and motherly care at that moment. Part of him dreaded facing her. He would have to endure her scolding, and then she would force him to return to the hospital, he was certain of that. He had to get moving and put this town behind him before she came driving along the highway on her way home.

One step at a time. Never had walking demanded so much effort and so much thought. The pain in his hip demanded that he stop. *Stop. Quit. Give it up. Be realistic. You cannot do this.*

In reply, his tenacity pushed one foot in front of the other. Again. And again. *Keep going. Maureen will be driving through here this afternoon and you do not want her to find you and take you back to the hospital.*

At the café up ahead he would have water and could gulp down one of the treasured pain killers. No, he could not wait for water. He unwrapped his cache and put one white tablet on his tongue, swallowing it as best he could.

Unaccustomed to gauging distance across such a flat

landscape, he nevertheless squinted ahead and judged that he would need fifteen or twenty minutes to reach the small gray building in the distance. That was probably the diner the taxi driver had recommended. He could rest there.

An hour later, he had made little progress. The hard pavement jolted his bones. He tried walking alongside the pavement, but then either tangled grasses or heavy dust grabbed at his feet with every step. Back on the pavement, he dragged his legs along, finally forbidding himself to look ahead at the flat gray building. Progress was too slow, and yearning after a goal that never seemed to move closer only opened the door to discouragement.

After one half mile that seemed like ten, he spread his blanket under a tree and eased his body down for a rest. Alarm flared up momentarily when he attempted to stand again and could not; then he reached for the walking stick and pulled himself upright. Pain shot through and almost collapsed his legs, but he gritted his teeth and clung to the stick. He would not give up—not just yet.

Much later, Johnny slid gingerly onto a stool at the counter in the gray block building that advertised FOOD with a flashing red sign on the roof. The clock on the wall announced twelve noon, but his body felt as though he'd been walking for days. Still, the exhilaration of freedom and one goal attained brought a grim smile as he propped the walking stick against the edge of the counter. He had done it. No one would convince him he could not walk home.

He ate, too, as though he had been on the road for days. The old cowboy on the next stool took note of the rapidity with which a huge pile of meat loaf and mashed potatoes disappeared, and he finally tilted his head toward Johnny as a friendly grin created even more wrinkles in his creased and weathered face.

"Good you got here when you did, young man. Looks like you were in danger of starvin'."

Johnny realized then what a picture he must have made. His face still showed traces of cuts and stitches, and one large bruise lingered along his right cheekbone. His walk was more of a shuffle, and even when he stopped, he could not stand upright. He bent over like an old man. All of that was packaged in Amish clothes and topped with a black hat. No wonder people stared. He decided, though, not to explain his appearance or situation. Because, really, where would he start?

"I'm headed toward Houston," he offered instead. "Can you tell me what I'll find between here and there?"

"Waaalll," the old cowboy drew out the word, "not a whole lot." His drawl, Johnny thought, sounded just the way Johnny had always imagined an old cowboy would sound. "You've got a ways to go, son. Victoria is 75 miles up the road. Guess you already know you want to take Route 59 from there. But if you're set to walk the whole stretch to Houston, you'll be on the road for days. That's almost 200 miles from here." The wrinkles around the corners of the cowboy's eyes deepened even further as he imparted this information.

While studying Maureen's atlas, Johnny had calculated that it would take several days to reach Houston, but when he heard *200 miles,* his heart dropped a bit. Even on this first leg, he had misjudged the distance. And from his experience that morning, he knew he had also misjudged his body's readiness for this walk.

"'Round here, you should be able to hitch most of the way," the man went on. "And there's a truck stop a few miles before you get into Houston. Right on the edge of Sugar Land. Take my advice; stop there and get a ride through town, for sure. That's one mess of traffic up there; no place to be walkin'.'"

"Thank you, sir. I do appreciate the information."

"Maybe he ain't goin' through town, Ned," said an equally old man on Johnny's left. "Maybe he's stoppin' in Houston."

Johnny felt the palpable expectation on his left and on his right as they waited in silence for his response.

"I'm actually headed home to Ohio."

More ears had tuned into the conversation, and now Johnny heard a buzz of comments and a few snorts of unbelief. The wrinkled cowboy who had first started the conversation spoke.

"Ohio." He seemed to study the word, rolling it around in his mouth and turning it over in his mind. "Sounds like you've got quite a trip ahead of you. Where do you plan to cross the River?"

He meant the Mississippi, Johnny decided.

"I don't really have a plan for that. Just thought I'd cross wherever I happen to be at the time."

The cowboy shook his head.

"That's the Mississippi you'll be lookin' at, son. Not that many bridges crossin' it, so you will need to plan a bit. Ask the truck drivers; they'll point you in the right direction."

Johnny laid several dollars on top of the bill on the counter and rose to leave. He winced and was sure the cowboy noticed.

"I'll do that. Thanks for the advice."

A chorus of voices wished him good luck as he pushed open the door and left the diner.

23

Maureen's anger dissolved the moment she caught sight of the bent figure shuffling along the side of the highway, leaning heavily on the walking stick.

Over the last two years, her reaction to the sight of hitchhikers had done an about face. At one time, she had been wary, almost afraid, of any bedraggled strangers wandering along the highway. These days, she always felt an impulse to pull over and offer a ride. *That is some mother's son,* her heart always thought. *Some mother's son, trying to get home. That could be my Dougie, on his way back home.*

She saw Johnny limping along, and then it was as though God pulled back a curtain and revealed a masterpiece He had painted. She suddenly saw the complete picture of God's plan, the reason He had saved Johnny's life. This explained why she had come upon Johnny now, walking along the highway. She had not even had to search for him; here he was, almost at her front door. God had caused this intersection of her story with Johnny's. The Almighty was finally sending His answer to her prayers. She had knocked and knocked and knocked at the door, and now He had opened it. Her eyes filled with tears of relief and gladness.

She slowed the car, giving herself time to blink away the tears before pulling up beside the pathetic form. Expecting to find a dejected Johnny, she was surprised by the face turned toward her: a face filled with excited freedom and resolute independence.

He recognized her and looked around quickly for some avenue of flight. *Like a cornered animal,* she thought.

"Are you the escaped convict that everyone was talking about today?" He didn't look at her, but kept walking. "Get in, Johnny."

"No. I'm going home."

"Johnny, home is thousands of miles away. You're not ready. And you probably haven't eaten all day, right? I live less than a mile away. At least, let me give you a solid meal and a good night's rest in a soft bed."

"No. I need to be alone."

"Look here, young man. If you expect to even have a chance of getting to the next town, you will do as I say. Get in. Now!"

"No. You'll take me back to the hospital. I'm not going back."

"Johnny, be reasonable. Look at you. You can barely walk. Let me cook you a few good meals. I promise I won't force you to go back. But take a few more days to rest before you go on with this foolishness."

She felt a small uneasiness as she heard herself pledging not to return him to the hospital. That must be the mother Maureen, taking control. The nurse Maureen would load him into the car, take a quick U-turn, and hightail it back to Corpus Christi.

He hesitated briefly, then apparently decided to trust her and opened the door. Neither of them said another word until, just five minutes later, she pulled into the driveway of a small ranch house and turned off the ignition.

"I'll get the garage door for you," Johnny offered. She knew he probably did not have the strength to open it.

"No. I park here. The garage is full. No room for a car."

She got out and searched in her bag for her house keys.

***

Johnny hobbled along the sidewalk after Maureen, like a duckling obediently following its mother. Her house was the last one on this side street, and beyond here the road simply stretched off through the fields to the horizon, straight and endless, like so many roads Johnny had seen in Texas.

The ranch house and small yard were bordered on one side by a grove of those short, stubby trees that Johnny could not name; and as he followed Maureen into the house, he could look straight through the living room and then the dining room to glass doors leading into the back yard. The small patch of grass there ended abruptly and gave way to more large fields. Off to the right, across the fields and toward Main Street, he could see a cemetery, with the rows of gravestones marching like foot soldiers over a slight rise in the flat landscape.

In the living room, family pictures hung on one wall and marched along a shelf. With a brief and almost unconscious glance, Johnny took in the sense of history displayed by the images of a proud mother and father and a little boy growing up, often in a baseball uniform and finally in Army green. The room was faded but tidy. Soft chairs and a couch had been molded by years of use, but they still looked clean and inviting to a weary body. Johnny thought he caught the lingering odor of fried eggs, a smell that reminded him of breakfast in his mother's kitchen.

All of his defenses suddenly collapsed. How long had it been since he had taken refuge within four walls of a home? He did not know. His family had told him he had left home on March 1. Had he really been wandering around the country, homeless, for almost four months? His resolve strengthened. His body was exhausted to the point of collapse, but he knew he must get home.

"Just make yourself at home," Maureen called out as she went into the kitchen. He heard her put a kettle on the stove and open the refrigerator door. He sat down in a dark red recliner and, leaning back into the softness, he closed his eyes.

***

"I always have tea and a tart to unwind at the end of the day. Hope you like lemon," explained Maureen as she came back into the living room with a plate in each hand. In the doorway, she stopped at the scene before her: Johnny, lying in Wayne's chair, already so deeply asleep that he did not move a muscle at the sound of her voice. She set the plates on the stand, gently drew an afghan over her sleeping boy, and sat down on the couch to sip her tea and watch him rest, contemplating what God had done.

Johnny slept, never moving or making a sound, until supper was on the table. The house was small, and Wayne used to complain that Maureen always seemed to be rattling kettles and dishes too loudly when he wanted to watch television. But Johnny slept undisturbed as she worked in the kitchen. Even when she tried to rouse him and tempt him with food, he was so exhausted that he showed no interest in eating. He opened his eyes, but they would not stay open. She let him sleep and ate a solitary supper.

***

The next morning she came into the living room and found the recliner empty. Johnny stood at the sliding doors in the dining room, looking across the flat fields behind the house. He held a glass of water, and Maureen thought he looked startled when she came up behind him, like a child who had been caught with his hand in the cookie jar.

"That cemetery over there reminds me of our family's cemetery on Strawberry Hill. A white fence around it. One solitary tree. Annie's buried close to the tree."

"And my Wayne is buried close to the tree you're looking at now," returned Maureen. "Guess it doesn't matter whether you're in Ohio or Texas, we all end up in the same way."

It seemed to her that Johnny was a new man this morning. Was he even standing straighter?

"You never told me your husband was gone," he said.

"You never asked, sweetie," she said briskly. She didn't want to talk about this now. "And right now, I've got to get you some breakfast and hustle off to work. Steak and eggs? Grits? Biscuits? Pancakes? How about some fresh fruit? What would you like?"

Johnny did not question her again about her intentions. He had accepted her promise not to force him back to the hospital in Corpus Christi, and he must have believed she would stay true to her word. As she drove into the city, she replayed their breakfast conversation and found no hint of mistrust on his part.

Maureen's conscience raised one small protest; Johnny was not ready to leave medical care. Her professional judgment objected loudly to giving in to Johnny's wishes. But Maureen stifled that voice. She was convinced that God's larger purpose had seized command and was now in control.

24

Left alone, Johnny spent most of the day alternating between naps and his self-imposed therapy. He slept on the recliner for an hour or two, then grabbed his walking stick and hobbled outside. Something about walking out into sunshine and easy breezes refreshed his soul and strengthened his body.

He explored the small yard, front and back, and the short, squat trees on one side of the property drew him in for a closer look. He knew every tree on the farm back home in Ohio, but this tree he could not identify. These trees grew close to the ground, as though afraid to reach too far upward. *Shaped like some people,* Johnny thought, *growing wider than they are tall.* The branches put forth creamy, brush-like blossoms mixed with long, hostile thorns that seemed to be protecting the flowers.

The small storage shed in one corner of the back yard held a lawn mower and a few other yard tools. The yard itself, though, looked as though it had not been mowed for weeks, and while the grass in the lawn grew sparsely in many spots, making the lawn look almost like a plucked chicken, the grass clearly flourished in the cracks of the sidewalk and in the gravel driveway. At some places, blades of grass or tufts of weeds reached almost a foot high.

The walk around the yard exhausted Johnny, so it was back to the recliner for another nap.

A few hours later, again refreshed, he went down a short hallway leading from the kitchen and opened a doorway to the garage. For a moment, he stood at the threshold in shock. He had never seen a garage quite like this one.

Maureen's statement the evening before that the garage was "full" had been a mild description of the chaos. Johnny edged forward carefully, working his way between boxes and bags, lawn chairs, a ladder, a garbage can, bulging black garbage bags, two bikes, a shelving unit that lay where it had fallen on the floor, flower pots, paint cans, tools, two partial bags of cat food, a folded cot, bedsprings, a mattress, a wheelchair, an empty bird cage, odd pieces of lumber, a few shingles, old license plates, oil cans, cardboard boxes marked "Christmas", a dirty barbeque grill, and small mountains of what could only be called trash. And all of that was only what was visible. What was *under* all of those piles?

Johnny stepped cautiously through the tumbled assortment. Mandy would never have allowed such a mess to exist in her house. John would not have tolerated it in the barn or shop. Johnny had never seen such a collection of … stuff. He could not help but smile, thinking that if his mother saw this, she would not be able to rest until everything was cleaned and organized.

The garage told stories of the lives that had existed in this house. Johnny wondered how much of this was still a part of Maureen's life. Or did she never open these doors? Were all of these things relics of a life now gone? He pictured her standing in the hallway with a bag in her hand, opening the door to the garage, and simply giving the bag a pitch onto the heap.

Johnny recognized something else that surprised him. He felt the impulse to straighten that pile of boxes, to carry out the bags of garbage, to set the shelf unit upright and organize the cans of paint and tools. He must, indeed, be Mandy's son.

But not just yet. He would start on that project tomorrow. Now it was time for another nap.

***

Maureen came home to find a new Johnny. At least, that's what she exclaimed when he greeted her from the recliner late that afternoon. He declared he felt a change in himself. Of course he had also rested in the hospital, but perhaps it was this freedom that made the hours of sleep so deeply restorative.

He was awake and alert when she came through the door. She soon discovered he was also restless.

"I'm ready to start, Maureen. I'm sure of it this time. You were right. A good meal and some rest was just what I needed."

She raised her eyebrows and wagged a finger at him.

"Now settle down, honey. You're not quite ready yet. You might have rested all day, but I'm not letting you out of here until you've got a little more strength in those legs."

He grinned at her with those teasing blue eyes that made him a different person altogether from the angry, sullen patient she had too often seen.

"Your food worked miracles, Maureen. Just one dose, and I'm ready to go. And you'd be amazed at what I can do when I've set my mind to it. Just ask my family."

She believed him; she had already seen his stubbornness.

"You admitted that I was right about a meal and rest. I'm right, too, when I tell you to take a few more days before you walk off. Please. Give yourself a little more time."

He sighed, but it was a good-natured capitulation.

"Okay. You're the boss. But you must allow me to do something here for you, if I'm going to be eating at your table."

Maureen had a brief thought that this might be the moment to tell him. But something held her tongue. No, not yet. It was not yet the right time. Besides, Johnny was telling her about his own plan.

"I thought I could mow your lawn. Maybe do some repair work for you. I am pretty good with tools and wood. And I took the liberty of ... well, I was in your garage." He sounded apologetic, as though he felt he had trespassed on someone else's secret territory.

But Maureen shook with laughter.

"And here you stand to tell me about it. You didn't get lost in there forever. Those piles of junk didn't trap you or swallow you up! You're a brave soul, Johnny, my boy."

"So it would be all right with you if I straightened up a bit?"

"Go to it, if you feel up to it."

She was happy that he had found a project. That garage would keep him busy for a week, and he would not be leaving tomorrow. She moved him into the guest bedroom and reclaimed the red recliner for her afternoon tea and lemon tarts.

25

Maureen had underestimated Johnny's renewed energy. By the end of the next day, she was surprised to find he had already cleared a wide path through the jungle in the garage. When she returned home from the hospital, he peppered her with questions about what she wanted to save and what she would discard. And how would he dispose of what she didn't want to keep?

"Garbage man."

She saw his puzzled look.

"Really, honey? You don't have garbage men in Ohio? We have a garbage truck that comes along every Wednesday and picks up anything we've set out at the edge of the driveway. Our trash just vanishes and we never have to worry about it again."

This seemed difficult for him to understand. The trash had to go somewhere, he reflected.

"The landfill, I guess."

"So everyone's garbage just piles up and sits there? Then what happens to it?"

"Goodness, I don't know. I don't really care. I'm just happy they take my trash away."

"But most of this junk you're discarding is metal or plastic or chemicals. Dad always says we are only stewards of the earth. I'm wondering what is happening to that land buried under a huge mountain of trash."

She could give him no answers. Just pile it all at the end of the driveway, she told him and then changed the subject.

When she came home the next day and saw an unexpectedly small pile of trash in the driveway, she suspected that Johnny was not throwing out everything that she considered trash. When she quizzed him at the dinner table, her suspicions were confirmed.

"I thought you might sometime find a use for many of those things," he offered. "If anything was salvageable, I cleaned it up and put it in a proper spot. You never know when you might be looking for a short 2x4 or will need a few shingles. And maybe you'll have grandchildren who will want those old bikes."

Maureen looked at him for a long moment. Busy spreading a piece of bread with strawberry jam, he did not notice.

"No. I don't think I'll ever go into that garage again, looking for something I need. Just pitch it all, Johnny. I don't want to be saddled with all of that. I don't want to be *bothered* even with thinking about it. You've seen how this place looks. I can keep up with my housework, but the lawn and buildings and even the garage ... it's all too much for me. Just please get rid of it, honey."

He looked up at her.

"I can't," he confessed. "Throwing everything away just seems too wasteful. But—if you really don't want anything out there—do you mind if I use a few things I found? There's a tent I thought I could use on my walk and a duffel bag. You are right, Maureen, a blanket, a stick, and a notebook won't get me very far."

Johnny had, it turned out, created a small pile of his own—items that he now asked to borrow. Maureen thought to herself that *borrow* was probably not an accurate word. She would never see the items again once they walked away with him. But then, she *had* told him to throw everything out; she did not want to save a thing.

Still, when he showed her the items he had gathered into a neat pile near the kitchen door, she felt a twinge of pain go through her heart. He had found Wayne's old Army gear. A pup tent, a duffel bag, a canteen. An old knife that Johnny had somehow sharpened. She had forgotten that those pieces of Wayne's life were still buried out there in the garage. Everything had piled up for years, once the wheelchair held Wayne captive. He had given up puttering at his workbench or fiddling with his tools. At one time, Wayne had kept a meticulous garage. Any time either of them needed anything, he could put his hands on it in seconds. "A place for everything, and everything in its place." She used to get so tired of hearing that, even provoked when Wayne reminded her. But then, after Dougie disappeared and her husband began to disappear in front of her very eyes, she sometimes longed to hear the old Wayne muttering his tired maxims.

"These were my husband's," she said finally. "I had forgotten they were still out here. But the war changed his life, so I guess he felt they were a part of him he couldn't let go."

"Your husband was in Viet Nam?"

"Oh, goodness, no, Johnny. He fought in the second World War. Before we were even married. We got engaged before he left; I promised him I would marry him when he came home. But the man who came home four years later was not the same one who had gone off to war."

"He was wounded?"

"Yes. But his physical wounds didn't seriously affect his life. It was another kind of wound that changed him. Something much deeper. Something he couldn't talk about. We did get married. But life was always a struggle. His personality had changed. He couldn't hold a steady job. So I went back to nursing school and went to work myself. Wayne had a series of odd jobs, but they never lasted long. We would have starved if I hadn't landed a job at the hospital."

Johnny had forgotten the pile on the garage floor. He was listening intently.

"And he … his mental state … he never recovered?"

"No. Our life was a long road of extreme ups and downs. The worst came when our son was reported missing in Viet Nam. That seemed to drag Wayne back to all the horror of his own war experience. For a while, he was determined that there *had* to be a way to find out what happened to Dougie. Wayne wrote letters and made dozens of calls. But nobody could help us. We were always told there was nothing more they could do. Eventually, some of the government offices wouldn't even take Wayne's calls. Finally, he gave up. And then he gave up on life, too. He just kind of shriveled up. Ended up in a wheelchair, but even then the doctors couldn't find anything physically wrong with him. Eventually, he grew so bitter and so tired of life that he … ended it."

Maureen stopped. This was far more than she had intended to tell Johnny. A long time ago, she had taken all the pain and boarded it up, like hiding a stash under the floorboards, except that what she had hidden away was not a treasure she wanted to protect—it was pain she wanted to forget. She'd nailed down those boards securely and vowed never again to take them up and let loose old sorrows that lay hidden away.

But now she was ripping up the boards, opening up everything that had been buried for years, and bringing out all the broken dreams for this stranger to see. No one else had ever opened her up like this. Was it because this boy reminded her so much of her son?

She regretted the words the moment they left her tongue.

Johnny searched for words.

"I'm sorry."

Maureen tried to blink away the tears, but they came too fast. She was angry that she was crying.

"Take it all, if it will be of use to you. No sense in my keeping it here."

She turned abruptly, walked down the hall to her bedroom, and shut the door behind her.

26

Johnny finished his project the next day. He had transformed the chaotic, dirty disorder into a clean and tidy garage with more than enough space for Maureen's car. Neat shelves held paint cans and bins of miscellaneous hardware. He cleared off Wayne's workbench and organized the tools. As much as possible, he brought order to the jungle of memories, boxing up everything from old cookware to what must have been some of Wayne's clothes. He marked all the packed boxes carefully and stacked them so their labels were easily read. The old bicycles had been washed and the tires inflated with a hand pump. Johnny tried riding one of the bikes, but the pain in his hip had protested, even cutting through the numbness induced by the pain killers.

Johnny had tried to ration his hoard of drugs. He had no way of obtaining more, and the small cache he had managed to smuggle out of the hospital was dwindling rapidly. On his first active day in the garage, he had promised himself he would not take any of the tablets unless the pain became unbearable. But he found himself thinking about that small heap he had hidden in a drawer in the guest bedroom. And even though the pain in his hip and ribs had dulled considerably, he was pulled back to the drawer. With each pill he took, he promised himself it would be the last for that day.

Just as powerful as the pull back to the dresser drawer was the fear of facing a day with no pain killers. That day was fast approaching, and then how would he get more drugs? The practical side of his brain told him to reserve the medication for the times when he truly was in agony; but the pull of the pills ignored the practical advice. The pills improved his mental state, he was certain. He wondered if Maureen could get him more of the medication. Then he wondered how he might ask without her suspecting his motive.

Maureen herself brought up the question that evening as she surveyed his finished work.

"How did you manage this, Johnny? You can't even walk without that stick. How did you manage to clean up this mess?"

"I rested often. Tackled it slowly."

"But you still have quite a bit of pain, don't you?" She looked at him knowingly.

"Yes. But ..." Oh, well, she might as well know. Maybe then she would help him. He put his hand in his pocket and withdrew the three remaining pills, opening his hand to show her.

"Hmm. You're a sneaky one, aren't you?" said Maureen.

"I was just planning ahead," returned Johnny.

"Is that all you have left? One more reason to stay here awhile. There's no way you'll be able to walk as long as you're having so much pain. And, Johnny," her voice softened. "I can't get more for you."

Johnny stuffed the pills back in his pocket. His disappointment was overshadowed by panic. What would he do without the pain killers? She had read his mind; she knew he would need more. He decided to make light of the situation.

"Well, then, you'd better hope I get that lawn mowed tomorrow before I'm out completely," he joked.

"Don't mow the lawn. Rest tomorrow. I think you're pushing your luck by working so hard, honey."

"Have to work. I can't just sit here thinking about things."

He saw Maureen's face change swiftly.

"What's wrong, Maureen?"

"For a moment there, you reminded me of my son. He said something like that before he enlisted in the Army. He had friends who were drafted and sent to Nam. He told me one night he could not just sit here and think about everything that was going on over there. He had to *do* something."

"Was he about my age?"

"No. He was only eighteen. He had just graduated with honors. And he was a star baseball player. As a boy, he was so excited when Houston's baseball team was named the Colt .45s. He thought that was a perfect name for a Texan team, and he wanted to wear that gun on his chest someday. It was a big disappointment for him when they changed the name to *Astros*. But he was loyal. His dream was always to play for Houston, no matter the name." She smiled sadly. "Come, look."

She took him back the hallway to the third bedroom, behind a door that had never been opened to Johnny before. The door was not locked, but Johnny had never entered; he knew instinctively that this would have been Doug's room and he would not trespass on that ground. Now Maureen swung open the door and motioned for Johnny to enter.

This room was neat. On one wall hung a bright blue pennant, with *Houston Colt .45s* and a gun illustrated in white. A barrel held half a dozen bats, and a glove hung over one of them. On a shelf, a prized baseball displayed a scribbled name written in tall, looping letters. Johnny bent his head to look closely, but he could not read the name.

"Rusty Staub. He was a first baseman for the Astros," explained Maureen. "That baseball was Doug's prized possession."

She paused for a short moment, then said softly, "My son is just a Texas boy who wants to play baseball. He just wants to come home and play ball."

"You talk as though you know he's alive," said Johnny.

Maureen nodded.

"I know he's alive over there somewhere, but Wayne could never have the same faith I did. He remembered too much—you know, about what he had seen himself in the war." She hesitated for a moment, as though not certain she wanted to go on. "But I know Doug's alive. I talk to him in my dreams."

Johnny said nothing. He waited.

"The dream is always the same. Doug was a rat, you know. He was what they called a tunnel rat. The Vietnamese dug tunnels and hid in them, and Doug and his men had the job of entering those tunnels and clearing them out. It was dangerous work. They never knew what or who waited for them in the dark. The enemy often knew they were coming and were ready for them. Their last mission—" Maureen took a deep breath, "was a trap. Six bodies were recovered, but my son's body was not one of them. Somehow, he must have escaped."

"But how can you believe he could have survived that?"

"I told you, honey, I talk to him. Almost every night. The dream is always the same. Dougie is standing at the tunnel entrance. But he's my little boy, about five years old. It's Christmas Eve, and he's holding a stuffed bear and a toy gun. 'Mommy, I'm so sorry. I opened my Christmas presents. Mommy, please, I'm so sorry. Come get me. I'm so alone here, Mommy. Please come get me.' I reach out to grab him and hold him and bring him home, and he's snatched away from me. He vanishes."

Maureen paused and took another deep breath. Johnny noticed how pale her face looked under the bright red hair. She had picked up a Christmas stocking hanging on the bedpost and was caressing the fuzzy head of a bear tucked into the stocking. Beside the bear,

Johnny could see the butt end of a toy gun and his eye followed the line of the barrel down through the stocking. Maureen stroked the bear's head as she went on.

"I wake up screaming for my little boy. When Wayne was alive, I'd scare the dickens out of him. Now I only wake myself." She gave Johnny a small smile. "But you haven't heard me screaming, have you?"

Johnny shook his head. He thought her smile grew brighter.

"That's because I can now tell Dougie that someone is coming for him. And that he'll be home soon. Ever since you arrived, in my dream I can tell my son that someone's coming to help him. And Dougie doesn't disappear. He smiles and says, 'That's great, Mom. Tell him to hurry.'"

"How are you going to find him? Who is going to help you?"

"You are."

27

Johnny thought he had misunderstood Maureen's words. Surely he had misunderstood. How could she think he was going to save her son? Maureen stood smiling at him, eyebrows up in expectation, as though she had just given him a gift or shared a wonderful secret and she was waiting for his exclamations of delight.

"Me? Why would you say that? Why would you think that, Maureen? I have no way to find your son."

"You might think you aren't the one for the mission, my dear," Maureen's voice was calm, convinced. "But God sent you to us. God knows where Dougie is, and He can supply everything you need to find my son and bring him home."

Johnny felt as though he were spinning through the air, losing control not only of the conversation but also of his own body. Maureen's remarks about God brought a snort of anger from him.

"God? Maureen, God hates me. Remember what I told you? I was dead. I was hand in hand with Annie, standing at the gate to eternal bliss. Then I was ripped from her side and woke up back here, cursed with life. Why would God do that to someone He supposedly loves? He denied me paradise."

Maureen gave a little chuckle. *She's laughing,* thought Johnny. *Is she insane? We are having this bizarre conversation—and she's laughing?*

"I did almost wear out my prayer beads, honey, bringing you back. I thought then that I was only praying to save your life. I didn't know until you showed up almost on my doorstep that God had bigger plans for you."

"Maureen, think about this. I'm Amish. I know nothing about the war or the military or the government or … any of those things I would need to know to find your son. I can tell you—I'm not the help you prayed for. God might be planning to save your son, but I am pretty certain He is not going to send you an Amish man to do it. I know this Amish man can't help."

"He works in mysterious ways, Johnny. I wasn't expecting an Amish man, either. But it's pretty clear to me—God sent you here to help my Doug."

"I wouldn't know where to start. I am just a farmer. We're a peace-loving people. We don't participate in the world's wars. And Doug has been missing for over two years. Perhaps God sent me, instead, to help you accept what has happened. Perhaps you need to accept that whatever happened to your son was God's will for him and for you."

The green eyes blazed and blotches of red appeared on Maureen's neck below the red hair.

"Don't talk like that! Don't even think such things! Dougie's alive and God sent you here to help me find him and bring him back home."

"I cannot, Maureen. I cannot be part of a war. I cannot be part of the military. I cannot put my faith in the government. I cannot use violence in any way. It would go against all my beliefs and the teachings of Jesus."

"Never? You would never use violence, even against evil? What would you do if someone threatened your wife? If you could have saved your precious Annie by shooting someone, you would have done it, wouldn't you?" She was firing accusations at him; they stung as they hit their mark.

"You have nothing to say to that, Johnny? You would have resorted to violence if it meant you could save Annie, right? This is my family, my son. I will resort to anything, *anything,* to get him home safely."

Johnny chewed his lip and dropped his eyes to the floor. What would he have done if he could have saved Annie? Maureen had him, and she knew it.

"I ... I don't know. I know we believe in non-violence and in Jesus' teaching to turn the other cheek. I don't think I could ever harm another human being."

"Answer my question, Johnny. What would you have done to save Annie?"

"I didn't have a chance to save her. And I've never been in the position to know what I would do in such a case ... it's never happened ... I don't know."

"We are fighting evil, Johnny. Are we supposed to let evil run rampant everywhere? I believe the Bible says we are to resist evil, does it not? Why can't you stand up against evil, Johnny? What a coward you are!"

Something within Johnny was beginning to churn and boil.

"Maureen, you believe in prayer, maybe more than anyone I've ever known. I'd pray for protection if my family was threatened. God can do anything, you know. He could protect us."

"What if *you* are the protection God has supplied for your family, Johnny? What if God's plan is that you stand up in His strength and resist evil and fight for what is right and good? How can you choose to stick your head in the sand and claim to be peace-loving when there is so much wrong going on all around you? Boys like Dougie are giving their own lives so you can have your safe, peaceful life! Mothers like me are giving up their sons!"

Maureen's voice had been rising in volume. The boiling in Johnny was rising, too, and his words came out harsh and loud.

"God's plan put me back in this life instead of letting me into Heaven. This might be hell. I may not have been good enough for God. If that's so, He can just go ahead with whatever plans He has without counting on me to help Him out. Obviously, He doesn't want me now. And maybe that's quite all right with me, too. Maybe I'm done with Him.

"I don't know what God is thinking about me now or what I'm thinking about God. But I will tell you one thing, Maureen—I am not your man! God did *not* send me here to rescue your son. I am positive of that! The only thing I'm going to do now is get back home. Someone else will have to rescue your son. I cannot do it, Maureen. I won't do it!"

Every shred of compassion and love that had cloaked the nurse Maureen was thrown off. Johnny was looking into the eyes of a tigress—a tigress who wanted to protect her son, no matter the cost. She would have killed to do so, he was certain. And now she was furious with him. So be it. He was furious with her, too.

She stared at him a moment with those burning green eyes, then turned into her own bedroom and slammed the door.

28

Maureen had already left for the hospital the next morning when Johnny open the door of the guest bedroom and stepped into the hallway. He had awakened earlier but stayed in bed until he heard the car back out of the driveway. Although some of his own anger had dissipated, he had no way of knowing if Maureen had also softened; and he did not want to discover her mood by way of another confrontation.

Was she crazy? Had her grief and the long years of waiting and uncertainty caused her to be so out of touch with reality that she would think an Amish man could find a missing soldier in Viet Nam? How could he ever explain to her that he would never take up arms against an enemy?

To be honest, he had to admit that he had never given the church's teaching on non-resistance much thought. He had accepted it, agreed that it was in line with Jesus' teaching, and had never met with anyone so fiercely opposed to his belief as Maureen had been last night. Her question came back, biting into him, *What would you have done to save Annie?*

As he lay in bed waiting for the sound of the car backing out of the driveway, he decided what he would do today. The lawn would not be mowed. He must leave before Maureen had any chance to take her crazy idea further. He felt certain that some of what Maureen had said the night before had come out of anger and frustration. He himself had said things he wished now he could retract. But one thing was clear: Maureen really did believe that God had a plan for Johnny to help her, and Johnny was just as certain that Maureen had completely misread God's intentions.

She had been so good to him, taking him in, feeding him, letting him rest, and honoring her promise not to take him back to the hospital. He thought about how much strength he had gained in the days he had spent at her home. She had been right; when she had first come upon him walking into Odem, there was no way he could have walked even to the next town. He had been too weak and the pain still too intense. He had been wise to give in to her wishes and stay here for a short time. But that time was finished. Now he had to leave before she could press him to proceed with her passionate plan to save her son.

He hobbled around the house collecting the few things he would carry. The army duffel bag, the canteen, the tent, and the knife—Maureen had said he was welcome to them. He stuck his own blanket and Annie's notebook in the bag. The old atlas lay on the desk in the corner of the living room. He picked it up for a moment, debating, then laid it back down.

He looked at the two remaining pills and wondered how he would get through the next days without more of the drug. Well, he would do it. He would have to. He thrust the two tablets deep into his pocket, picked up the duffel bag and his walking stick, and, with a feeling of relief, shut the door behind him and walked away from Maureen and Doug.

***

"Maureen? Oh, it's so *good* to hear your voice! How are you? How are all our friends at the hospital?"

Maureen felt caught. This, too, was someone she had grown to love. Maureen knew exactly why Audrey was calling, and she was not yet prepared to have this conversation.

"I'm fine, honey, just dandy. I saw your horse run in the Derby. Thought he was going to win for sure."

"We did, too, Maureen. We were very optimistic. Secretariat was just a little better horse that day, but we'll catch him sometime soon. Those two will meet up again, and Sun Dancer will remember him. Sun Dancer loves to run."

"I know nothing about race horses, honey, but it sure looked like that to me," Maureen wanted to prolong the chit-chat, but she was running out of ideas. She knew what—or who—was on Audrey's mind.

"Maureen, you know I wanted to get back there as soon as I could after the Derby. But we couldn't get away from all the parties and appearances in Louisville, and then when we got back home, I had my graduation ceremonies, and then my mother requested my company on a trip to Mexico. I promised the Millers I'd let them know how he's doing, but I could not get back to the hospital as soon as I wanted to. We know you're taking good care of him, though, Maureen. So how is he doing?"

Oh, dear Lord, what do I tell her?

"Well, honey, I guess it's a little good news and a little bad news." No, she had not said it correctly. There was silence on the other end of the line.

Then, in a more subdued voice, Audrey asked, "What's the bad news, Maureen? Have there been more complications?"

"No, no, honey. Don't go jumping to hasty conclusions and thinking the worst. I should have given you the good news first. He is much improved. Walking all around the hospital without assistance. Getting sassy and playing some tricks on us. Seems he was beginning to be his old self again."

"*Was?* Maureen, you said he *was* getting back to his old self.

What happened? Did he have a relapse of some kind?"

"There was no relapse, Audrey, honey. Truly, he is progressing better than expected. It's just that ... well ..."

"What? Maureen! Tell me! What happened?"

"Johnny just up and walked out of here one day last week. He said he was going to do his therapy by walking home."

"Oh, Maureen, no! Oh, no! How does he imagine he's going to walk home? How would he even get out of the city?"

"As I said, he is much improved. Truly, Audrey, he is. He's been pushing his walker everywhere and getting around pretty good on his own. And he spent a lot of time planning this, honey. He had his nose in an atlas and asked us about routes and towns. I think that boy has a good head on his shoulders, and I'm sure he'll get rides when he can. I don't like the idea any more than you do— I even told him it was foolishness when he first started talking about this plan—but you know as well as I do how stubborn he can be. So one day he just slipped out while most of us were in report."

Audrey was silent. Maureen felt her hands trembling. What she was about to do was wrong. It was wrong.

"Maureen, do you know what direction he's headed? Do you think we should try to find him?

"Maureen? Are you still there?"

"Yes, honey. I'm just thinking. Of course, he's headed north. He's headed home. But how in the world would we know where to look, dear? There are so many routes he might have taken. We could be running all over eastern Texas and Mississippi. And he might be hitchhiking or taking the bus ... I think it's pretty useless to go after him, don't you agree?"

"I guess you're right. And Johnny's so stubborn anyway that even if we did find him, he would probably refuse our help. But tell me, Maureen, what shall I tell his family? Can I tell them that he is much stronger and that you think he's ready for this? Will that be the truth, Maureen?"

"Yes, dear. I think that is the truth. Johnny is much stronger. He's resourceful. He'll rest when he needs to, and he'll find his way. But remind them, Audrey, that God always knows where His children are and always holds them in His hands."

"I know, Maureen. I know. It's just that … I don't want to think of Johnny out there on the highway alone, trying to walk a thousand miles."

"I told him it was foolishness, but he's a stubborn one. Tell his parents I'll be praying for him, too."

"Thank you, Maureen. You've been so good to us. We are so glad you were there. And please let us know if you hear anything at all from Johnny."

Right then, Maureen wanted to weep. What was she doing?

She said, "I will, honey. Say hello to your dad for me."

29

The Army duffel was outfitted with two straps that gave Johnny the choice of either carrying it like a suitcase or hanging it over his shoulders. He experimented with both ways and saw immediately that he could not carry it in his left hand. All of the weight on one side of his body threw off his balance. He shifted the duffel to his back, and that seemed to work, although the added items he had brought from Maureen's garage, especially the tent, seemed like far too much weight to carry. Still, Maureen was right—he would be foolish not to be prepared for bad weather.

He limped down the wide main street. Should he have left a note? His conscience nudged him. He should have left a note. How could her personality have changed so abruptly? Yet he had to admit that he, too, had shown drastic mood swings recently.

She was convinced God had sent him to help her. He remembered the mother and daughter he had seen in the chapel just before he left the hospital. The mother had told her little girl that Johnny was a man of God. Or had he just imagined that? And had he imagined the name *Annie?*

And now he remembered a Christmas Eve, an evening that seemed like decades ago, although it had been less than two years.

He was certain this memory was real; this had happened, and he was not imagining it. He remembered Christmas Eve, the night he had asked Annie to marry him. And Annie had said *yes*.

That night, as they sat in the tree house high above their valley, listening to the carolers and watching the moonlight on the snow, Annie had seen a vision of the future. He remembered her words: "Johnny Miller, you are going to be a strong leader, a wise and kind Christian man that God uses in many ways. I can see it, Johnny! I don't know what troubles or joys lie ahead, but I see God working through you to bring peace and healing to many people."

The skin on his arms and neck prickled as he remembered Annie's words. He had made some comment about her being right there beside him through all of their future, and she had not replied. Now here he was, without Annie. Had she seen that in her vision, too? That night, did she somehow know already then that their future together would not be forever?

The future she had seen—had God changed His plan for that future? Johnny did not feel wise or kind, and nothing he was doing now was bringing peace and healing to many people. Too preoccupied with his own slow healing and void of peace, he was walking away from one opportunity right now. But surely God did not intend for him to help this family; this was a situation beyond his ability and his resources.

He should have left a note. He was beginning to regret leaving without making some kind of apology to Maureen. He had never spoken in that way to any woman. She had prayed for him and cared for him, and he had repaid her with his anger. He could not go back, but perhaps he would write a letter.

The weight on his back soon sapped what little strength he had. He had walked less than an hour, but he needed a break. After the break, he walked an even shorter distance before his body demanded that he stop again. Finally he found a rhythm, walking fifteen minutes, then taking a ten minute break.

"At this rate," he muttered to himself, "I'll be an old man when I finally reach home."

"Hey, soldier, where ya headin'? Need a ride?"

A pickup with many dents and scrapes pulled over and waited for Johnny to walk up to the passenger side door. He could see nothing more than a hat on the driver's seat. Between him and the driver sat a monstrous beast of a dog, almost filling the cab.

"Not a soldier, just out walking ..." he began through the open window. Then he realized folks looked first at the duffel, and seeing the *U.S. Army* on the side, they assumed he was a soldier. Well, that assumed identity might bring him more rides. He could hitchhike if and when he wanted to do so.

"I'm heading up toward Victoria. I'll get 59 there to go to Houston," he said to the dog.

"Well, that's farther than I'm goin', but jump on the back and I'll get you twenty miles closer. I'm headed to Refugio to the grain mill. Find a comfortable spot back there."

With considerable difficulty, Johnny swung himself onto the bed of the truck and settled in among bags of grain and the comforting aromas of farm life. He closed his eyes and pretended he was home, scooping feed from bins to distribute to the dairy herd. When this mixture of grain was ground up with molasses, the scent was even more pleasing. His memory imagined the smell of it, and a great longing for the life he had left behind rose in his chest. But even if he reached home, life would never be the same as it was with Annie. And would his body ever obey him again? The aching in his body and the blackness of his loss closed around him. For a moment, he lay back on the bags of grain with his eyes closed and thought there was no reason to go one mile farther.

Something within refused to surrender to the darkness and pain. He opened his eyes to bring himself back to the Texan countryside and watched the miles slip away behind the pickup. He imagined Maureen's car coming up the highway, right up to the back of the pickup as he sat there. Would she come looking for him? She was the type of person who would not give up easily. Her husband had given up. He had given up so completely that he decided death was better than life.

But hadn't Johnny thought the same thing many times in the last two months? Just a few minutes before, was that not the thought that had tempted him?

He wished again that he had written Maureen a note. He regretted some of the things he had said to her, even though she had been so irrational. How could she possibly believe God had arranged all of these events to bring Johnny to her home and to her aid? But if he had not run off this morning and had waited to talk with her again this evening … maybe they each could have understood the other a little better.

With the sun on his face and the aromas of home around him, Johnny drifted off to sleep. He awoke to sounds he immediately recognized—the whine of gears and wooden pulleys driving leather belts. He knew the truck must have arrived at the Refugio Farmers Mill, but part of him, still sleepy, wanted to believe he was home. He wanted to be home, hearing his dad ask him to hitch up the work horses. They'd back the wagon up to the corn bin and shovel cobs of dried corn on the wagon, then drive to the Milford Elevator. He wanted to be home, with a body that could do his share of the work—but he knew none of his wishes were reality.

"Well, soldier, this gets you closer. Another 40 miles to Victoria, then a bit over 100 miles, and you'll soon be back home in Houston."

"It's … I'm …" started Johnny, then he decided it wasn't worth the effort of explaining. "Thanks for the ride, Mister."

"Good luck to you, soldier."

Seeking food, Johnny wandered down Alamo Street. He had not walked enough to work up an appetite, but he must be prepared for the rest of the day. He was quite pleased to have come this far in such a short time, but forty miles to Victoria would take many more days, unless he was fortunate enough to get more rides.

In answer to his questions, the clerk at the counter of the small grocery store told him there was "nothing" between Refugio and Victoria. He purchased several sandwiches, crackers, apples, two cans of soup, and a package of cookies and stashed them in his bag. At a small table in the back corner of the store, he sat down and pulled Annie's notebook out of the duffel. Like wisps of smoke from a campfire, pieces of scenes drifted back. He saw himself sitting with this notebook after long days of biking, reading the thoughts Annie had tucked away in those pages. The memories came into sharper focus as he recalled how he could hear her voice speaking her written words.

But ever since he had seen Annie at the gates of Heaven and then had been torn away from her again, he had not opened the notebook. Now he turned to the back of the tablet, to blank pages well beyond where he knew Annie's neat handwriting marched across the pages. He tore out a blank page, closed the notebook, and stuffed it back into the duffel.

He asked to borrow a pencil and began a letter. *Dear Mom, Dad, and Naomi.*

The note was brief. He had started his walk home, he told them. He was doing well thus far (he didn't tell them he had ridden most of the miles he had already traveled) and would keep them posted on his progress.

The post office just down the street sold him an envelope and a stamp, and he dropped the letter into the mail slot, feeling as though home had just moved hundreds of miles closer.

Back on the shoulder of the highway, he berated himself for not choosing his food more carefully. The added weight slowed him even more, and the cans of soup kept shifting around in the bag. During his first break, he tried to rearrange everything and pack more tightly.

He acknowledged that he was thankful for the morning's ride, since it had put distance between him and Maureen quickly. But he decided he would not accept rides for the next few days. This journey home was about healing of mind and body, and too many rides would bring his body home ahead of his mind.

He slogged through the afternoon. The warmth of the sun on his back gave him some measure of comfort. So did the thought that every step he took brought him closer to home and recovery.

Twice he stopped and, clutching the walking stick tightly to maintain his balance, he bent over to pick up an object lying by the road. The first was a screwdriver that looked almost new. How did a tool like this come to be lying on the shoulder of the highway? His first impulse was to look around, to locate someone who might have dropped the screwdriver and return it to them. Then he realized the foolishness of that thought: cars flew by, but he was a solitary pedestrian on this highway, and there were no homes in sight. The deep-seated frugality of his family's lifestyle prompted him to slip the tool into his bag. A small thought rose up and reminded him: this was more weight to carry. Yes, he acknowledged that. But a good screwdriver was often useful. And after all, he was holding it in his hand—he couldn't very well just toss it into the grass, could he? That would not be right, either.

The second thing he found was a broken basket and a scattering of peaches, beautifully brushed with color but already showing bruises from their fall. He pushed several around with the tip of his walking stick until he found two that had suffered little harm. Those went into his bag also, along with the broken slats of the basket. *Kindling,* he thought.

Once or twice he found himself so lost in thought that the pain in his hip faded to the back corners of his mind. But that only happened for short periods of time. Then the pain in his body pushed to the forefront again and demanded all his concentration. For most of the afternoon, a battle for dominance raged: escape from body pain meant succumbing to mind pain. Back and forth went the battle.

At all times, he battled one thing more: the call of the two white pills in his pocket. When all he could think of was burning pain in his body, the pills promised relief. When his mind dwelled in the dark torture chambers, the pills promised relief. But he had only two left. He would wait as long as he could before taking one.

During the mental jousting, he was besieged by remorse about his treatment of Maureen. At other times, he replayed the scenes while he was dead. Was there any clue in what he had seen or in what Annie had said that might explain why he was now here, burdened with this suffering body and unreliable mind?

Once during the afternoon he allowed his mind to linger on the people who had gathered around his hospital bed: the two men who were total strangers to him and the auburn-haired young woman always with Naomi. The sight of Audrey with the red horse at the Kentucky Derby had brought brief images of a sunny, pleasant day. He did remember the day had been pleasant. Why could he not remember exactly what it was that had been pleasant?

He wondered where these people belonged in his life and how they fit into the weeks his mind seemed to have lost. But he had learned he could not force his memory to give up its secrets. He wondered briefly, and then he let those faces go.

30

All day, Maureen carried a heavy load of sorrow for the way she had treated Johnny the night before. And she had not apologized. Their heated words burned in her heart all day, and Audrey's phone call had added to her turmoil. Everything was getting too tangled.

She rebuked herself. *Fires of hell, Maureen, that's what it is. The fires reserved for liars are already burning in your soul.*

It had been a long time since she had carried such a heavy load of guilt to confession. Technically, Maureen had not lied to the young woman, but neither had she told her the entire truth. She had made her decision in a second; she could not tell Audrey that Johnny was at her home. Even though Maureen liked Audrey immensely, the young woman could not come into the picture and deter Johnny from his mission now. For the rest of the afternoon, she tried to justify what she had done—and had not done.

But the guilt still burned.

Maureen had no doubt that God had sent Johnny to help her find Doug, but she admitted she had done nothing to aid God's plan when she attacked Johnny last night or when she lied (yes, she would acknowledge that word) to Audrey. She would go home and apologize to Johnny. She had hurt him with her remark about saving his precious Annie, and she had regretted those words as soon as they had left her lips.

She must make Johnny understand, though, the urgency of finding Dougie. She must make Johnny see that God had saved him and put him in *her* hospital and then her home for a reason.

By the time Maureen pulled into her driveway, her planned apology was genuine and her spirit calmed. She would ask Johnny's forgiveness and they would be friends again and God could get on with His plans.

Then she opened the front door to an empty house. When no one answered her call, she swore—something she had not done for many, many years—and then immediately prayed, "Oh, dear Lord, forgive me, forgive me. But look what he's done. He's gone off and run out on me again!"

***

Several times that day Johnny felt the ground tremble beneath his feet. The first occurrence alarmed him; he thought perhaps he had pushed too hard and dizziness was overtaking him again. A few seconds later, he relaxed when he heard the rumble of a train.

In many places, the railroad track ran parallel to the road, to his right and down over an embankment. Johnny found himself looking forward to the long trains, reading the lettering on the cars, and wondering if those names represented towns along the line. He tried to realistically assess his chances of slipping aboard one of these trains. He had read about hoboes who rode the rails. Perhaps he would meet one such character along the way and would be able to glean advice about how to hop aboard. Traveling by train was permitted in his church.

But would his conscience permit jumping on board unseen and without a ticket? Was it honest? Or was it cheating?

He would soon need to find a place to camp. The evening sun sent his shadow far down the road ahead of him. Both his sense of distance and his awareness of time had been distorted by the unfamiliar topography and his struggle to make his body obey. He must be traveling at about one mile per hour. That meant he had only traveled six or seven miles toward Victoria.

Ahead, a cluster of trees huddled close to the road. These were the same trees he had studied at the edge of Maureen's lawn; she had pronounced them mesquite trees. Behind the mesquite grove, the land dropped away to the railroad bed, and on the other side of the rails lay a flat grassy area offering a perfect spot for his camp.

He had experimented in Maureen's back yard, erecting the tent several times until he was certain he could do it in darkness if necessary. (He had thought of that preparatory exercise—why had he not thought to bring a flashlight or lantern?) The tent was not much more than a canvas draped over a frame and fastened to the ground. A pup tent, Maureen had called it. At least, it would keep him dry.

The tent went up smoothly and quickly. Johnny hoped the musty odor that unrolled with the canvas would not linger. He collected small sticks in the mesquite grove and combined them with two slats from the broken basket, and his fire sprang up easily and burned hot. The wood gave off a sweet and pleasant scent, and he hoped it would saturate the musty tent. Mesquite trees dotted the landscape, he had noticed, and he would have no problem finding wood for fires.

Johnny took the screwdriver he had found and punched several holes in the top of the soup can. Carefully, he set the can between two burning logs. The darkness closed in around the circle of firelight as he waited for his supper to heat. Then, with a stick, he eased the can away from the flames and, holding it wrapped in one corner of his blanket, he sipped the hot liquid.

As he drank, the hot soup revived his entire body, his soul, and his spirit. The flames danced, their warmth reaching out and embracing him. He tilted back his head and gazed a long time at the thousands of stars strewn across the dark sky. It was good to be outside. He had lived in the hospital world for too long. Now the arch of the sky and the aromas of farm country and the sight of green growing things reminded him of who he had once been.

For the first time since he had awakened to find himself back in the world, he recognized a few moments that could be called peace. Was this the beginning of his coming back to himself and to life as he had known it? Strange, at one time, life as he had known it had not been enough for him. He had run away from it. Now, he wanted only to reclaim that life. He was on his way home, back to his old and known life.

Ensconced in his pup cocoon, Johnny was soon dead to the world. The ground was much harder than Maureen's guest bed, but his weary body craved rest, and sleep came quickly.

A roar jolted him awake. The whole world was shaking.

Where am I? What's happening?

His groggy mind could not put the strange smells and pitch darkness and quaking earth together. Was death coming back to claim him? That would be good news.

The sharp whistle of the train screamed from the darkness and the clacking of the wheels on the tracks became distinct and hypnotic. He had camped close to a railroad crossing. He peered out into the darkness and saw the vague shapes of train cars sliding by. The shadowy line melted away into the dark night. Within minutes silence settled again, and soon he wondered if the train had been only a dream. Red embers glowed in the circle where he had cooked his supper, their pulsing heartbeat assuring him he was not totally alone.

He shifted his weight carefully on the hard ground. The ache in his hip had spread to nearly every other part of his body. *I've got to find a softer place to sleep tomorrow night. And more drugs.*

That was his last thought.

31

In the morning, Johnny found flickers of life lingering in the embers. He stirred them to greater life, filled the canteen cup with water, and pushed it into the fire circle. Soon a twirl of steam rose from the cup. He had failed to think of breakfast while buying food. Cookies would have to be sufficient. Cookies and hot water.

The steaming water displaced the chill that had seeped into his body during the night. Water should not be a problem, he decided. The previous day he had seen numerous windmills and pump systems used to water cattle. And if it was necessary to drink from a stream, he would do so without a second thought.

One concern must be addressed, though. The previous day his body had felt off balance at almost every step. Shifting the duffel bag to his back helped to distribute the weight he carried, but still his body fought for balance. He needed another walking stick, a fourth leg.

Rising from a seated position by the fire was a challenge in itself. His knuckles whitened as he clung to the carved intricacies of Jim's walking stick and pulled himself upward with a groan. Was it possible that there were even *new* aches? Maybe those new pains were signs of progress, signs that his body was stretching itself to new limits. He chose to believe that.

As he steadied himself, he thought about where he *could* have been—with Annie in pain-free bliss. Instead, here he was, without Annie and with a body imprisoned by pain. Maybe Maureen was right. Maybe this was extreme foolishness. And what did he have to go home to, anyway?

No. This was a bright, clean, new morning. He would not let his thoughts go down that dark path.

"Find another leg, Johnny. Get going," he said.

In the mesquite grove, he marveled at the twists and turns taken by most branches of the strange trees. He knew of nothing back home in Ohio that grew in such an awkward fashion. But the strange shape was to Johnny's advantage—branches grew low and were within easy reach. He tested a few, wondering if he'd be able to break off a branch of the thickness needed for his walking aid. The sharp thorns would have to be trimmed off, too. And could he find a branch straight enough?

Then, there it was, like a gift laid before him: a branch already broken from the tree, long enough and almost straight enough. The hard wood resisted his old knife. He managed to cut off most of the small branches and the thorns, although little knobs remained. The screwdriver also had no effect. The stick would have to do, though, rough knobs and all.

"Sorry, but I've got to be going," he said to the red embers as he spread them out and splashed water over them. They hissed in reply. "Thanks for keeping me company last night."

He hoisted his bag and took a stick in each hand, testing his new balance.

"Yup, you're exactly what I need," he told the mesquite stick.

It would be a good day. He felt as if he had grown a new leg.

***

Maureen had been wrong. This was not foolishness after all. Each day Johnny felt stronger. Each day he pushed his body a little further. Although the road always ran ahead of him, flat, unending, and disappearing into the far horizon, he knew he was making progress. And he still had two pills in his pocket.

The store clerk who had told him there was "nothing" between Refugio and Victoria must have been counting only buildings and traffic. True, there were very few structures along this stretch of highway. Johnny passed solitary businesses and glimpsed houses down long lanes. He saw even fewer people.

But he considered that there was much to see between the two towns. He enjoyed strolling along vast farm fields, attempting to detect what crops had been planted there. Some of the crops were foreign to him, but other fields looked much like the Millers' fields at home—except that everything here was so flat. Where the land was not tilled, some acreage was covered with long grasses and punctuated by the waving, twisted arms of mesquite trees. Johnny had assumed these were pasture lands until he realized on the third or fourth day that he had seen no livestock of any kind.

Traffic was light, but several friendly drivers stopped and offered rides. He turned them down, determined to build up his strength.

He was content to keep walking because, finally, he was in charge. Buoyed by the knowledge that he had taken back control of his days, he settled into a cheerful and optimistic mood. At last he was doing something that made a difference.

His strangest roadside find on the highway to Victoria was a child's fuzzy blue and white blanket. It rested on tall grasses, as though it had drifted down from the sky. He picked it up, thinking it would make a wonderful pillow. But a few yards past that spot he came upon a long-legged, stuffed rabbit with a sad look. This toy was obviously well-loved; its fur was worn thin and one eye was missing. Johnny could imagine the dismay of some small child when he or she discovered the blanket and rabbit missing. He dug the blanket out of his bag and hung it on a small bush, like a flag. Under the bush, he tucked the rabbit in a sitting position, watching the road with its one eye, waiting for its child to come find him.

His soon established his routine: walk, rest, take nourishment, repeat. He kept tight control of his thoughts, and concentrated on the landscape around him. It was only when he walked too long without rest or food and water that thoughts about Annie and all he had lost crowded back into his mind; then the tight control loosened and he felt himself poised at the edge of that familiar pit of black despair and discouragement. He learned it was best to stop and make camp early, before he was overly tired or hungry. Supper and a night's sleep helped to keep him from tumbling over the edge into the depths of that pit.

And for a few days, the old Johnny grinned at the sun, whistled with the birds, and grew stronger.

32

Johnny had dreaded entering Victoria, expecting he would have to navigate heavy city traffic. But his route skirted the southern side of the city, and with the exception of a few large factories and businesses along the highway and the smell of the city to the north, Victoria did not infringe on his peaceful walking.

At times, Johnny thought the highway always looked the same, running on and on and on, flanked by the flat, flat fields and covered by the vast blue dome of sky. At other times, he marveled that, in this land that never seemed to change, he yet found new and interesting things to watch each day.

He often stopped to watch hawks in flight. By the third day he began naming the engines that went by. The cars they pulled changed, but the same engines ran back and forth past him. As each profile came into view against the sky, he recognized it as one recognizes the shape and gait of an old friend approaching at a distance. Small towns triggered his curiosity, especially those with unusual names like Edna and Louise. And every now and then he did encounter someone along the highway—a farmer tightening his fence, a woman at her mailbox, a truck driver fixing a flat. Then simple good mornings made him smile and reminded him how much he missed his family at home.

Sometimes the highway shoulder dwindled to inches, and he stepped off the pavement and walked through the grasses along the highway. Walking on uneven ground was much easier with two walking sticks, and he relished the sensation of being in the fields again. Would he one day walk through his own fields? Annie had loved wandering over their farm …

No, he was not going to think about that now.

At times, when he needed to distract his thoughts, he concentrated on the pain in his hip, fighting it and willing it to subside. The physical pain was still insistent, still too sharp to be ignored; but he would rather fight the pain in his body than the acknowledge the pain afflicting his mind and heart.

On one evening when the hurt of losing Annie hovered precariously close, he felt panic creeping in. He had walked too long that day, and many sections of the highway had narrow shoulders; he had been forced to walk on uneven ground much longer than usual. In one stretch of grass, he caught the tip of his mesquite walking stick on a hidden rock, lost his balance, and fell flat on his stomach. The ache in his hip exploded and left him lying paralyzed by the agony. After a few moments of gritting his teeth to keep from screaming, he fumbled in his pocket and shoved a pill into his mouth.

Walking had been much slower after that fall. He was no longer walking; he was shuffling. Two cars had stopped and offered a ride, thinking he was hurt. Dusk was settling over the flat landscape, and he had not yet found a camping site.

He smelled the mesquite campfire at the same time he saw the smoke twisting up from behind a row of trees. Limping across a stretch of grass and stepping carefully across the railroad tracks, he followed the scent and the smoke but could see no one until he finally came through the few trees that sheltered a man squatting beside a small fire.

"Welcome," said the stranger, without looking up. "Dinner's almost ready, and I'm willing to share it with good company."

"I did not mean to disturb you, sir," said Johnny.

The face turned toward Johnny was bearded and ringed with long hair.

"No disturbance. And I'm not a *sir*. I'm Sam. Some folks call me Slick."

Slick, thought Johnny. *If he'd cut his hair, clean up, and put on a suit, he might be a slick salesman.* It was the voice and the smooth way he talked, Johnny decided. No trace of a Texan drawl flavored his words. Johnny could detect no accent of any kind. Every word was pronounced clearly and perfectly. The man sounded like a preacher, Johnny thought, like someone who had been trained in public eloquence. The voice came as a surprise and did not belong to the faded clothes, scuffed boots, and long hair.

"I'm Johnny Miller."

"Welcome to my humble abode, Johnny Miller." The man waved his arm, sweeping the surrounding area. Johnny looked around but saw little more than a duffel bag much smaller than his own, a log drawn up to the fire like a bench, and a small kettle hanging over the flames. Mouth-watering aromas came from the kettle and Johnny realized how hungry he was.

"As a rule, I like to avoid crowds, but please, be my guest tonight," the man said as he stood and offered Johnny a hand. Even in the twilight, Johnny could see the cleanliness of Sam's hands. Not a trace of dirt lingered under the long fingernails. Johnny brushed his own hand over his pants leg before grasping Sam's.

Very few times in his life had Johnny been speechless. This was one of those times.

"I … thank you."

He shuffled around the fire to the log and almost fell into the flames as he tried to lower himself onto the seat.

"Whoa, there. Are you all right?" Sam reached out a hand to

steady him, but Johnny had already thudded down onto the log.

"Yes. It's difficult getting up and down sometimes," he said.

Sam eyed the two walking sticks.

"Where are you from, Johnny? Do I detect a German accent?"

"Ohio. Yes, I grew up speaking Pennsylvania Dutch."

"Ah," said Sam, stirring whatever it was that smelled so wonderful in the kettle.

"Do you by any chance have a plate with you, Johnny? Or a fork or spoon?"

"No."

"Well, I'm sorry I don't carry enough kitchen wares to entertain regularly. We'll eat in shifts. Here. Enjoy. It's my own secret recipe."

Sam had scooped out a large portion of something that looked like stew. Johnny recognized potatoes. Meat of some kind. Whatever it was, it was hot and far better than most of Johnny's meager suppers. He had stopped at a diner one day and ordered fried chicken, but nobody could make fried chicken like Mandy. He had not finished that meal.

Sam handed him the bowl and a fork.

"Go ahead. Eat up. There's plenty."

Johnny felt uncomfortable eating this stranger's food while his host waited, but the first taste broke through his reservations. The food was delicious. He could almost feel strength pouring back into his body.

"From Ohio, eh? And where are you headed?"

"Back to Ohio. I've been … traveling the West. Now I'm headed home."

Sam said nothing for a moment, and Johnny felt the man was measuring him.

"Well, if you're tired of traveling, home is always your best destination. And if you're in a hurry to get there, Johnny, I can have you back in Ohio by the day after tomorrow."

Johnny paused between bites.

"How is that possible?"

"I can get you to any place in America from here, Johnny. To Ohio? Catch the 2 a.m. train coming through here tonight. Jump on board at the road crossing up ahead. In Houston, slip over to Track 7 and take the Western Express for San Antonio."

"West? That's the wrong direction for me. I need to be heading north and east."

"Ayuh. You do. But sometimes, Johnny, you have to go far away from home to get back to home."

Sam paused, again looking at Johnny with eyes that looked as though they could see a person's thoughts.

"In San Antonio, find Track 10. That will take you to Dallas. You'll need to be careful in Dallas. I've never been caught there, but many others have." A white grin broke through the beard. "I've earned my nickname, although there have been some close calls.

"Track 5 in Dallas has a run all the way to Nashville, and from there up to Columbus."

Johnny's fork had stopped as he listened to this itinerary.

"How do you know all that?"

Sam smiled.

"I travel a lot."

"Are you …" Johnny searched for a polite way to ask the man if he were homeless or a hobo or, maybe, a fugitive from the law.

"*Hobo*'s the word most people use," said Sam. "I'm a traveler, just like you. You dropped in just in time to see me off. Tomorrow morning, I'll be catching the 4 a.m., heading up toward Minnesota. Texas is great in the winter, but too warm for me right now. I'm a bit late getting started north this year. Come fall, I'll be heading south again, just like the birds."

"Where's your home?" asked Johnny.

"Right now, this beautiful little spot of green."

"I mean, your home—a place with walls, a roof, and family."

Johnny heard his words hang in the air and wished he could reach out and pull them back. In the light of the fire, he thought he saw moisture gathering at the corners of Sam's eyes.

"Well, Johnny, I'm sorry to say, that is the one place I cannot get to from here."

He stood and reached for the bowl.

"If you're finished, I'll wash up and have my dinner. Feel free to pick any spot you like for the night."

Johnny handed him the bowl and fork and thanked him, then sat in silence while Sam ate his own meal.

Just about the time Johnny began to feel uncomfortable with the silence, he remembered the cookies in his duffel. He dug out the bag. Some had crumbled into small pieces, but he found three whole ones and offered them to Sam.

"Dessert?"

"Ah, a treat! Thank you, Johnny."

More silence. Then Johnny spoke up again.

"If I were to hop a train, I'm not sure I could remember all those connections."

"There will always be someone to guide you," Sam assured him. "You just need to take that first step, and then help will come along the way as you need it."

In his pup tent, Johnny felt the 4 a.m. train before he heard it. He peered out into the darkness and saw a shadow moving on the other side of the low fire.

In the morning, all traces of Sam were gone except for the glowing embers of the fire he had built. *Like a part of his life he left behind*, thought Johnny.

33

Although Sam's hot stew had refreshed Johnny, the fall had not only bruised his body but had also punctured his spirits. As he broke camp the next morning and picked up both walking sticks, he found himself thinking about Sam's directions for getting back to Ohio. Even by train, getting from Texas to Ohio would be a complicated matter, and the enormity of his undertaking swept over him.

What am I doing? Walking all the way home is crazy. I might still be walking when the snow flies. You don't even have a map, Johnny. Just give it up. You have nothing to go back to, anyway.

And that sad comment to himself opened the door he had kept barred for the last few days. What *would* he do when he returned home? Life without Annie had been unbearable; that was why he had begun his bike ride in the first place. Why was he going back to that life? Why was he here and not in Heaven? Why had God sent him away? Those questions led to thoughts of Maureen and her passionate belief that God had sent him to rescue Dougie. *I'm no use to her and her son. No use to anyone. Why did I think going back home would make any difference? I am crazy, just like Maureen said.*

Perhaps he had not seen and talked with Annie at Heaven's gate; perhaps it had all been a dream concocted by his unconscious because he missed her so much. In the morning light, unsure of his own mind, he wondered if Sam really existed. The conversation with him had been at dusk, as the world hung between light and darkness, and now in Johnny's mind Sam seemed like some shadowy ghost moving in the flickering light of the campfire. The entire scene of the night before seemed more illusion than reality.

The sun shone hot and bright that day, but Johnny plodded along in darkness.

***

At noon, Johnny browsed through the maps at the truck stop. The last days had brought a dawning awareness of the vastness of the country that lay between him and home. He had studied Wayne's old atlas, but those tattered pages had not conveyed the magnitude of his plan as effectively as had the last days of walking less than twenty miles between sunrise and sunset. Dreaming from his hospital bed, he had chosen what he thought an obvious route home; and because he had always had a knack for numbers, he had been certain he would remember each planned leg of the journey. Now he could not even recall the states he must travel through. His first goal had been Houston, but what after Houston? All those route numbers and town names he had memorized had left him, and he felt like a dandelion seed, carried along by changing winds.

As he had walked that morning, the light traffic on the highway had grown heavier, and more and more commercial properties lined the highway. When he passed the entrance to a large medical facility, he thought about the one pill in his pocket. But could he just walk in and ask for drugs? He was certain there would be questions. He would have to come up with a plan.

Surely this was Houston. Even though some fields showed signs of coming crops, Johnny could tell that the city was growing outward and devouring the farm land. Uneasy about the heavy traffic flying past within a few yards, he left the pavement and walked in the grasses or along the edge of business parking lots. A large sign welcomed him to Sugar Land. He was disappointed that this was not yet Houston. But someone had told him to stop in Sugar Land ... Or had he imagined that, too?

A line of parked trucks soon came into view; Johnny was relieved that at least he had remembered the conversation about the truck stop accurately. That encounter in the diner had been real. The cowboy had advised him, too, to find a ride through the city.

"Headed home, soldier?" asked the man at the cash register as Johnny laid the maps on the counter. Johnny opened his mouth with the automatic response, "I'm not a soldier; I'm Amish." But some impulse changed his words.

"Well, actually, I'm on foot and trying to figure out a way through Houston without getting run over."

A big man with a bulging wad of tobacco in his right cheek waited patiently behind Johnny. Now he gave something like a snort and spoke.

"That's more dangerous than anything you saw in Nam."

Johnny turned to the man who was more than a head taller than he. Should he try to explain? *No, use it to your advantage.*

"How far the other side of Houston you goin'?"

"Anywhere, as long as it's north or east. I plan to end up in Ohio sometime."

"Well, buddy, I've got a load goin' down to Laredo. I'd be happy to give you a ride, but I'm goin' the wrong direction."

Laredo. That name struck a chord. The curtain pulled back just a bit further. Johnny felt as though he were about to enter a room; and somehow he knew that the room would be familiar and reassuring. He did not know how he knew this, but *he knew.*

"I recall a man—Bill ... Mac ... I'm not sure of his last name. He had some connection with a plow company."

"You know Big Bill McCollum? Sure, I haul loads in and out of there every month." With those words, the burly man and Johnny were kin. "Hey, Danny," the trucker yelled across the room. "Where you headed from here?"

At the counter, a gaunt young man with a long ponytail turned away from his plate of food to answer Johnny's new friend.

"I got a load of steel heading over to Alexandria. Got a small drop off in Livingston up on 59, then over through Jasper into Louisiana. Taking Route 28."

"You got room for my buddy here? Fresh out of Viet Nam and goin' home. He knows Big Bill down in Laredo."

"Any friend of Bill's is a friend of mine. Happy to have someone to talk to."

"There you go, buddy." The big man put a giant hand on Johnny's shoulder, and Johnny thought there were tears in the man's eyes. "And thank you for what you did over there."

Thank you?

The man turned away and began paying the cashier before Johnny could decide how to explain.

34

In another lifetime, before the accident and the bike ride, Johnny had never been at a loss for words. Now, seated high in the cab of the semi, he felt unsettled and awkward.

Danny, the young driver with the ponytail, seemed far too frail to be maneuvering such a big rig. His scrawny arms were like thin threads attached to the steering wheel, and his chest caved inward beneath his tee shirt. Johnny turned down the offered cigarette and focused his attention on the city as they rolled along in the steady stream of traffic on the interstate.

Their conversation started and stopped many times. Johnny did not want to talk. He did not care if he appeared rude or unfriendly. He was thinking about how different this place was from their valley at home; he felt like a foreigner here. The last few days of slow progress and Houston itself had now opened his eyes: he *was* a long, long way from home. And his body was not growing stronger. He had embarked on an impossible journey. His plan was foolish. Should he give up walking? Take a bus home? Part of him resisted that alternative; he knew he was not yet ready to be home, as much as he longed to be. But why not? Where else could he go? He did not belong anywhere else.

When Danny asked about his time in Viet Nam, Johnny had had enough.

"No!" he exploded. "I am not a soldier. I'm an Amish man, and we Amish would never think of joining the Army or going to war. Look at me! Do these clothes *look* like a soldier? Why must people jump to wrong conclusions?"

"Sorry, dude, I didn't know," answered Danny. Johnny's irritated outburst had not ruffled him. "It's just that you're carrying that bag, and I assumed it was yours. So you're Amish, huh? Have to admit, I did wonder about those clothes you're wearing. I don't know much about the Amish, even though I drive through some communities up in Missouri sometimes. I've heard you live without electricity. Is that true?"

For some reason, one question was all it took to open Johnny's well of homesickness. His anger died away as quickly as it had flared up, and he began to explain to Danny the Amish way of life; vivid and detailed descriptions of the home and family he had known came pouring out of him.

"Sounds like a good life," Danny said when Johnny paused. "If you don't mind my asking, why leave all that?"

"My wife died. Life didn't make much sense after that. I went to the west coast and started a bike ride across the country, wanting some time to think through everything and try to put the pieces of my life back into place. But I found out you can't do that when the most important piece is missing." He heard the bitterness in his own voice.

"I know where you're coming from, man," said Danny. His ponytail was bouncing in the wind from the open window. "My wife left me. Took my kid and disappeared. I got home one weekend and they were gone. She left a note. Said she didn't want to live this way anymore. But this truck driving, it's all I know. I don't know what else to do."

For the first time in a long while, Johnny felt the pain of someone other than himself.

"I'm so sorry," he said.

"Me, too. But I found out you can't go back. Can't put the pieces back together to fix that old picture. It's gone. All I can do is go forward."

Johnny stared out the window. He could hear his heart thudding and he felt as though someone were sitting on his chest. He remembered someone else saying those words. He was standing in a little garden cottage. Audrey, looking up at him, was saying almost the same words: "It's not possible, you know— putting things back together. You can't go back; you can only go forward." He remembered. He could hear her voice.

That reminded him, too, that he had not heard Annie's voice since he had come back to this life. Before his accident, he often heard his wife's voice in his head. He had known her so well that he knew exactly what she would have said in most situations. He had conversations with her voice. Now he searched his memory, trying to recall when she had last spoken to him. It had been at the gates of Heaven. He had not heard her since.

Danny broke their silence.

"So that's when you met Bill McCollum? On your bike ride?"

"I'm not sure. I can't recall. I had an accident; I was hit by a truck. And Bill was in my hospital room when I woke up. They tell me we had just met a few days before, but my recollection of those days is either fuzzy or completely gone. Sometimes I think I can almost reach out and grab a memory or two, but then it just evaporates and I lose it again."

"Well, Bill's pretty well known in these parts for that huge cross he put up down by Crystal City. He does love that cross. He'll talk about the cross every chance he gets, to anybody who will listen. Lots of folks have heard his story."

"Yes," Johnny said as the curtain pulled back further. "Yes! I do remember that! Bill told me the story of how the cross changed his life."

"Yup. That's what he claims. He likes to say the cross has the power to bring us from death to life. I ain't too religious, so I never quite figured out what he means, but that's what he likes to say."

Johnny saw the cross rising from the Texas countryside. He saw the battered old truck that Bill had been driving. He recalled sitting at a picnic table with the cross towering behind them and Bill telling his story, the story of almost drinking himself to death and the way the cross had saved his life. He recalled the feel of the sun on his body, the cross against his back as he sat at its base and basked in the words that had brought him hope: *Everyone who calls on the name of the Lord will be saved.* That was the day he had been certain of his hope.

He remembered that day.

35

When they pulled up to the docks of the busy plant in Alexandria, Johnny said goodbye to Danny with reluctance. For a few hours in that cab, with Danny smoking one cigarette after another while his ponytail flapped in the wind and the two of them talked, Johnny had felt safe and protected. Now he was pushing off again on his own, and he had no idea exactly where he was going or how to get there. They had crossed into Louisiana and he was finally out of Texas, but the unknown between him and home loomed formidable and even impassable.

He thanked Danny, and as he walked away the skinny young man called after him.

"Hey, where are you crossing the Mississippi River?"

"I suppose I'll cross that bridge when I get to it," answered Johnny, stopping and turning around.

"No, it's not that simple. There are only a few places to cross. You certainly can't swim; it's too dangerous. But you'll be at the river in a few days, and it would be smart to have a plan."

"What do you suggest?"

Danny took off his hat and scratched his head.

"I guess it depends on where you want to be once you've crossed. In Vidalia you can cross over to Natchez, Mississippi, or you could follow the river north to Vicksburg, or you could go all the way up to Greenville, Arkansas. Maybe Natchez would be your best bet. You can get on the Natchez Trace Parkway there, and that goes all the way up to Nashville, Tennessee. You'll have beautiful scenery. Commercial trucks are banned and the speed limit is lower, so it might be a safer route for walking. You'll find lots of campgrounds, too. Yeah, Natchez would be a good choice.

"And by the way, there's a motel about five miles up the road. Reasonable. And clean. I don't know if you can get there before dark, though. And if you ever need a place to sleep, find a cemetery." Danny grinned. "No one's going to disturb you there."

"Thanks for everything, Danny."

"Sure thing. Good luck, Johnny."

Danny had studied his own map and given Johnny a suggested route out of Alexandria. This city, although nowhere near the size of Houston, seemed just as threatening and foreboding. Johnny kept to side streets and residential areas, but he felt stifled by the traffic and buildings and parking lots. He did not belong here, and darkness was falling rapidly.

He had not walked at all that afternoon, but exhaustion set in as evening progressed and the town began to turn on its lights. Darkness gathered around him, and in the darkness lurked apprehension and grief and anger, all released anew and given more strength by his recounting of it to Danny. The nostalgic descriptions he had painted for Danny had intensified his longing for home and his old life.

He was so tired—tired of an aching body, tired of wandering, tired of being without Annie, tired of trying to hope that at the end of his journey he might find life bearable again. He wanted to drift away into sleep and forget about everything, but he was walking along a residential street and there was no motel or place to camp.

As he walked along the sidewalk, he caught glimpses of life within the homes. Families at the supper table or watching television. Children playing with a dog. One man on a stepstool changing a light bulb and a woman with a baby on her hip. He was a homeless man walking in the midst of all these homes lit within by life and love. And even if, by some miracle, he reached home, his house would be dark. His life and love were gone.

If only he could walk fast enough to escape all these dark thoughts. He reached into his pocket. One pill left. He had been able to resist swallowing it, thinking that he must save it for some future day when his pain was unbearable. For the last few days, his fear of being without any pain killers had been greater than his desire to escape mental and physical anguish. He wished he had saved many more of them. Tonight, of all nights, he wanted to dull every kind of pain assaulting him.

A small corner store threw welcoming light across the sidewalk. He stopped and peered through the window. The interior reminded him of the old general store at home in Milford, with shelves holding small quantities of many necessary items. With no specific plan, he walked in, propped his walking sticks against a wall, dropped his bag, and shuffled down the aisles while perusing the shelves and wondering what might ease the agony he felt. Aspirin would help his aching hip. He found cough syrup that listed codeine as an ingredient; he had heard that term in the hospital. He took one of those bottles off the shelf. He collected three cans of soup, three packages of cookies, two chocolate bars, and half a dozen apples.

With his arms full, he looked for a basket or some counter where he could set his purchases while he finished shopping. At the very back of the store, more memories broke loose. The six-packs of beer were old friends calling to him. He remembered this pain killer. He had used it on a temporary basis when he was a troubled youth, in his "wild" days before Annie. And beyond the beer he found an array of options that promised to be far more effective than aspirin or beer: vodka, whiskey, rum, gin. He had never used any of this type of liquor, but he had seen plenty of the bottles at drinking parties up at the quarry.

It's wrong, whispered one thought. *You don't do this anymore.*

It might work, whispered another. *And what difference does "right" or "wrong" make now?*

Johnny reached out one guilty hand and picked up a bottle of whiskey. He stood silent for a moment as his memory took him back to the tree house on the hill, his sanctuary as a youth. Then, beer had comforted him. Now he did not want comfort. Tonight he wanted oblivion. This might silence not only the pain but also the conscience. He took another bottle from the shelf.

The cashier never raised an eyebrow or gave a questioning look as he rang up Johnny's assorted purchases. Johnny stowed everything in his bag, picked up his walking sticks, and limped out into the darkness. The duffel was growing heavier every day.

In less than a mile, he stood outside a white fence surrounding a cemetery. Neat rows of stones gleamed in the moonlight. Well, this would have to do for the night. He had no idea how much further he would have to go to find the motel Danny had mentioned, and it was unlikely he would find a camping spot. As Danny had suggested, no one would disturb him here.

A paved driveway led down the middle of the cemetery, and Johnny was surprised to find that this was not a small family burial ground such as he knew at home. The rows of grave markers ran on and on, as far as he could see in the soft moonlight. He hobbled almost a quarter mile beyond the entrance until he was surrounded by the cemetery.

An impressive white stone mausoleum drew his attention. The building sat fifty yards back from the driveway, against a row of bushes. Two steps rose to a dark door framed by round columns.

This would provide a safe place to sleep. The bushes would screen him from view in the back of the cemetery, and the building itself would hide him from the driveway. He did not expect anyone to come along here in the morning, but if someone did, he would be out of sight.

A gravel pathway leading to the building lay a few yards ahead, but he ignored it and cut between the gravesites in a diagonal line, headed for the mausoleum. Surely no one else was here, but for some reason he felt as though he were trespassing. As his walking sticks felt the way through the darkness, his eyes darted to the left and right to be certain he was alone.

He almost fell when his left stick found nothing but air. Off balance, he twisted and jerked backward. At his feet lay a dark, gaping hole. Piles of ground on the opposite side of the hole told him that this grave had been recently dug.

He had almost fallen into the pit. The imagined sensation of falling brought another memory. He had lain in Annie's grave, looking up at a bright blue September sky.

Shaken, he felt his way carefully around the back of the mausoleum; very little moonlight reached the few square yards between the building and the bushes. Dropping his sticks and bag, he slumped against the wall and slid to the ground.

The stones still held the warmth of the sun. He had done this before, he knew. He had slept in another cemetery. That mausoleum had been brick. The red bricks had also held the sun's warmth, and he had slept well that night. Johnny wondered if that was the last night his mind and his body had been sound and if it was the last night he had slept in peace.

Supper was a pain pill swallowed with one gulp. The second gulp downed a few aspirin. Dessert was whiskey. The warmth spread throughout his body and pushed out all aches; numbness stole over his mind and pushed out all pain.

36

Car doors closing. Heavy feet marching along. A few words barked into the quiet morning.

The unexpected sounds finally cut through heavy sleep, and Johnny groaned as he rolled over. Aches in his hip and legs and ribs had diminished. Now the pain all centered in his head. He did not want to open his eyes; even a slight roll of his eyeballs under closed lids felt as though it might burst open his skull.

But even through closed lids he could tell that the sun was much higher in the sky than it should be. He had slept hours later than usual. He had never put up his tent, only covered himself with the orange and yellow blanket and huddled up against Wayne's duffel bag before sinking into unconsciousness.

Now here he was, caught.

Cars. People in the cemetery. Rhythmic footsteps that sounded like a parade. He would have to force his body up. Would have to get out of here before someone discovered his trespassing.

He managed to raise his body far enough to crawl on all fours to the corner of the building and peer around the edge.

A short distance away and up a slight rise, a small crowd had gathered around the open grave he had almost stumbled into the night before. Now a casket draped in a flag hung suspended above the waiting pit. A young woman in black stood before the casket, her head bent over a baby held in her arms, causing her long, shimmering blonde hair to fall forward like a curtain across her face. An older man and woman stood protectively on each side of her, and behind the trio, a small group of mourners waited in somber silence.

How could he have slept so long? He had meant to be up and gone before there was any chance of someone finding him here.

Off to one side, five uniformed soldiers stood straight and motionless, guns all perfectly outlined against the sky, gold buttons gleaming, and the whiteness of their hats and gloves so intensified by the high sun that Johnny had to look away. The brilliance hurt his eyes.

The young woman with the baby raised a pale, strained face to the casket. Johnny thought she must be even younger than Naomi.

He did not wish to be trapped here during this funeral. He was angry with himself. The flag, the gold braid, the rifles—all brought back images of Maureen's house and pictures he had seen there. Her voice came, too, sharp, spitting out the words in her frustration. *They're giving their lives so you can have your safe, peaceful life.* He did not want to be reminded of those words. He did not want to think about Dougie in a jungle prison. He did not want to recall the anguish and anger in Maureen's eyes when he refused to help her.

But how could she ask me to do something that would go against all I believe in?

Maureen had been unreasonable. Unreasonable and unfair and crazy, with her ridiculous insistence that God had planned for Johnny to help her. But she was not here for him to rail against. The only person here was God. And now it seemed as though even this scene, making him an unwilling witness to this funeral—this was all God's fault, too. Why was God subjecting him to all this? Why was he being reminded again of Dougie?

God, isn't it enough that you've taken away my wife and my health? You wouldn't let me into Heaven and sent me back here. Why are you tormenting me now? Why can't I just walk home and go back to my old life? Could you not give me at least that one comfort? I gave my life to you, but everything's going wrong. Why are you making it all so hard? Are you punishing me?

He wanted to vent his frustration, but once he had done that, he really did not want to think more about God or Heaven or Maureen now. He must get out of here, get moving, no matter how much agony he suffered with movement.

He had no camp to break, only roll up the blanket and stuff it into the duffel. Bracing himself against the brick wall, he straightened and hitched the bag over his shoulder. Grasping his two walking sticks, he turned away from the sight of death and flags and gleaming uniforms and started around the opposite corner of the building. The cars parked along the pathway would offer a partial screen for him to slip away unnoticed.

But he turned the corner and there was yet another crowd standing in his path.

On this side of the building, less than fifty yards away, another group had assembled. Almost a dozen young men stood in a row facing the funeral group above them on the slope. There was no mournful black in this group and no smart uniforms. Instead of guns outlined against the sky, angry black letters shouted from cardboard signs. And instead of respectful silence, Johnny heard a low undercurrent of muttering. They were talking, debating something among themselves.

He stopped. His first impulse had been to shrink back behind the building again.

Come on, Johnny. What's scaring you today? They haven't even noticed you. You're just minding your own business. Walk by them and go on your way.

What *was* wrong with him?

Starting forward again, he read some of the messages on the signs. END THE WAR NOW. LOVE NOT WAR. BRING THEM ALL HOME NOW. GET OUT OF VIET NAM. And one that made him hurt for the young woman with the baby: DEAD. WHY?

They stood at the edge of the paved pathway, and he would have to pass them. He could hear a bristling anger and resentment in their low conversation. But he was just a passerby, and no one had noticed him. He walked on the opposite side of the pavement.

As he passed the group, he glanced past the signs, up the slope one more time. Would Maureen one day be standing next to a casket covered by a red and white flag? But what could he do? Why did God put him back in this world, in a place he did not belong? He had no kinship to this world. If God was going to send him back to earth, why did He not at least send him back to their safe valley? Here, in these strange places, his life had no purpose or meaning.

In that one brief moment, as the red and white of the flag burned into him, he felt the simmering anger toward God begin to rise again. Then one of the sign-bearers turned and their eyes met. Anger stared hard at anger.

"Guys. Another one." The words were clipped, hostile.

The rest of the group turned to look at Johnny, and the one who had spoken took a few steps across the pavement.

Johnny continued walking, but the crowd of signs drifted toward him, edging closer, moving like an unstoppable tide that was going to wash over him. He kept walking.

Finally he stopped and faced them. He was not going to run. More irritation rose; why should they even bother him? He was only walking by, minding his own business. Fine, if they wanted a confrontation, he would not let them bully him. The pounding in his head was building.

The man who had first seen him seemed to be their leader. He was at the front of the pack, within three feet of Johnny, when he stopped and the wave behind him stopped.

Someone in the middle of the forest of signs hissed, "Baby killer." The man who seemed to lead the crowd stopped staring at Johnny ... and spit on him.

Johnny looked down at the wet stain on his chest. Then his arm swung in a swift, strong arc, and the mesquite stick cracked across the face that had spit on the shirt Annie had made.

The young man fell back, hands to his face, and blood dripping through his fingers. The forest of signs fell to the pavement as comrades reached to help their fallen.

Johnny's stick clattered to the ground, too. He had felt the impact of hard wood hitting bone, and the shock of that blow drained all his anger. He threw the stick away from his body. Stunned and shaken by his own action, he could do nothing more than watch as the youths helped their wounded leader back across the pavement, leaving signs scattered on the ground and casting anxious glances back toward Johnny.

The swinging mesquite had sliced into the group and broken its unity. Pandemonium ensued. The young men were arguing and some were shouting. He understood none of their words; he heard only a dim roar and felt the pounding that was about to break open his skull. His arm shook as his body remembered the feel of his walking stick meeting the young man's head.

Then, rising above the babble, a clear command rang out from the slope.

"Present arms!"

Gunshots split the morning.

Fear shot through Johnny. Before he even had a thought, he was crouched behind a tall gravestone. But as he cowered there, he realized the gunshots had come from the uniformed men on the hill. No one was shooting at him.

Melancholy notes from a single bugle drifted out over the cemetery as Johnny huddled behind the gravestone and tried to quiet his pounding heart. The guns were not firing at him. But he had struck someone. He had raised a weapon and, in anger and malice, he had smashed the face of another human being. *He had wanted to smash that face. And he had done it.*

His anger was gone, replaced by shock and remorse. He was, in fact, sick with remorse. How could he have done such a thing? His actions had been wrong. Wrong. Wrong.

He must make amends.

He still had Jim's walking stick in his hand. He clung to it as he struggled to stand, then looked around for his mesquite stick. It lay a few yards away. He had dropped the duffel, too. He hobbled over and picked up the stick, then started across the pavement. Signs lay forgotten, and the group still seemed to be arguing among themselves. The young man with the bloody face sat on the ground. Someone had given him a tee shirt to hold over his wounds and catch the flow of blood.

All that John and Mandy and the church had instilled in Johnny propelled him toward the group. He must ask forgiveness. He had been wrong. Something had been broken, and he must repair it.

But several of the young men saw him coming, with both sticks in hand, and they sounded the alarm at once.

"He's coming back!"

"He's crazy! Let's get outta here."

They all ran. None of them bothered to help their bloodied friend. In spite of his injuries, he sprang up and sprinted after the rest of the group.

Johnny, hobbling toward him, called out. "Wait! Please. I want to …"

"Stay away from me!"

Johnny watched them as they scattered and ran through the rows of grave markers, leaving behind the signs lying on the driveway.

He knew there would be no mending of the broken.

What was done was done.

37

So this was the Mississippi. Johnny stood on a small bluff overlooking the wide expanse of water. Danny had been right. He would not be able to swim across. But it did not matter now.

In the fading light, the river was a living thing, moving and changing, oblivious to any other force because it knew it held more power within itself than anything along its shores. If it would choose to break loose, even the embankments and levees could not hold it back.

Johnny eased himself down on a stump and stared at the dark water. It was dusk of the second day after he had smashed the face that had spit on Annie's shirt.

So this is the Mississippi.

That was his only thought. Lights were coming on down along the shoreline to his left and to his right. Straight ahead, he saw only deep darkness. The stench of the river was like nothing he had ever smelled before. If he had tried to sort out the components of the rank odor, he might have detected hints of fish, diesel fuel, sewage, mud, grasses, and chemicals.

Johnny was not thinking about the smell. He had not bothered to build a fire or put up his tent. His bag lay on the ground beside him. He stared at the water and thought only, *So this is the Mississippi.*

He had seen nothing of his surroundings the last two days. The first day, he walked in fear, often looking around to see if he was being pursued. Would the assault be reported? Would the police be looking for him? After a few hours, he shrugged off the fear. If he was arrested or if the man he had attacked decided to hunt him down and retaliate, well, so be it. He deserved punishment for what he had done.

For two days he had plodded along, watching only the tips of the walking sticks meeting the ground and the toes of his Red Wings as one foot stepped ahead of the other. He saw a flashlight lying in the grass by the roadside, but he never paused. The cotton fields, so different from his corn and wheat fields at home, did not entice him to stop and study. Friendly folk sometimes called out a hello, and he did not look up or reply. He turned down offers of rides. As he walked through one small town, a boy who could not have been more than seven looked at him curiously and said, "Mister, you look awful weary. Shall I get you a glass of tea?" Johnny shook his head and walked on. And as he napped in the noonday sun, a Monarch butterfly had rested on his mesquite walking stick. Annie had loved Monarchs, and usually every appearance caused Johnny to reminisce. But that day, awaking, Johnny had simply brushed off the annoying insect and picked up the stick to struggle onward.

He bought more pain killer in a bottle and ingested many more doses at frequent intervals. He had not eaten that day. What was the point of eating?

Once, he had lost his balance and rolled down an embankment. He lay on the ground, with no desire to move. Immediately a car stopped on the shoulder above him and a woman appeared at the top of the bank.

"Are you all right, sir? Shall I call for help?"

His anger flared up, irritation that she would disturb his resting for a moment.

"No! I'm fine!"

He struggled to his knees, looking for his walking sticks.

"Here," she said, gently sliding his mesquite stick down the slope. "Are you sure you don't need help?"

"Leave me alone!" he snarled. She hesitated a moment, then disappeared, and he heard the car drive away.

He had no recollection of how he had finally arrived at the river. He thought perhaps he had asked directions once or twice, but he might have imagined those encounters. He did not recall the names of towns he had been through or even where he had slept the night before. He could not remember.

But here he was. Staring at the Mississippi River. And thinking about Maureen's husband. He had thought about Wayne often as he walked the last two days. He was beginning to understand Wayne.

He saw how darkness could overtake a person and make life hopeless. He imagined Wayne, sitting in his wheelchair, enveloped in the same darkness through which Johnny now walked. He had a visual image of Wayne from photographs at Maureen's house, and the more he thought about Wayne, the more he felt he knew the man as one knows a friend.

He imagined a few conversations with Wayne. Johnny had spent the last two days with the same thoughts playing over and over in his head, and when he had tired of swirling in that maelstrom alone, he had talked to Wayne because Wayne would understand.

This plan to walk home was ridiculous. Useless. Stupid. He was torturing himself—and for what? For nothing. He did not know if he could ever farm again. How could he walk behind a plow, pitch hay, or clean out stalls? There was *nothing* to walk home to or for. Why had he imagined he would find answers there?

Why would he want to go back to the farm, anyway? His mind kept calling up the warm family scenes he had glimpsed in lighted windows of homes as he walked through the dark streets of Alexandria. There would be no such scenes in his house. The light was gone. All that anyone walking by his house would see would be a man eating supper alone, trapped in a battered body.

His family would try to help. They would say they were happy he was home and assure him they loved him. But they all had their own lives. Naomi and Paul were looking forward to a happy future. They would soon be married and starting their new life together. Mandy and John had each other. His brother and older sisters all had their own families. In the midst of his family, he would be alone.

Just as he was alone now. They were all going on with their lives back home, oblivious to what he was going through out here. Come to think of it, if they knew the things he had done they would probably be ashamed to acknowledge him as their own. He had dishonored the good name built by generations of Millers.

The church would certainly not want him back. He had also dishonored the name *Amish* by violating one of their strongest and most cherished teachings. He had smashed the face of another human being. And he had *wanted* to smash that face.

He was beginning to see who he really was. Even in his drunken and depressed haze, one part of him had been shocked by the ugliness of his voice when he shouted at the woman who had wanted only to be kind and helpful that day he fell. Mandy had always claimed that her Miller men made good choices. He was not a son worthy of such a claim. Instead, he was a man too weak to deal with pain without drugs or alcohol. He was a man who could not control his anger. He was a man whose body would not work and whose mind was unreliable. He was a man who *wanted* to smash another person's face.

How could he go back to the life he had known? There in that peaceful valley, all of life was centered on family and church. He could never pretend; he knew now what he was: he was a fraud and he was worthless. Worthless to his family, his church, and himself. And surely, worthless to God. That was why he was not in Heaven with Annie but here, staring into these dark, sinister waters.

He understood Wayne. He understood how Wayne's life must have been overwhelmed by despair even darker and deeper than this river. Wayne had escaped the hopelessness and despair. Maureen had never said how Wayne had escaped; and Johnny had thought, one time when a semi roared past him and the wind of its passing almost knocked him over, that if he just stepped out into the highway at the right time …

Would it be wrong? Would he be buying a ticket to hell? Maybe. Or maybe Annie could plead for him. She might still be able to get him into Heaven. But if God would not have him, then what did it matter if this was wrong?

Did anything at all *matter*? This walk was hopeless. He was walking home to nothing. He was nothing. He knew what he was, and he could never make himself good enough for God. Jim had told him he had a second chance at life, but this second round had proven beyond a doubt what he was—and what he was not. Here he was, drunk, with the blood of another man on his walking stick. He was a worse person now than he had ever been before.

The last faint threads of daylight melted away in the western sky. The darkness grew stronger, coiling around him and squeezing any lingering rays of light from his mind. Soon all would be black, he thought. He would suffocate.

He understood why Wayne had escaped.

He sprang up with arms thrown upward, fists hard, and screamed at Heaven.

"Why didn't You let me die? God? Do You hear me? I don't want to live!"

38

"God, I want to live!"

The echo came back to Johnny from across the water.

No. That was not an echo. It was a call from out there somewhere in the middle of the dark, ominous waters.

Johnny leaned forward, straining to see through the darkness. Alarm clutched his throat when he saw a human form bobbing along in the current. One long thin arm raised up as though reaching to Heaven for help as the white head disappeared under the murky water, only to reappear again in seconds. The man was trying to swim toward shore but the current was too strong and was rapidly pulling him past where Johnny stood.

Before he thought, Johnny pulled off his shoes and shirt and plunged into the river. The slap of water against his body came as a shock, and as he swam away from the shore, the strong current caught him like a monstrous hand grabbing his body.

Only then did he have a thought, and that thought was *What am I doing? I can't swim this river.* He had spent many evenings in the pond up at the quarry, but he had never tested his strength against the power and dominion of such vast waters as these. He had been foolish. He and that man out there would both die.

Of course you will die if you fight the forces of nature. Don't fight it, outsmart it.

He knew the voice in his head. The words were from Wandering Willie, the wanderer he had met on a beach while he was on his bike ride along the California coast. Willie had told Johnny it was useless to fight rip tides. *Stay calm, use your head, look for the weak outer edges of the current.* Johnny had no idea if there were rip tides in a river as huge as the Mississippi, but he knew he must stay calm.

Strength pulsed through his body, and he was soon alongside the drowning man.

The man's frantic eyes peered out from between matted clumps of long white hair clinging to a gaunt face and neck. He saw Johnny coming and clutched at him, pulling him underwater for a moment. Johnny broke loose from the bony fingers grabbing at his shoulders. *Use the current, don't fight it. Otherwise, you'll both die.*

"Stop fighting!" Johnny shouted, grabbing the man's arms. "Let me help you! Fight me, and we'll both die."

For just a moment, Johnny felt the tension in the man's arms, then something like resignation swept through him. He went limp.

Johnny grabbed him under the arms. The thin body felt like a bag of bones, but there was no more resistance. Whether the man had lost consciousness or was fully trusting his rescuer, Johnny did not know. They floated with the rapidly moving current, and Johnny looked around, desperate for some clue on how to reach the river bank. The weight he pulled along at his side soon drained away that surge of strength he had felt. He swallowed a few mouthfuls of water, and his lungs felt as though the river were rushing into them, forcing out all air.

How foolish he had been! In the expanse of dark water, they were pushed about like two pieces of straw, small and helpless. Here and there on the riverbank, far ahead, Johnny could see small spheres of light. But no one would ever hear a call for help, and Johnny wasn't sure they could even stay afloat long enough to reach the lights. They would both drown. His family would never know what had happened to him.

"God! Help us!" he cried out.

The dark waters caught them and pulled them into a dizzying, swirling eddy. Johnny pushed down the urge to fight his way out of the turbulence. He concentrated on keeping his hold on the limp body. Then, abruptly, the river spit them out, and they were drifting in peaceful, shallow water within a few yards of the bank.

Johnny's feet found muddy ground, and he stopped swimming and began to plod through the mud and water. The stranger was still floating behind him and Johnny wondered if he could be dead. Gasping for breath and with trembling knees that threatened to buckle under him, he dragged the man up a short bank, dropped him on his stomach in the tall grasses, and fell beside the still form.

The man lay quietly, the thick, wet, white hair hiding his face. Johnny had no idea what to do. He did not know how to revive a drowning victim. He stared at the man, looking for movement or a sign of breathing. Reaching out a hand, he lifted one shoulder to turn the body over.

"Are you dead?" he asked.

"No. Not quite," came the reply.

39

The stranger crouched close to the fire, clutching the yellow and orange blanket tightly around his shoulders. Johnny could see the thin body shivering, even under the blanket. He himself felt no cold, even though he was drenched. After they had both rested on the bank of the river, he had helped the stranger up and half-carried him back to the campsite. He had built a fire in the small clearing between the river and a stand of trees, and then he began scouring the surrounding area for more dry branches. The bedraggled stranger said nothing. He sat quietly staring into the flames and trying to soak up the heat.

Johnny gave little thought to the man's silence. Instead, his mind was busy recalling the words that had come to him as suddenly as the slap of cold water when he dived into the river. Wandering Willie had talked with him about his grief and about finding the way home. He had given Johnny three pieces of advice: Don't fight the rips. Lighten your load. Dig deeper.

Johnny remembered meeting Willie on the Pacific shore. He remembered their conversation. He remembered giving one of Samuel Cohraine's twenty dollar bills to Willie, who had passed it on to Lizzie, the homeless woman. He remembered that Willie had a blanket just like the one Johnny carried. The practicality of Willie's blanket had prompted Johnny to buy one of his own from Sydney and Lisa and those two lived on a communal farm where Johnny had taught them to milk goats and rig up a system to bring water from the hills, and Sydney designed clothes, and he was making Johnny BarnDoor pants …

He was remembering it all.

His mind pounded from one memory to the next, running here and there in excitement and triumph. He remembered.

He had gathered wood automatically as his mind traveled again through California, Arizona, New Mexico, and Texas; he had started a fire and wrapped his blanket around the bony body while his thoughts rekindled friendship with Willie and Samuel and Audrey and Sydney and Lisa and Big Bill. A dam had broken, and memories of the last few months came gushing forth.

Then he forced his thoughts back to caring for his guest.

With a large pile of branches stacked next to the fire, Johnny used one stick to nudge a can of soup from the flames. He dug in his duffel bag and pulled out one wool sock he had found along the road. Wrapping the sock around the can, he passed the hot soup to the stranger.

"I'm John Miller," he began, breaking the silence.

The stranger took a tentative sip of the soup and finally spoke.

"I thank you, John Miller." His voice was surprisingly deep and firm. For some reason, Johnny thought, the voice did not fit the emaciated body. He had expected a thin, weak voice from that scrawny chest. "You were sent by God tonight, John."

"I just happened to be here at the right time," replied Johnny.

One of the silver eyebrows went up.

"Ah, my friend, there is no such thing as coincidence. God has His purposes in everything."

Johnny poked at the fire with the stick he was holding.

"I was taught that. Heard it preached all my life. But lately,

I've found it difficult to believe."

"Difficult to believe in God? Or difficult to believe in His purpose and sovereignty?"

Johnny used the stick to roll one log over, and sparks burst upward. He was not certain he wanted to think too deeply about the answer to that question. He admitted to being a little afraid of the answer.

"Everything that's happened to me in the past year … if God really is sovereign … I don't understand why He would allow all those things to happen."

The stranger took a sip of his soup without looking at Johnny. His eyes were on the fire when he asked,

"If you don't mind my curiosity, what has happened?"

Johnny did not mind at all. He was a naturally gregarious person, and he had spent weeks now without speaking freely and honestly with another person. And this stranger did not know him or his family or his background. He would probably never see the man again. It would feel good to talk.

"I had everything a man could want—even more," he began, poking the stick among the glowing logs. "Then my wife died suddenly and unexpectedly—there was an accident on our farm— and I had nothing. When I lost her, it seemed that I lost my whole life. And I did not know how to get it back, how to put it back together again. I guess I didn't want to put it back together. There was no point in anything I did.

"So I embarked on a journey. I thought if I took time away from the farm and the home we had shared that I could sort out everything and decide what I was going to do without her. So I took a long bus ride to the West Coast and started a bike ride across the country. I'm not sure what I was looking for … answers, maybe. An understanding of who I was without my wife. And hope. Hope that I could go on living, that there was something to live for. That life would be worth living.

"Then a few months ago in Texas I was hit by a truck. They say I died," Johnny hesitated. Should he tell the stranger about seeing Annie at Heaven's gates? "They revived me, and I lived.

"This life, though, is even worse. I've spent weeks in the hospital and still can't ..."

He paused.

"Can't what?" A small smile moved the corners of the stranger's mouth.

"Uh ... I was going to say that I can't move without pain. That I'm a cripple. And that my mind doesn't work like it once did ... but ..."

The stranger waited, watching Johnny. Johnny looked up at him with astonishment on his face.

"But I just realized that I've been working around camp here and I'm feeling no pain at all. None! And I am remembering everything I thought I had forgotten. I ... I'm not sure what's happened. I could not remember ... I knew months had passed, but I had no memories of anything from that time. My life had all these blank pages. Now, all of a sudden, those pages are filled with stories." Johnny's mouth hung open in wonder at the things he heard himself saying.

"How can that be?" he asked.

The blanket was still draped over the stranger's head, but Johnny could see him shrug his shoulders as he smiled and raised one silver eyebrow. He only repeated Johnny's question.

"How can it be, my friend?"

Silence hung between them, and Johnny almost forgot he had a guest as he poked the fire and pondered the miracle. Could it be true? Could he have been healed instantaneously?

The man's thin body shuddered with a coughing fit. Johnny jumped up and began to set up the tent as a small protection for the stranger. Then the thrill of new strength surged through his legs, and he thought triumphantly, *I'm up! Without any help!*

40

As Johnny worked at the tent, the stranger drew a knife from his pocket and wiped it dry on the edges of the blanket. Without getting up, he reached over and picked through the pile of branches Johnny had collected for the fire, chose one about twelve inches long, and began whittling. Within minutes, the shape of a slender canoe emerged from the stick.

While he shaved and carved and sculpted, the stranger began humming quietly. As the canoe emerged, so did the music, and before long the humming gave way to a strong bass voice that carried over the dark waters, singing the words of a hymn Johnny recognized. He had heard the song many times, but out here, far removed from any church service, the words came afresh to his ears. He stopped his work and listened. He was no longer in familiar settings where he had grown up, no longer with the people who had defined his life. Here, the words drifted up like the smoke of the fire and came to rest in his soul. Even the stranger seemed to melt away into the darkness on the other side of the flames.

"When I survey the wondrous cross
On which the Prince of glory died,

My richest gain I count but loss,
And pour contempt on all my pride. "

My richest gain was Annie, Johnny thought. Annie had brought him life. When he lost Annie, he had lost life. What did the cross have to do with that terrible loss?

"Forbid it, Lord, that I should boast,
Save in the death of Christ my God!
All the vain things that charm me most,
I sacrifice them to His blood. "

A sacrifice? The things he had held most dear—the person he had held most dear—would God require him to sacrifice Annie? How could God ask such a sacrifice?

"See, from His head, His hands, His feet,
Sorrow and love flow mingled down!
Did e'er such love and sorrow meet,
Or thorns compose so rich a crown? "

He remembered feeling the blood flow down. As he sat at the foot of the cross that Big Bill had built, he had felt the love of Christ as the Savior's blood flowed down and cleansed him. That day he had been certain of God's love for him, and he had been reluctant to leave the cross. He understood why Bill loved it so.

"Were the whole realm of nature mine,
That were a present far too small;
Love so amazing, so divine,
Demands my soul, my life, my all. "

Annie had been his soul, his life, his all. Now she was gone.

Did God take her from him? The song ended, the strong voice fell silent, and the silence felt empty.

"Do you know the song that begins, *'I must needs go home by the way of the cross'*?" Johnny asked.

"I believe I do," said the stranger with a smile as he set the carved canoe on the ground. "I've led that a time or two in church services." And he launched into the hymn.

> *"I must needs go home by the way of the cross,*
> *there's no other way but this;*
> *I shall ne'er get sight of the gates of light,*
> *if the way of the cross I miss."*

Johnny found himself humming along. When the song was ended, the stranger asked, "Is that a favorite of yours?"

"Your song about the cross reminded me of this one—I was singing it the day of my accident."

"The way of the cross. It is the only way to get home, John," said River Man. The stranger had never offered a name, and Johnny had begun to think of him only as River Man.

"At one time, I thought the cross stood for salvation and Jesus paying for my sins," said Johnny. "But I met a man on my bike ride—they called him Big Bill—who showed me that the cross also means hope for a new life."

"That it does," said River Man, nodding. "The cross and the empty tomb. Christ died, then came out of the tomb, resurrected to a new life. And anyone who believes in Him dies to the old life and is given a new life. Like a kernel of wheat that is planted and dies so that it can produce brand new life. That's part of 'the way of the cross'—dying to the old and walking into the new."

"That's exactly what my wife believed with all her heart!" Johnny's face lit up as he talked. "The Monarch was one of her favorite creatures; she was fascinated by the transformation of a worm into such a beautiful butterfly. She loved to talk about Christ doing that for us—changing us from worms into things of beauty."

The stranger smiled. "Yes, Annie loved Jesus very much, didn't she?"

"She owed Him her life. But then, God took her life. I don't understand …" Johnny shook his head. "And now she's with God and I'm left here … alone."

The silver eyebrow went up again.

"John, you are also with God. That's another thing the cross did for us. God came to us on earth, and what Jesus did on the cross ripped away all barriers between God and us, and now it's possible for us to live in the very presence of Almighty God. That's the whole reason for Christ's coming. He's right here now, with you. And you are as much with God as your wife is. He is holding both of you very close to Him. Annie is further along on the journey than you are—she's just a little ahead of you."

Johnny was silent. He was thinking about walking hand in hand with Annie toward the gates of Heaven. She had said the rest of the family would be coming soon, too.

I was there, with Annie. We were side by side on the journey. But I was forced to turn back.

"Are you a preacher?" he asked the stranger.

"No, my friend. But I enjoy bringing good news to people."

River Man reached over and picked up Jim's walking stick that had been lying beside the rough mesquite stick, both unused, on one side of the fire. The fingers that had coaxed the canoe from an ordinary branch now ran over the carvings on Jim's stick, the large eyes of the owl and the delicate feathers, the peak of the mountain and the date below it. His finger followed the curves of *David, Robert, James;* he paused at *Shiloh,* and then he felt the end that had pounded the ground for many miles.

"This was once someone's companion and treasure," he said reverently. The carvings had meant nothing to Johnny, but they must have had meaning for River Man.

"A patient at the hospital gave it to me. He said it had belonged to his grandfather."

"Carvings like this tell us stories. These were all done by the same person, but at different times of his life. I'm sure you've heard of totem poles? Those were carved to remind families or entire communities of their history and their stories. I wonder what this mountain represents. And who or what Shiloh was," River Man mused.

"I thought totem poles were … well, like idols or … part of witchcraft," said Johnny.

"No, they're works of art, a reflection of a people. Just as paintings and sculptures and even written words on a page tell stories, a totem pole will tell you something about both the creator and his or his community's past." The stranger was still thoughtfully running his hands over the carvings. Then he laid the stick down on the ground and picked up Johnny's rough mesquite stick. "And this one?"

Johnny grinned. "Well, that one should tell you the story that I was desperate for help in walking and I didn't have a sharp knife."

"You chose an extremely hard wood. This would take an exceptional knife to carve. Let's see if we can smooth it out a bit." His knife took a few quick cuts, and some of the burls that had been irritating Johnny's hand slipped away.

"What would you carve on your walking stick, John?" River Man asked as he worked.

Johnny thought about all the places his journey had taken him. If someday his grandson looked at this stick, what images would remind him of grandfather's stories?

"I'd have to think about that. We Amish don't create pictures or sculptures."

"Ah, but you do create other beautiful things, don't you? Creations that reflect the craftsman?"

"Yes, but …" Johnny was at a loss to explain how building furniture or piecing lovely quilts might differ from carving a story into wood.

"Everyone leaves behind something of their own story," said River Man. Johnny noticed that strips of bark were flying as the knife met the mesquite. "It's worth thinking about. Decide what it is of yourself you want to leave with those who have known you."

Johnny had to admit that up until now he had given very little thought to anything he might give to the world. His life had been pretty much focused on what he was receiving from the world.

Some of the words River Man had sung came back to him. The songwriter spoke of God's amazing love and the Prince of Glory dying for him. That love and sacrifice instilled so much gratitude and a love so large that the writer vowed he would hold back nothing, nothing, in this world from the Savior.

Johnny had felt the love of the God as he sat at the foot of the cross Big Bill had built. He had been certain of God's love that day, but he had wandered a long way from the path home. He wondered how one could love the Savior so much that everything else in this world took second place. At the same time that he questioned, he also felt a fierce longing—a longing to love that much himself, and a longing to know that He was held in the hands of a God who loved him.

The stranger was still cutting at the hard wood. With his eyes on his knife as it met the walking stick, River Man asked, "John, do you love Annie more than you love Jesus?"

This startled Johnny. Had he been saying aloud what he was thinking? He did not think so. How had the man known the questions and longing that were echoing through his head and soul? And it suddenly occurred to him that this was the third time River Man had used Annie's name. Johnny was certain he had never spoken her name to this stranger.

"Who are you?"

River Man smiled.

"I am a man with a new life, John," he said with a twinkle in his eye. "You gave that to me tonight when you pulled me from the river. You are a man with a new life, too.

"My name? I haven't yet decided. Names are important, don't you think? A name says something about who you are. And I'm not certain yet what my name will be in this new life."

Leaning heavily on the mesquite stick, River Man pulled himself upright, slowly unfolding his long length. He stood for a few seconds, as though his body was trying to remember how to stand. With one hand he pulled the orange and yellow blanket from his shoulders and handed it to Johnny.

"I think I am dried out. Thank you for this comfort."

Johnny had no reply. He had never had such a puzzling conversation. Taking the blanket, he wrapped it around his own shoulders, wondering about River Man's enigmatic statements.

The stranger let the mesquite stick drop gently in the grass, turned away from the fire, and hobbled crookedly away from the circle of light.

Johnny jumped to his feet. "Wait!"

The dark form crowned with silver did not speak a word or turn around, but melted silently into the shadows of the trees.

41

The steady throb of a motor awakened Johnny even before the first chirp of the earliest bird the next morning. He opened his eyes to see a small aluminum boat skimming over the water, cutting through the gray ribbons of rising mist. Above the far riverbank, a faint pink lit the sky. Watching as purples and blues deepened above the pink, he thought that surely *sunrise* was one of God's loveliest ideas.

Indeed, the whole world was quite lovely this morning.

The pup tent stood empty. He had erected it last night thinking it would shelter the wet and shivering stranger. But the stranger had limped into the night and had not returned. Johnny, with mind reeling from the astonishing conversation by the fire, had simply pulled his blanket more tightly around his shoulders and laid back on a patch of soft grass. Watching the night sky for a long time, he felt his very small presence in the universe and the very large presence of an almighty God. Eventually, with an unshakable conviction that his God kept watch over him, he had drifted off to a deep and refreshing sleep.

He was in no hurry to be off this morning; he wanted to soak up as much of the surrounding beauty as he could and carry it with him throughout the day. The sun rose above the eastern horizon and a pathway of glittering light rippled across the river.

He marveled at how *good* his bones and muscles felt. He rolled over in one direction, then back again. He stretched his legs and flexed his feet. He sat up and leaned forward to touch his toes. Yes, the pain was gone.

Was that possible? Could a miracle somehow have occurred? He had come to the river last night feeling suffocated by the ever-present pain. Now he rolled over on the hard ground and felt not one ache. River Man had talked of Christ giving new life, and Johnny understood he had been speaking of spiritual life. Was the giving of a new life something as miraculous as this healing of a broken body and bestowing of new hope?

He finally rose, stretched again, and went about the business of breaking camp. Every movement was slow and savored. What he had always taken for granted was now a gift, and he relished the thought of moving ahead and conquering the challenge of whatever distance or obstacle was still between him and home. The road could be mountains or valleys, rivers or plains, two hundred miles or two thousand miles—it did not matter. He could do it.

He took down the tent and packed it up, along with the blanket, the sock, and the soup can. He would find a trash can somewhere to dispose of the soup can. But when he picked up the half-empty bottle of vodka, he knew he could not put it back into his bag. Turning it upside down, he watched the liquid run down into the grasses and then drew back his arm and fired the bottle across the water. A small, distant splash gave him immense satisfaction.

The walking sticks lay in the grass where River Man had placed them the night before. Both would still be helpful in his walk, but they were no longer artificial limbs—now they were only walking sticks.

River Man's knife had transformed the rough mesquite staff.

Stripped bare of bark, the striking grain of the wood was apparent. Even before he stooped to lift the stick from the grass, Johnny saw its beauty and was thinking about the finishes on the shelves of his shop at home; he would find just the right one to deepen and enhance the reddish hues of the wood.

Picking up the stick and running his hand over the smooth length, he turned it and saw that River Man had not only stripped the bark, he had then carved something into the mesquite. Where before there had been only rough edges and irritating bumps, the bare, beautiful wood now displayed the graceful shape of a cross. At the base of the cross lay a sheaf of wheat. In careful and minute detail, River Man's knife had captured the long, flowing lines of the stalks and the heavy fullness of each ripe head. The detail was so exquisite that Johnny could almost feel the weight of the grain in his hand, remembering moments he had stood in his own wheat fields checking the coming harvest. Looking more closely, he saw the outline of a butterfly resting at the bottom of the sheaf.

Johnny could not have put into words what he felt, but the carving resonated deep in his soul. This was his story, even though he could not yet say why or how he recognized it. He had the sensation that River Man knew him well—and perhaps knew his story even better than Johnny himself did.

He gripped the mesquite staff, raised it at arm's length above his head, and said firmly, "I am going home."

42

Highway 65 had seemed like an easy route north, but Johnny soon surrendered to the lure of the Mississippi River and the varied and unpredictable traffic on its waters. He wanted to see as much of the river as he could, and 65 veered off away from the water scenes. Stopping at a gas station, he bought maps of both Louisiana and Mississippi. It might take a few more days, but he would seek out secondary roads where he could get to know the river better.

The land was flat, and the sky was wide, and Louisiana was bursting with all shades of green. The farmer in Johnny noted the rich dark soil and recognized many of the same crops he grew in Ohio: wheat, oats, and corn. Creamy white and pink leaves framed blossoms on endless rows of dark green plants. His curiosity finally prompted him to stop and ask what this crop was; cotton, the farmer told him. In a few days, the bolls would emerge. That was a sight Johnny would have liked to see, but he could not wait.

Farming life he knew, but the life built around the river was foreign and intriguing. Sometimes his road was so distant from the river that the Mississippi was only a silver ribbon beyond the flat fields. Other times, he walked for miles with trees on either side of him; he could smell and hear the river, but he could not see it.

He heard the traffic on the river, too. At those times when he walked in full view of the waterway, he sometimes sat and watched the various crafts as they went by. And because river life was so unfamiliar to him, he found that many times he could only guess at the purpose of a boat. He marveled at the loads of grain, coal, and steel carried by the barges, daydreamed about floating down the river on a houseboat, and waved at several brave folks in canoes. Once he watched an old-fashioned steamboat cruise down the river, and the scene was so nostalgic that he almost expected to see Tom Sawyer or Huck Finn come floating along on a raft.

He also quickly learned that choosing secondary routes meant he would bypass the larger towns and much of the traffic. Most of what he walked through was farmland to his west and trees and river to his right. This also meant that he needed to plan his supplies carefully. He was never sure when or where he would find a grocery to replenish his food supply.

Camping spots, though, were easily found either in the heavily treed areas or on the shores of a lake. As he studied his map, he saw a great number of strangely-shaped lakes—their blue space on the map curled away from the Mississippi and curved like loops of ribbon laid out on the page. At the marina on one of these lakes, Johnny questioned the clerk about the odd configuration.

"These lakes are oxbow lakes, sir," said the young man as he rang up Johnny's snack purchase. "We've got a lot of 'em here along the River."

"Oxbow lakes? I've never heard of them. What are they?"

"At one time they were part of the Mississippi, curves in its natural course. Over time, for one reason or another, the river cut a new, straighter channel, and these curves were no longer part of the river but became lakes."

The lakes drew Johnny even more than the river. Their natural beauty, with clean water, acres of forests, and sometimes unusual birds and wildlife, seemed oases of peace promising reprieve from the hot pavement warming his shoes and the summer sun baking his shoulders and back. He missed his summer straw hat; it would have been so much cooler than the black hat his family had sent to the hospital. He'd seen caps and hats for sale at the small stores and gas stations, but he was reluctant to give up the hat that spoke of his life at home.

At noon on the day he entered Arkansas, he rested on a bank by a small pond and ate a sandwich. A long-legged water bird hunted for its own lunch in the shallow water, and Johnny wished for the bird book on his shelf at home. He had seen many interesting birds in the last few days, but had been unable to identify them.

When the bird flew off, he removed his shoes and socks and waded into the shallow water. The cool water over his feet and ankles was so refreshing that he took a quick look around and wondered if this place was private enough that he could strip down and take a swim. Then he saw the alligator lying in tall grasses and watching him with beady eyes. Johnny kept his eyes on the alligator, too, as he hurriedly put on his shoes and gathered up his bag and walking sticks.

This was the first gator he had seen. He was reminded that he knew little about the wildlife in this part of the country. He began to choose his camping spots more carefully, looking for places that seemed unlikely to be visited by evil-looking creatures. Then again, what did a farmer from Ohio know about the nocturnal habits of gators?

***

The night he camped in Lake Chicot State Park, deer grazed unafraid in the campground. He had decided to take a short detour to camp in this park partly because of the sheer beauty of the lake and partly because he hoped that, with a greater human presence here, there would be less chance of a nightly visit from gator.

His tent went up on a site surrounded by tall trees that were unfamiliar to him. The gentleman cooking supper on a Coleman stove in the next site told him that these were pecan trees.

Johnny sat on a wooden deck at the edge of the lake and watched the sun set. He reflected on all he had learned in the last few days. This was a different world than his farming valley in Ohio. Walking through it was like reading through the pages of a book, each mile bringing some new thought or experience.

He thought how different these days had been from his drunken stumbling between Alexandria and his first view of the Mississippi on that dark night when he had come so close to dying in the river. He remembered little of those days walking in darkness, but what memories he did have were all in black and gray. There was no light at all in those images. Now, his days were vibrant with color and brimming with life. He woke each morning eager to see what encounters the day would bring. Every evening, he was satisfied that he was closer to home.

What had changed? His body, of course. Every day, he felt a sense of awe at the strength coming back into his body and he rejoiced at the absence of the old pain. He had been given the gift of a miracle, he was certain of it. Every day, he thanked God.

The encounter with River Man puzzled him. He did not know who the man was, how he had come to be drowning in the river, or why he had disappeared into the night when the sensible thing would have been to rest by Johnny's fire. Johnny could still hear the rich voice singing about the cross. They had talked of the way of the cross and of Jesus bringing new life and healing. Strange. Johnny had experienced healing that night, but apparently River Man had never been given the same miracle. Johnny remembered how painfully he had limped away from the fire into the darkness.

His eyes were on the sunset, but his thumb traced the carving on his mesquite staff. The cross. The sheaf of wheat. The butterfly. What meaning had River Man cut into that piece of wood and left for Johnny to ponder? The butterfly reminded him of Annie, and River Man had spoken of her and known her name.

Johnny did not want to dig deeper into the things the stranger had said about Annie. He had chosen to keep those gates closed. He was not yet ready to open up the walls of his fortress. For now, he would rather focus on the unexpected joy of being alive and seeing all these new things.

The next day, he would cross the Mississippi River. The truck driver Danny had been right. One did not find many bridges across this mighty river. He would cross at Lake Village, over to Greenville, Mississippi. The next bridge would be another four or five days' walk north, and Johnny was more than ready to turn eastward. Although either route would move him toward home, somehow the words *turning east* felt as though he would be making more progress than *walking north* for another week.

43

Johnny had walked for a week along the mighty river, yet he was still unprepared for the sight of the Benjamin G. Humphreys Bridge. Its lacy steel rose high against the sky in a scalloped pattern. Huge cement piers supported the span, and yet it looked frail and delicate as it soared through space. The approach to the bridge rose in elevation; and as the surrounding area fell away below him, Johnny had the strange sensation of walking up into the sky. Far below, the river moved ceaselessly.

He had been nervous and apprehensive under the watchful stare of the alligator, but now he was terrified. Never had he felt so precarious and so near death. Only two lanes crossed the bridge, and there was no shoulder. A narrow ledge ran between the highway and the guardrails of the bridge. Johnny walked along that ledge, but it was such a small space and so close to the traffic speeding by that Johnny doubted it was meant for pedestrian traffic. The guardrail was low and constructed like a simple board fence at home; Johnny felt completely exposed and unprotected. One stumble, and he would fall either into the path of an oncoming vehicle or over the rail, to plummet into the waters far below.

He could feel movement and vibrations in the bridge, even

when there was no traffic passing him. Hung high above the water, he felt as though he had lost all sense of balance and contact with solid ground. Cars flew past within a few feet. He was careful to keep his walking sticks and duffel bag close to his body, out of danger of being caught by a wide load. He did not want to look at the river far below, and he did not want to look at the traffic bearing down on him, just a few feet away.

And so, walking with his eyes on the cement underfoot, he did not see the pickup truck until it came to a stop beside him and a woman's voice called out.

"Young man, what are you doing out here? Get in! We are going to save your life!"

He looked up to see a door opening and a round face framed by white curls beaming at him. The speaker was a tiny but very plump woman of at least seventy-five, and she was sliding across the seat of the pickup to make room for him.

Behind the stopped pickup, Johnny saw a tractor-trailer rig approaching. He heard the engine shifting down and the blare of the horn. He hopped into the cab of the pickup, pulled his bag and sticks in with him, and slammed the door. Tires squealed as the driver accelerated in the fastest getaway Johnny had experienced since his teenage years.

He caught his breath, and looked over at the driver who was every bit as old as the tiny woman. The man was grinning, enjoying every moment of the daring rescue the two had just pulled off.

"Thank you, but ... well ... I was headed to Mississippi," he began, rearranging his bulky duffel and the walking sticks.

"Oh, we know," chirped the woman. "We were headed over to Greenville, too. But we saw you on the other side of the road ..."

"... and she said, 'George, we can't let that boy out there. Turn around. Let's pick him up and get him across that bridge.' So I whipped this thing around and we snatched you from certain death." The driver finished his wife's story. He was clearly enjoying the adventure of saving Johnny's life.

"Thank you," said Johnny. He wasn't sure what else to say.

"I'm Millie," said the petite woman. "And this is George."

"I'm John Miller."

"Where are you heading, John?"

"Ohio, eventually. Today I was heading to Greenville. Or as close as I can get."

They were off the bridge, on the same side of the river that Johnny had just left. George took the first road to the right, found a wide space, did a quick U-turn, and headed back toward the bridge.

"We're off to Nashville," said Millie. "We've always wanted to see the Grand Ole Opry, and this is our fiftieth anniversary present to ourselves."

"Just a few years late," George said with a smile. He glanced over at Millie with eyes brimming with affection. "We intended to take this trip year before last, but life sent us a few detours. Now we're finally going."

His wife's tiny hand patted his knee.

"We've only been on the road a day and a half, and already it's been worth every penny and every year we've waited and dreamed," she said. "It's the trip of a lifetime. And now we've even saved a life. We were sent as your guardian angels, I think."

Johnny wondered if her round pink face wore that beaming look continually.

"I will confess that I'm much happier to ride over this bridge than to walk over it," said Johnny. And though he was sitting safely in the truck, he did not look through the railing toward the water as they passed over the highest part of the span. He gave a sigh of relief as they came down the other side of the bridge and continued onto a safe, grounded highway.

"You'd be welcome to ride with us a ways," George said. "We are going all the way to Nashville, and if that's the way you're heading, we'd be glad to give you a lift."

"Thank you, but no," Johnny answered before he even gave it a thought. "I'm walking. You can just pull over here and I'll get back to my walk."

"Are you sure? Ohio's a long way to walk," Millie said.

"Yes, I'm sure. I'm … well, I am enjoying the journey." Johnny smiled as he thought how true this statement was. Yes, he was enjoying himself tremendously.

George eased the pickup over to the side of the road. Johnny opened the door and climbed out.

"Thanks again. And have a wonderful trip," he said.

Now he took his first good look at the pickup. On the bed of the truck was a miniature house, complete with painted clapboards, chimney, and window boxes filled with cheerful red flowers.

"Oh, we will. Bye! Be careful!" Millie waved a small hand, and did not bother to slide over to the passenger's door. She stayed right where she was, nestled up next to her George.

***

The Benjamin G. Humphreys Bridge carried Route 82 from Arkansas to Mississippi, and Johnny knew that this highway would take him through the state to the Natchez Trace Parkway. He remembered what Danny had told him about the Parkway, that it would be more scenic and safer than most highways. Highway 82 to the Natchez Trace seemed like a good plan.

At the edge of Greenville, he spent one night in a motel. He did not want to navigate the city in the dark or look for a camping spot in this urban area. Besides, he needed a long shower and a good rest in a real bed. He washed out his clothes in the sink, as best as he could, and hoped they would dry by morning.

He set out the next day with renewed vigor and determination. The route across Mississippi to the Trace would take almost a week. So be it. He would enjoy the journey.

In Mississippi, endless rows of cotton were whitening with ripening bolls. Walking by miles and miles of fields of green corn and golden grains, he wondered what it would be like to farm such vast fields. He chuckled to himself. Certainly couldn't plant and harvest such fields with a horse!

The longing for his own soil and harvest grew stronger as he walked surrounded by the richness of growing things. As Mandy would have put it, he felt a growing itch to get home.

44

The itch flared into a full-blown malady of homesickness on the Natchez Trace. Here, at last, were hills! How long had it been since he had seen green hills? Months, but it seemed like years.

From the moment he entered the Parkway, he was aware of the endless treasures to be discovered along this road. Hiking trails, waterfalls, antique homes, monuments, ruins, historic sites, and traces of people who had lived here centuries ago—all were here for the exploring. The first day on the Parkway he had stopped several places, but the urge to dispense with more miles each day soon overruled his inquisitiveness. He kept his eyes open to all around him, but he kept his feet moving northward.

He felt stronger and healthier than he had felt since … when? Since Annie had died?

And it was a good thing that his strength was returning, because his duffel bag was growing heavier every day. Walking for weeks along well-traveled highways means that one finds many, many useful items either lost or discarded. He had found tools, clothes, a blanket, one lawn chair, food, and even money. His thriftiness had prompted him to pick up a perfectly good garbage bag. It was still neatly folded and unused. As he shifted the

growing weight on his back, he reasoned that he had not kept
everything he had found—only those things that might prove
useful at some later point. At one campground, a family of six
camped next to him; and when he noticed the smallest girl in tears,
he had discovered he had the tool necessary to fix her tricycle.
Walking through one small town, he had pulled a jacket and two
caps out of his duffel and dropped them into a Goodwill collection
box. And of course he did not carry the lawn chair along with him.
He set it up under a tree, as a wayside rest for some other
wandering soul. Still, each morning he found it necessary to
rearrange and pack his bag in more creative ways so that the tent
would fit back into the duffel.

His thriftiness paid off on the morning he began the short
stretch of the Natchez Trace that cut through Alabama. Daylight
had never fully arrived. Heavy clouds obscured the sun and
seemed to grow lower and more threatening with every mile. At
the Freedom Hills Overlook, Johnny took the time to climb to the
top of a hill and take in the views from what was proclaimed the
highest point on the Trace. Ordinarily, he would have rested at the
dramatic spot and admired the views across the mountains, but an
ominous sky prompted him to turn around and hurry back down
the trail. Drizzling rain started as he descended.

He did ask himself *where* he was off to in such a rush—he had
no idea where he would find shelter from the coming storm. He
stopped to take out the garbage bag, cut a hole for his head, and
pull it over his upper body. It would afford a measure of protection
against the downpour that was sure to come.

Less than a mile down the road, he saw a familiar house, the
little house built on the bed of a pickup truck. George had pulled
over into a grassy area beside the road and he was working at the
back left tire. Millie stood next to him, trying to shield him with a
ridiculously small, pink-flowered umbrella. She was maneuvering
in a kind of dance around her husband; when the umbrella was

over George, she was unprotected. And if she tried to stand close enough to share the shelter with George, she was constantly in the way of his elbow or knee.

Johnny knew they were all going to be drenched soon, but he smiled at Millie's flowered umbrella and her little dance.

"Hello," he shouted. "Can I help?"

George and Millie both jumped. They had not seen him approach. And he was sure he looked silly in his garbage bag raincoat.

"It's our boy John!" shouted Millie, and Johnny thought that her face beamed even when soaked by a downpour.

George looked up and grinned.

"We have a situation here. Having a little trouble with this tire. These old bones don't work quite like they used to."

"Let me have a go at it," offered Johnny. Pulling the garbage bag over his head, he gave it a few vigorous shakes. "And here, put this on. We're all already wet, but it will be some protection."

A few twists by his younger muscles, four confident hands replacing the flat tire with a new one, a few more quick twists, and the tire was changed. Millie stood under her flowered umbrella, rain running down her legs and soaking her shoes. But once the job was finished, she was in charge.

"Into the camper, both of you," she ordered.

Johnny took two steps up, through a wood cottage door, into the tiniest house he'd ever seen. On his left was a kitchen work area, consisting of a two-burner gas cooktop and a row of shelves narrower than Millie herself. To the right was a small refrigerator, a tall pantry cupboard, one very small stuffed sofa (Johnny thought that it would be a very tight fit for George and Millie both to sit on the sofa), and more drawers. At the front of the "house," against the back of the truck's cab, a built-in bed frame held a mattress covered with a quilt and six pillows, one of which was embroidered with *Home Sweet Home*. In one corner stood a compact kerosene heater. George lit it and moved it to the center of the very small space in which they all stood. Then he sat down on the edge of the bed and offered Johnny a seat on the sofa.

"I'm soaked," Johnny began.

"Don't worry about it; it will dry out," Millie reassured him. "This small place warms up quickly."

And it did. In a matter of minutes, Johnny felt as though he were being steamed like a hot dog. It seemed odd to be gathered around a heater when the day outside was warm and rainy. But sure enough, their clothes were drying quickly.

Millie put together several fat sandwiches, turned on the burner under a tea kettle, and took a pan of Jell-O out of the refrigerator. George pulled two small folding stands from beneath the bed and set one in front of Johnny and one in front of his own seat on the bed. Millie bustled about, putting food and hot tea on the small tables in front of them. The rain drummed on the roof and blew against the windows, framed by yellow-checked curtains, on either side of the house.

"I was surprised to see you. I thought you'd be in Nashville by now," Johnny said, trying to speak over the sound of the downpour.

"We're taking our time, enjoying everything along the way. We stopped whenever we saw something that interested us, and we took time off the Trace Parkway to visit some friends we met years ago. Then we camped a few days beside a lake so I could fish. Looks like you're making better time than we are," answered George with a grin.

"This is our time to enjoy each other and whatever we meet along the way," added Millie. "We decided we weren't going to rush through this trip. Who knows what we might miss if we do that? And you—you were our guardian angel today, John. We thought we were saving your life on that bridge, but it turns out you were here to help us today."

"I'm no angel!" The words slipped out with a bit more

vehemence than Johnny intended.

"Perhaps John doesn't believe in angels, Mill," said George mildly, taking a bite of sandwich.

"Of course there are angels!" came Millie's firm declaration. "The Bible speaks often of angels sent to protect and help us. Some people even entertain angels unaware, Scriptures say. Me," she smiled as though she knew a secret, and there was an added sparkle in her eye, "I'm keeping my eyes open for all the angels along my way. I don't want to miss them!"

Johnny watched as Millie took her cup of tea and sat down next to George. George was just as tall and bony as Millie was short and round. Yet they seemed completely in tune with each other. *They shall be one,* the Scripture said of the marriage of a man and woman. These two, seemingly so different, had become one over the years. For just a moment, Johnny allowed himself to think about what he and Annie might have looked like on their fiftieth anniversary. *Annie would not be quite that round. She is so petite* ... Then he felt the ache begin, and he quickly slammed the door on those thoughts.

"Do you know how close we are to Nashville?" he asked.

"We had thought we'd get there tonight," Millie answered. "But with the rain and the flat tire ... What do you think, George?"

"We may still get there tonight. With this downpour, we probably won't stop too often for sightseeing. I reckon we have about 130 miles to go," George offered.

"That's five or six days for me," Johnny realized that he was ready to be done with this stretch of his walk, no matter what spectacular scenery or fascinating sites lay ahead. He had already decided that he would buy a bus ticket in Nashville and ride the rest of the way home. Maybe he would even arrive home in time to help with the last of the harvest. They would probably be into the third cutting of hay, and maybe the wheat and oats were in—but hadn't Naomi said everything was late this year due to heavy rains? At least he could be home for corn picking. He was fairly certain of that.

Millie picked up on his rueful tone.

"Ride along with us! We'll get you there faster, even if we do make a few stops. You don't want to walk in this downpour anyway. Please, John, come with us."

Johnny hesitated for a moment, considering. But it was only for a moment.

"Sure. I would like that."

***

The downpour continued for the next three hours. George drove slowly through small rivers washing over the highway. He sat hunched forward, gripping the steering wheel, and peering through the rain battering the windshield. His intense concentration on his driving and the sound of the raindrops pelting the roof of the truck discouraged conversation, even though the three were tucked snugly into the cab. Every now and then, Millie would venture a few thoughts about some subject, but Johnny could not hear everything she said, and George was focused on the road and did not reply.

They were soon in Tennessee and passed several sites that Millie declared they *should* have visited, but no one wanted to stop or walk about in the torrential rain. As a result, by late afternoon they began seeing signs that told them they were nearing Nashville. About that time the rains also lessened, and Johnny caught sight of patches of blue sky.

"Do you have a place to stay tonight?" asked Millie.

"No. I usually walk until I find a good camping spot. Every now and then I've stayed in a motel. And if I can find a campground, that's ideal."

"Come with us. We'll find you a motel close to our campground, or perhaps you can get a campsite there, too." Johnny thought that this was the greatest number of words George had spoken since they started driving in the rain.

"We'd offer you a bed, but this place was only built for two," said Millie. She patted George's knee. "George has been a builder all his life, and he built our little home on the road with his own hands. Made it just perfect for us."

"Last big project I was able to finish," said George, his eyes straight ahead.

"I agree; it might be a little tight for three of us," said Johnny. "I do appreciate the ride. But I would like to walk the last few miles into Nashville. I haven't set foot on Tennessee ground yet, and it looks like this is beautiful country. I'm almost there. I will be buying a bus ticket in Nashville and riding the rest of the way home, so I'd like to take one long walk here in Tennessee before I do that," he explained.

"I think you have about twenty miles to go," George offered.

"You can't make it before dark," Millie protested.

"That's okay. I'll find a place to camp. I think the rain's over."

"George, we can't let him …" began Millie.

"Yes, Mill, we can. Remember your guardian angels? Our boy will be fine."

They stopped at a picnic area and Millie had supper on the folding tables in minutes; then Johnny said goodbye, bending over when Millie stood on tiptoe to hug him and kiss his cheek. He wished them a happy anniversary—a few years late. As he watched the little house drive off, he was thinking about guardian angels and how sorry he was that his time with George and Millie was over and he would never see them again.

45

The patches of blue sky had deceived him. Less than ten minutes after George and Millie's house disappeared around the next curve, clouds once again obscured the sun and a slow drizzle started. Johnny hunched his shoulders against the rain and wondered where he could find shelter.

The days on the Natchez Trace Parkway had been beautiful but lonely. Very few of the advertised attractions and scenes were visible from the roadway; signs pointed away from exits, and Johnny had decided not to chase too many of those detours. Even many of the scenic views were obscured by long stretches of forest. Every now and then a break in the trees had given Johnny a glimpse over hills and valleys and forests.

The Parkway offered no shoulders for walking, and most of the time Johnny trudged in the mowed grassy areas along the roadway. Many bicycles and motorcycles and even other walkers passed him, and nearly everyone was friendly. A more relaxed pace prevailed on this highway. This was indeed a beautiful area, and Johnny was glad he had chosen this route; he only wished he could see more of the surrounding countryside.

And now, with the rain soaking his shirt and running down his back, he also wished for a roadside diner or a motel or even a gas station. But his experience on the last two hundred miles of the Trace told Johnny that probably all he would find ahead of him would be more highway winding through the trees—and nothing with a roof.

One exit sign pointed west and promised a town. Johnny had no idea what he might find in that town, but he had a few hours of daylight left and decided he would have to take this detour and find a place to take shelter.

He turned down the exit. Not far down this new road, though, he glimpsed a white steeple rising through the treetops on a hillside. The narrow, winding, unpaved driveway leading away from the highway and up the slope beckoned him to follow. He turned and followed it through a tunnel of trees.

In a small clearing near the crest of the hill, an old church building welcomed him. A sign in great need of paint proclaimed this to be the Mountaintop Holiness Church where the FULL gospel was preached every Sunday. Johnny's first wry thought was that apparently other churches in the area were missing out on some parts of the gospel.

Two steps rose to the front door and were covered by a small roof that was more decorative than functional. It offered little refuge. Johnny walked around the building, hoping to find a protective nook or even an outbuilding of some kind. *They might preach the full gospel here*, he thought, *but what I really need now is shelter for my FULL body.*

At the back of the building, an overhang reached out and promised sanctuary. Johnny saw that a flight of steps led downward to a basement door. Well protected by the ample roof, the concrete landing looked large enough for him to lay out his blanket and perhaps even spread the tent out to dry. The old wooden steps creaked loudly as he descended.

On an impulse, he checked if the door was locked. The knob

would not turn. He realized, though, that the door was not latched; and with only a slight push, it swung open.

He stepped inside, wondering if this was a sin; then the thought came to him that he had not even tried the front door of the church. Surely any congregation believing in the full gospel would have open doors, offering shelter to all sojourners on their pilgrimage toward home.

He was standing in the furnace room. Obviously, this was also the storage room and the workshop. The furnace reigned in one half of the room, but at the end of the other half was a workbench with tools neatly hung on a pegboard above it. Shelves lined one wall, and they held everything from cleaning products and boxes of odd mixtures of nails to church papers, a vacuum, and a small stack of plastic trays and silverware. In a corner behind the furnace, a few chairs and one wooden table were folded up and tucked in, awaiting their call into service.

The room was tidy and spotless and spacious enough that Johnny decided immediately he would settle in here for the night. One basement window on the far wall was opened slightly, allowing fresh air and the gentle sound of the rain to flow through Johnny's new abode.

Another door led into the general basement area where tables and chairs were already set up. Johnny stepped out to the water fountain along one wall and took a long drink of what tasted like fresh spring water. Restrooms were down a short hall; stairs led up toward the sanctuary. The church was small and old; the block walls had seen generations of church life, but the current emptiness felt eerie. Johnny retreated into his cozy room and shut the door.

He was well aware that this was Saturday night. Tomorrow, the church would not be so empty. But he was an early riser and would be miles down the highway before the first congregant arrived to hear the full gospel preached at the Mountaintop Holiness Church.

46

Johnny awoke, dazed and confused. As the rain continued a soft patter on the window, a calm and peaceful rest had overtaken him, and he had slept deeply and undisturbed.

Familiar words now reached his ears and brought him from sleep. "Amazing grace, how sweet the sound, that saved a wretch like me ..."

The aroma of coffee and Mandy's breakfast was not yet in the air. Why was Dad singing so early in the morning?

Where was he?

The deep voice did not belong to his father; the words were sung with a lyrical southern accent. He was not home. He was in a church furnace room and the service had already started. He jumped up, grabbing some of his clothes that he had hung to dry the night before. What if someone needed an extra chair or those church papers and opened the door to come face to face with their overnight guest? Was escape possible? Could he gather everything and slip out undetected? Or perhaps, instead of slinking away, he would walk up those basement steps and join the Hilltop brethren in worship. No, he had been in only a few English church services as a youth and wouldn't quite know how to act.

His startled mind flitted from one possibility to another for a few minutes, then he calmed enough to assess his situation. He had not yet been discovered, so he would slowly and quietly pack everything and make his escape. But he remembered how noisy those outside steps had been when he first descended them the night before. He would have to leave during the singing.

The old church building had seemed so small the night before, and now it sounded as though the walls must be bursting with a packed-in crowd. How these people could sing! Johnny recognized some old hymns, but this congregation sang with such gusto that the songs were transformed. Even the old block walls in the basement seemed to pulsate with music.

He was mesmerized by the vigor of the singing and found himself humming along with familiar tunes. He slid into a seated position with his back against a wall and the half-packed army duffel beside him—he would listen for just a moment—and let the music flow through his body as memories of family singings drifted through his mind. It would be so good to be home again.

A few more lively songs started, and now the ceiling above him shook under stomping feet, and occasionally a jubilant clapping and enthusiastic shouts drowned out the words of the songs. The Mountaintoppers were really getting into their worship. As unfamiliar as this service was to Johnny, he found himself thinking that he might like these lively people if he would only have the courage to join them.

The song service ended, and Johnny strained to hear what was taking place next. He tried to open the basement window a little further; apparently the windows upstairs had all been opened and everything that was happening above drifted down to this basement room.

Some type of money-giving came next. An offering. To help a church in Africa. Then a woman's voice called children forward, and the shuffling above was lighter and quicker. Johnny was sure some of the little feet were running. This was something new. Johnny had never been in a service where the children were singled out and given a special spot in the program.

The woman called attention to the beautiful sunshine pouring through the windows. "Why do we need sunlight in this world?" she asked. A little voice spoke up; Johnny could not hear what was said, but the congregation chuckled.

"Yes, that's right, Charlie, but what would this world be like if there were no sunshine at all? That's hard to imagine, isn't it? Have you ever awakened in the middle of the night when everything was dark and the toys and furniture in your room looked very different, sometimes even scary? That's what it would be like if we had no sunlight in the world. It would be like the middle of the night, all day long! We would always be in the darkness, unable to see unless we have a light of some kind.

"Now is there any other reason we need light?"

Apparently no child could think of any other situation necessitating the presence of light. The woman paused for a moment and then went on.

"Look at this beautiful bouquet of flowers I picked from my garden this morning. Here is an ear of corn that's almost ready to eat. And look how green and lovely these leaves are on this little branch. I could have pulled up a handful of grass and brought it into church, but instead, let's all look through the windows at how thick and lush the grass is on the lawn outside.

"Now, how are all those things different from …" Johnny heard her pause. "… this?"

Ripples of laughter floated through the church, and one young voice shouted, "That's dead!"

"Yes, Timmy, this poor plant is not doing well, is it? I think it is almost dead. I planted corn seed in this pot at the same time I planted the seed for this juicy ear of corn in my garden. But after they had both sprouted, I took this pot with the tiny plant and I shut it up in a closet. I watered it every now and then, but why do you suppose this sad little thing did not grow up to be a big stalk of corn like those in my garden?"

Timmy had caught a glimpse of the lesson. He knew the answer. "It didn't have any sunlight," he shouted in reply. Johnny smiled at the boy's uninhibited enthusiasm.

"That's right. This plant did not have the sunlight it needed. God created plants in such a way that sunlight is one of the things they must have to grow. Without light, they will look like this poor plant in my pot. Or perhaps they will never even sprout.

"Did you know that God created us like that, too? We need light to grow and to blossom and to be healthy. The light we need is Jesus. Jesus said He was the light of the world. He came to this world to bring God's light to us, and the Bible says that when we belong to Jesus, he moves us from a land of darkness to His land of light. One verse even says that God transplants us to His own courts. Your momma probably transplants some of her flowers from time to time. A flower or bush might not be doing well where it is planted, so we dig it out and move it to a place we think it will grow better. That's what God does. He transplants us to His own home or gardens where His light shines on us. And there we grow and are healthy and strong like these flowers and corn and trees.

"Jesus brings the light of God to shine in our lives and we come alive. We do not shrivel up and die like this sad little plant. God's light is what gives us life."

Johnny sat on the bare floor, his back to a wall, and gazed at the beams of sunlight streaming down through the narrow basement window. He knew well the importance of light to growing things. Long before he was a farmer, he had been a boy fascinated by trees. But to be truthful, he had also been a boy who had heard dozens of times those words of Jesus, *I am the light of the world*—yet he had never given them deep thought.

He remembered that dark day, when he first arrived at the

Mississippi River. The heavy clouds of pain and despair and guilt seemed to have obliterated all light in his life. He had wanted to die that night. At least, he had not wanted to live.

Something had changed between that black hour when he stood on the riverbank and screamed his frustration at God and the next morning when he opened his eyes to the loveliness of color and light in the eastern sky. What had happened that night?

And what was happening in his life now? He'd been thinking about the darkness of the last few months and the darkness that had shrouded him wherever he went. He saw that he had used and mistreated people, unable to break through the gloom of his own pain and anger. But since that first morning light on the banks of the Mississippi, the colors of his days had been vibrant. He had rejoiced in the light. He was beginning to enjoy being alive again.

There remained only the one room of darkness—that room with the closed door, the room of his loss and grief. He was still unwilling to open that door and face the darkness within, and yet at the same time, he knew he lived inside that room. He imagined that his life in that room was something like the shriveled little plant deprived of sunlight. Could Jesus bring light even to that room? Tears filled his eyes.

"Could you, Jesus?" he whispered.

47

The sound of his own voice startled Johnny and brought him back to the basement and the sounds of the service above. The minister had started reading from the book of John, the first chapter.

> *"In him was life, and that life was the light of all mankind. The light shines in the darkness, and the darkness has not overcome it ... The true light that gives light to everyone was coming into the world.*

"Those are John's words about Jesus coming into this world," the preacher began. "Jesus came to bring life and light to everyone, and no darkness can ever overcome the light He brings. Keep those words in mind, and let's turn to this morning's text in Matthew 20. While you're turning there, let me tell you the story.

"Jesus and his disciples have created quite a stir among the people. They've been traveling from one town to another in Galilee and Judea, and by the time they leave the city of Jericho, a crowd is following Jesus to hear His teaching and see what miracles He might perform. We know there are some in the crowd, too, who are looking for ways to trap Jesus or silence Him. He is rocking their boat, challenging the established religion; so they are following Him about, hoping to find ways to squash His growing popularity and His teaching.

"So Jesus and his disciples leave Jericho somewhat like the Pied Piper, with a large crowd of the locals following them as they leave town.

"On the outskirts of town, sitting by the roadway, are two blind guys. They are probably regulars at that spot, day in and day out. Their blindness makes it impossible to work, and so their only recourse is to beg for money.

"They've heard the large crowd approaching and know that something unusual is happening. They pick up the news that this is Jesus coming by. And as soon as they judge, in their blindness, that the crowd is within shouting distance, they begin yelling, 'Lord, Son of David, have mercy on us!'

"Now, doesn't that strike you as an odd way to address Jesus? To use the word *Lord* might have been common at the time, much like we might use *Sir* to show respect and esteem. But to address Jesus as the *Son of David* is to acknowledge His kingship, and in that Jewish world, they are calling Him the Messiah, the great Deliverer who God had promised!

"So they are going to make themselves heard! This Jesus is powerful, He is kingly, He is the promised One who would heal the blind and release the prisoners. They are not going to miss this opportunity to appeal to Him for help.

"The locals are embarrassed that Jesus has to encounter these undesirables. They shout at the blind men to be quiet. But the beggars just turn up the volume and call all the more loudly.

"What are these two pathetic dudes hoping for? Do you think they are hoping that this kingly, powerful man would show them mercy and grant them a large sum of money to live on? Do you suppose they have heard of the miracles Jesus was performing and are hoping to be healed of their blindness? At this point in the story, we are not told what they are thinking, but we do know they are persistent. They shout even louder. I can imagine this ruckus—some in the crowd are yelling at the two to shut up, and they are yelling even louder, determined to be heard above the criticism of those trying to keep them quiet.

"'Lord, Son of David, have mercy on us!'

"And then we come to the question that hits home, the question that is the focus of today's meditation because it is the question we also have to answer. They do get Jesus' attention. And Jesus asks them, 'What do you want me to do for you?'

"Every day, these men station themselves beside the road. Every passerby knows, as soon as they see the men, that these two are there to beg for money to live on. How easy it would have been for Jesus to tell his treasurer to give them money. Isn't that what was expected?

"But these two have recognized that this Jesus is a man with power and was sent from God. They may have heard about His miracles and know He can do amazing things.

"And Jesus knows that their need goes much deeper than financial resources. He wants them to recognize their need. He asks them the question: 'What do you want me to do for you?'"

Johnny was far ahead of the preacher. He knew exactly where this was leading. Or maybe it was the voice of Jesus Himself saying, "Johnny, what do you want Me to do for you?"

What did Johnny want from Jesus? He continued to gaze at the sunbeams, already slanting at a different angle through the window. His first reaction to the question was, "I want Annie back. I want my old life back."

But was that really what he needed?

If Jesus really is Lord of the heavens and earth, as I say I believe, then what do I need most from Him?

"I need light, Jesus. I need light. I want to see. I want to live." He said the words aloud, and as he said them, the door to that darkest room swung open. He felt a quiver of fear at finally opening the door, but he was desperate for the light.

"Lord, I want to see. I want to see why you took Annie. I want to see why you did not let me into Heaven. I want to see why I've had to go through that accident and those months in pain. Lord, I see only darkness when I look at all of that. Where was your light while all of that was happening? Lord, I want to see!"

While Johnny was answering Jesus' question, the preacher had finished the story of the healing of the blind men. They knew they wanted to see. Jesus felt great compassion for them and touched their eyes, and immediately they were given sight.

"Can you imagine," he was asking the quiet congregation, "never being able to see before, and now suddenly you see light and colors all about you? And what was their response to this miracle of sight? They didn't go running to tell their families—no, they followed Jesus. They did not insist upon going home and gathering a lot of stuff to carry along; that was all unnecessary. What was most important to them now was just that they could be with Jesus and follow Him.

"Wherever you are in this Mountaintop Holiness building today, Jesus is asking you the same question: *What do you want Me to do for you?* You may be able to see with your eyes this morning, but you are spiritually blind—so blind that you need a good shot of mercy. Cry out this morning, 'Jesus, Son of David, have mercy on me. I want to see, to understand, to discern.'

"And when the great light of understanding enters your being, you, too, will want to follow Jesus, the one who brings life and light. And you, too, will want to spend time with Him, because just as Miss Marybeth explained to the children this morning, light is necessary for growth. The light of Jesus will bring growth and life will flourish. Without that light, we cannot truly live."

Johnny took a deep breath. He could already feel something new stirring in his soul. Was it new life? Was it life, sweeping away darkness? Whatever it was, the preacher was right. Once you can see, once the light begins to shine, then the one thing you want most is to follow Him who brings all light and life.

When you have that light, then you can *truly live*. Annie had used that phrase, too.

"I will follow you, Jesus," he breathed. And he realized that he did not care what the cost would be to banish the darkness in that last room. Whatever would be required, he would be willing. He craved the light. He was desperate for life.

48

Johnny sat immobile as light bathed his heart, mind, and soul. Then he was suddenly aware that the crowd above was standing, paging through hymnals, and beginning another song. He jumped up and snatched a few more things that he had spread out to dry.

The second verse began, punctuated with hearty hallelujahs and shouted praises. Johnny paused in his packing. Words floated back to him from Wandering Willie: "You are traveling too heavy. Get rid of everything you don't need." He was indeed beginning to feel as though he carried too much excess weight. Willie had told him if he let go of stuff, he'd be surprised at what could happen.

And, thought Johnny, *this will be a symbolic letting go. If I am going to follow Jesus, I will not hold on to too much stuff.*

He started removing things from his duffel—a hat, miscellaneous tools, a jar of baby food (peach pudding, he had thought when he found it left behind at a picnic area, might be a good snack), a flashlight with no batteries, the sock, and even—in one moment of greater faith—the food supply he had purchased for the next few days. Only his blanket, Wayne's tent, canteen, and knife, Annie's notebook, and his wallet remained.

The sight of his wallet reminded him of the single twenty-dollar bill still folded and waiting in a small slot. It was the last of the five twenties Samuel Cohraine had given him as a reward for returning his own lost wallet. Johnny had wanted to refuse, but Samuel had been insistent and Johnny had heard Annie's voice saying, *Take it, and give it away*. Over the next few weeks, her voice had prompted him when to give away the twenties.

But now, without a word from Annie, Johnny withdrew Samuel Cohraine's last twenty and tucked it under the jar of peach pudding. An offering for Africa.

The fourth verse had started. He had no idea how many more verses there were in this hymn, but surely the song would soon be finished and the service over. He must get out of here. He scanned the cozy room that had been home to him. Other than the "stuff" that had weighed him down and was now lined up on the worktable, he would leave no sign of his presence here.

The door opened easily and soundlessly, but the stairs creaked loudly. Johnny took three at a time and hoped the stomping and clapping covered the noise of his escape. At the corner of the building, he swung out in a wide arc along the edge of the gravel parking lot now filled with cars, hoping no one could see him.

From his vantage point on the small stage, Reverend Jeremiah Dixon breathed a prayer for the soldier he saw slipping away into the woods.

49

Johnny walked with a lighter pack and an even lighter heart. He felt as free as the Monarch that fluttered along beside him for a few moments; he was floating through those Tennessee mountains. The Natchez Trace Parkway did not call him back; although he had been looking forward to seeing Nashville, he was not quite ready to enter the city. The serenity of green hillsides and forests pulled him away from the towns and traffic, and he decided to enjoy another day of carefree walking without the intense push to reach his goal. For the rest of Sunday and the next day, he would follow the small back roads and simply delight in God's nature.

The moments in the church furnace room, when he had seen clearly that following Jesus would be new life for him, had infused him with a new energy. Now the hours of ambling along winding dirt roads brought even more healing to his spirit. He knew that, back in the furnace room, he had also dropped his burden of sorrow. He still loved Annie. The void in his life still ached. But he would be able to live with the void now. He felt strong and unfettered. Free.

The door to that locked room in his heart had swung open, and liberating, life-giving light was cleaning out the dark corners.

He was also beginning to see, and one new thing he saw was that God had been with him every step of his journey. Even when he was running away, God had been there, guiding his steps to bring him home.

He thought about Millie's assertion that God sends guardian angels to help people. He was not sure whether he believed that, but he did know that God had brought people into his life at just the right moment when he needed them. He would have a conversation with Dad about angels, once he was home.

He was startled to realize that Annie might have believed in angels. It was there in her notebook.

He had pulled the tablet out of his duffel bag as he sat on an enormous rock at the top of a mountain overlooking the surrounding countryside. Nashville lay off to the northeast. He judged that he could walk there in less than a day, if he chose. He would rather sit on this mountaintop, though, and admire God's spectacular handiwork. As he sat there, some inner prompting reminded him of Annie's notebook.

He drew it out of his bag and held it for a long moment. Since his accident, he had not read anything she had written. He had told himself that he could not bear to read her thoughts and see her neat handwriting and know that he would never hear her voice again. But now, he was ready to open the notebook once more.

In the months following Annie's death, he had read all of her journal entries dozens of times. Many of them were so familiar to him that he could almost recite the words from memory. Still, he now noticed things he had glossed over before.

She wrote of mundane details: which fields the men were sowing or harvesting, what vegetables she and Mandy had canned that day. She wrote her prayers. And she wrote of her own dreams: children, the home she and Johnny would build together, the family she had come to love as her own. In one small line in the account of an ordinary day, Johnny found the words: *Send your guardian angels, Lord, to protect them.*

Johnny remembered the day. He and his father had been helping his brother Jonas with a logging operation in the next county. They were working under a tight deadline, and Johnny's dad had cautioned them about pushing too hard; accidents were much more likely when crews worked under such pressure. All had gone well. Now Johnny read that Annie had prayed for the protection of guardian angels as they worked.

But if one believed in guardian angels, then there would always be the question of *why.* Why was Johnny hit by a truck? Why was Annie killed in a freak accident? Where were those guardian angels then? Why did God allow such things to happen?

He had told God he wanted to see. He had wanted to see God's plan, to see God's reasons for the things that had happened to him. He had wanted answers.

God was giving him new eyesight, but what Johnny began to see was that most of these answers belonged only to God and not to him. What did belong to him, though, was the sure knowledge that he was not alone in anything that came into his life. Jesus had promised He would always be with Johnny. He would never walk through anything on His own. Whatever God had planned for Johnny's life, Jesus would walk beside him, or, if He must, He would carry Johnny through.

Under a brilliant blue sky, with the hot sun warming the back of his neck and the magnificent views below him, Johnny flipped through the pages, smiling at the little ditties Annie had written and sung to the butterflies. She had loved the story of Monarchs, how they were transformed from worms into beautiful creatures. Annie always said that was the story of what Jesus could do in even the ugliest, most tainted and twisted life. He brought transformation and new life.

The story of the butterflies' migration was fascinating. Three generations of Monarchs lived only a few weeks, but the fourth generation lived seven months, to fly thousands of miles to a mountainside in Mexico, overwinter there, and then start the long journey north again the next spring, headed back to the place they had been born. The fourth generation, Annie had always noted, was a generation with a special mission. And then she would remind Johnny that he was the fourth generation to live on and farm the Miller land. "I wonder what special purpose God has in mind for you, dearest," she would muse.

Johnny's thoughts went back to the morning in Texas when a Monarch butterfly had landed on his hand as he rode down the highway. That slight distraction had caused him to swerve into the path of the truck.

He did not dwell on that memory. Already, the hospital, the long recovery, and the dark walk to the Mississippi seemed in the remote past, in another lifetime.

He found a prayer Annie had written: *Because of your wounds, I am healed. Because you died, I have new life. Thank you, dear Jesus.*

The words held new meaning for him. Whenever he thought about his own miraculous physical healing, he thought about the words of the stringbean stranger in the hospital chapel: *Jesus suffered terribly so we all could live. And heal.* Those words had come back to him many times since the river, whenever he marveled at the strength now in his body. He suspected the healing of the cross would reach far deeper than his leg and ribs.

Turning the pages, he knew what he would soon read. He had read this many times before. The last page filled with Annie's handwriting held her final words, written to him the night she died. As he lay sleeping, she had left those words for him. He had read them the next day in the hospital. She had known she was going to die. And he had been sleeping.

Dearest Johnny,

It is after two o'clock, and I'm afraid that soon I won't be able to think very clearly. I can hear you breathing in the next room and want so much to come in and hold you and tell you how much I love you.

Don't ever lament that we didn't seek help last night. It would not have made any difference. Things are as they are supposed to be. I never told you this, but when I was a child, I often dreamed I would die at an early age. Lately, those dreams have returned. It's as if God has been telling me it's about time to go home. I do love you with all my heart, but I love Jesus more. If He calls, I must go.

Johnny felt as though his heart had stopped beating for a moment; he couldn't breathe as Annie's words burned into him: *I do love you with all my heart, but I love Jesus more.*

River Man's question echoed in his ears, *John, do you love Annie more than you love Jesus?*

Tears filled his eyes and he bowed his head. The tears dropped down on Annie's pages as deep sobs shook his body.

Yes, he loved Annie more than he loved Jesus.

River Man had known. The stranger had seen into Johnny's heart, had seen that he held Annie as everything and all. Johnny had thought Annie was life for him; he had thought losing Annie meant losing everything.

Even now, after he had promised to follow Jesus, he still loved Annie more.

He fell forward, crumpling to the ground, wracked with grief-stricken sobs. This grieving was not for Annie or for himself. This grieving was for the hurt He had caused the One who promised him new life. Johnny had put Annie above the One who had died so that he, Johnny, could heal and live.

"Forgive me, Jesus!" he cried. "Forgive me! I was blind and did not see!"

***

For a long time, Johnny lay prone before his God. Tears poured out and cleansed him. His grief at his betrayal of Jesus purged the last vestiges of self-pity and anger.

Finally, as the day faded away, he rose, picked up the notebook, and put it back into the duffel bag. He knew without a doubt that there was something more in those pages that he must read. But not tonight. Tomorrow.

Tonight, his heart and soul and mind had been split open, creating wider spaces than he had ever thought possible. And those spaces were filling with a new love.

50

The next morning, before beginning the day's walk, he again opened the notebook. This time, he did not desire to read Annie's thoughts or hear her voice. Instead, he knew, with an inexplicable assurance, that God meant to show him yet one more thing in Annie's last letter. He did not question the thought or think it strange; he simply knew there was one more message.

> *I have had it all. The most wonderful man in the world accepted me and loved me unconditionally, just as Jesus accepted me.*
>
> *I am so sorry for the pain you will go through now, but just remember how very happy I will be. I will look for you every day and will meet you at the gates when you come home, too.*

Yes, Annie had been waiting for him at the gates of Heaven. He had almost entered paradise with his beloved. Was that why he had been denied entry—because he had loved Annie more than Jesus? His heart burned with shame as he now recalled how, these last few months, he had been angry because he was not permitted to be in Heaven with Annie, and not once had he thought about being in Heaven with Jesus.

> *You have my blessing to remarry. You need a good wife, dearest. Someday, you will be ready, and a special lady will be very fortunate to share life with you.*

Surely this was not the message God had for him. He thought immediately of Audrey. No, he was certain this was not the message he was meant to hear this morning.

> *I think I can hear angels singing. I really think they are coming for me. Don't forget to release this last butterfly when it hatches.*
> *Oh, Johnny, one last thing, Christine is going to need some ...*

There! The line faded away in squiggles; Annie must have lost consciousness right at that point. These were the last words she had written. Now it was as if Jesus Himself—or, Johnny thought with a smile, one of His angels—pointed with a heavenly finger and said, *There! That's it!*

Christine. Annie knew she was dying, and she somehow knew that her little daughter Christine was going to need something from Johnny. What? When?

Christine was being raised by Annie's sister. Annie had given birth to the little girl before she had met Johnny; and, as a young, unwed mother, she had been forced to give her baby to her sister. Johnny knew the story, and he knew the sadness it caused his wife.

The words brought back his last conversation with Annie. He remembered every word, and he could see the freckles on her face and hear the timbre of her voice. It had really happened. He no longer doubted it. He *had* been with Annie at the gates of Heaven.

And now he finally remembered her last words.

As he left the earth after his accident, Annie had met him. She had welcomed him joyously, had taken his hand, and had said, "Come with me. We're going home." They had walked, hand in hand, toward paradise.

Then Annie had suddenly stopped, as though listening to something or someone.

"What?" Johnny had said.

She had looked at him with a clear, strong look in those lovely dark blue eyes, a look that held no sorrow or pain, and she had said, "Not yet."

"What do you mean?"

"Not yet, Johnny. It's not yet time for you to be here. I've just heard: You will need to go back."

"No! I'm here with you now. We're together, and I don't want to lose you again. I don't want to go back! I won't go back!"

"Yes, dear, you will go back. Christine is going to need you."

He could not bear to lose her again.

"No! I cannot leave you."

"You must." Her voice was firm. "Don't despair, Johnny. Your journey will soon bring you here, too. I was just a little ahead of you on the road, coming home first. But once you are here, time will mean nothing. There is still work for you to do on earth before you come home.

"And remember this, dear Johnny: You are never alone."

With that, Annie had vanished. He had felt himself falling away from the light, and darkness had swept in as he screamed against the grip of pain and sorrow that took hold of his body.

***

So that was the answer: Christine would need him. His journey was not yet done, and he would be needed here on earth. That was why he had been sent back.

Johnny remembered the look on Annie's face. There was no sorrow or anger at parting again. She had been serene and confident as she told him his journey must continue.

Annie had also told him he would never be alone. He recalled Jesus' words, spoken thousands of years before to all who would ever follow Him: *I am with you always.*

He had not been alone, from the farm to the edge of the ocean, over the mountains and through the cities and the desert, in the depths of pain and darkness, and even in his blindness—he had never been alone.

Well, then, apparently he still had a journey ahead of him—but he would not walk alone and so he could walk without fear.

He slung the duffel onto his back and picked up his walking sticks. He had work to do.

51

He didn't know how it had happened, but somehow he had managed to reconnect with the Natchez Trace Parkway just as it ended on the outskirts of Nashville. In less than a mile, he again left the Trace for Highway 100 and almost immediately spied a small white house with a sign that proclaimed it to be a café. Apparently the food was good there; the parking lot was full, even though it was early for the supper hour. Johnny had had no lunch, and he was ravenous.

Seated at a small table covered with a red-checkered cloth, he looked at the Loveless Café's menu. Fried chicken. Oh, to be sitting down to one of Mandy's fried chicken meals! Perhaps he should try the Southern-fried catfish. No, he was so close to home, and his taste buds wanted to taste home, even though he knew the chicken would not taste like his mom's.

Soon the waitress put a heaping plate of food in front of him.

"There you are, sir. Enjoy your meal."

Johnny looked up at her.

"Did I order these biscuits?"

"We serve them with every meal," she explained. "They're Annie's famous biscuits."

"Annie's?"

"Yes, she and her husband were the original owners. Annie Loveless. She was famous for her biscuits, and we still serve her original recipe."

Johnny could only shake his head at the irony as he dug into the delicious meal that left him fully satisfied. While he ate, he studied a gallery of famous faces; the walls were covered with signed photographs of country music stars.

"How far am I from the Grand Ole Opry?" he asked the cashier as she took his money.

"Not far. It's only about twenty-five miles. Although with the city traffic, it might take an hour to get in there. Are you goin' to stay in Nashville for a show?"

"No. I won't have the time. It will take me most of the day just to get downtown. I'm walking."

She looked up from the cash drawer.

"What? You're walkin'? All the way to downtown?"

Johnny smiled at her.

"Yes. All the way to downtown."

"Say," she began, looking at him more closely. "Are you goin' to be performin' there? You a singer?"

Johnny laughed.

"No. Just passing through. But I did want to see the Ryman Auditorium before I left town."

She was still studying his face.

"You wouldn't put me on, would you? You *look* like some big star … with that beard and those blue eyes and those clothes …"

Johnny was astonished at the ridiculous suggestion. The barber who had cut his hair when he left home had said he looked like Paul Newman. That had not meant too much to Johnny, but apparently the barber thought it was big deal. And what did this woman now see in his Amish pants and shirt that caused her to think he was a celebrity? He answered soberly.

"No, ma'am. I would not put you on. I truly am just an ordinary person, passing through. See?" he pointed to the duffel bag and walking sticks he had left in a corner by the coat rack. "That's my gear."

"Well," she began doubtfully, as though not quite sure she could believe him, "if you're walkin', you'll never get there tonight. You'd better just walk on over to our motel and take a room. Go downtown tomorrow."

"That's a good idea. Thank you," said Johnny, and he made his escape from the scrutinizing and suspicious eyes of the cashier.

He settled into the small motel room. With no tent to set up, no supper to cook, and all the extra baggage he had been carrying left behind at the mountain church, he had little to do to make camp for the night. He unfolded his orange and yellow blanket and spread it on the bed.

Then he lay back, with his arms behind his head, looking at the ceiling. His thoughts were sorting through tomorrow's chores. Find the bus station. Buy a ticket to Columbus. Pack up Wayne's gear and send it back to Maureen. Visit the Ryman Auditorium. Should he buy a ticket and see a show? Here he was, in Music City. Could he pass up the opportunity to see live performances of stars he had listened to for years? But that would mean staying one more night before he could board the bus for home.

Call Big Bill.

The thought came out of nowhere and was so unexpected that Johnny sat up.

"What?" he said aloud.

Call Big Bill. He can do things you cannot. He can find Doug.

Of course. If anyone had the resources and the contacts necessary to find Doug, it was Bill McCollum. He hobnobbed with powerful people in Washington. Politicians and big businessmen came to him for advice. He ran an international business. And he had once told Johnny that his private jet would be available to take

Johnny anywhere in the world. Of course. Bill might be able to help Maureen and Dougie.

Johnny was on his feet, going to the desk where he had laid his wallet. As he pulled out the green card with Bill's number on it, a small white card fell on the desktop. The name on the second card caught Johnny's eye: *Samuel Cohraine, Attorney At Law.*

The name alone sent a jolt through Johnny. Surely Audrey knew by now that he was no longer in the hospital in Corpus Christi. After she and Naomi had both gone home, she had called Maureen several times to check on Johnny's progress. Maureen had slyly told him about each call; but then, when he had no memory of the time he had spent with the Cohraines, the calls were only puzzling to him. Now he wondered if Audrey was still in contact with Naomi. Had they continued their friendship? Where was she now? What was she doing this summer? Did she ever think about him and wonder where he was or what *he* was doing?

He took a deep breath, shook his head, and laid the card face down on the desk. Thinking about Audrey was useless. He remembered the powerful attraction of her presence when they first met, but there was a long list of reasons why he should probably forget about the day they had spent together. He remembered stopping his bike to toss away all the contact information she had given him. But he could not so easily discard the memory of the sparkle in her eyes when she talked of her dreams of changing the world for impoverished children. Whenever he tried to sort out the thoughts and feelings triggered by Audrey's name, he found himself going in endless circles.

He knew of only one person who might be able to help him understand those thoughts and feelings—Naomi. His sister knew him well, she had loved Annie dearly, and she was one of the most sensible young women he knew. He would not think about Audrey until he was home. Then he *might* talk with Naomi about the situation. She could help him sort it out.

He picked up the phone, followed the instructions to make an outside call, and dialed the number on Bill McCollum's card.

The phone rang only once, and Bill's hearty "Hello!" boomed over the line.

"Mr. McCollum ... Bill ... this is Johnny Miller." He had not thought what he would say.

"Johnny! How are you, my friend? Where are you? I heard you are walking home."

"Yes. Well, that's what I set out to do. But I am so close to home—I'm in Nashville, Tennessee—and I'm so ready to be back on the farm that I'm buying a bus ticket tomorrow."

"That's great news. Your folks will be so happy to see you. How are you doing?"

"I am doing fine, Bill, just fine. Really. I've had some incredible experiences along the way, and I've had a miracle of healing, and I've learned so much about the cross and what it brings to our lives. I can't begin to tell you everything. But I'm calling now to ask a favor."

"Sure, Johnny. Ask away."

"Remember I gave you a twenty-dollar bill, thinking you were some poor destitute soul?"

Bill's laugh resounded through the earpiece.

"Yes I do remember that. My wife got a good laugh out of that, too. And I told you your twenty dollars would buy a ticket on my jet, anytime, anywhere."

"I want to redeem that ticket, Bill. For someone else. You remember my nurse, Maureen? She has a son who has been missing in action in Viet Nam for two years. Her husband tried everything he could to find him, but with no success. Every government agency told him there was nothing more they could do. But I thought if anyone could find their son, you might be able to do it. What do you think? Is it possible?"

Bill was silent as he considered Johnny's question.

"That's hell on earth over there, Johnny. So many people have simply disappeared without a trace. We've got at least two thousand men who are unaccounted for. I'm not sure where I would start."

"But if anyone can do it, you can."

He could tell Bill was smiling.

"I guess you're right about that. If any private citizen can accomplish such a miracle, then I admit, I stand a better chance than most. Tell you what. Give me Maureen's number, and I'll give her a call. We'll talk, and I'll see what I can do."

"Thank you, thank you! You will be an answer to her prayers."

"I can't guarantee anything except that I'll talk to her and then look into possibilities."

"That's all I ask, Bill."

"What's her number?"

Johnny realized he did not have any way of contacting Maureen.

"I don't know. I haven't been in contact with her. But I suppose you could call the hospital."

"Sure. That's a good idea. I probably can't talk with her until next week. I'm going to be in Washington for a few days for some hearings, and those days will be pretty crazy. When I get home, I'll give her a call."

"That's good, Bill. If Doug's still alive and God intends for you to find him, then God will keep him safe for another week, I'm certain of it. Thank you again."

"Glad to be of help, Johnny. I'm coming up there one day to see you and your father."

"Okay. We'll look forward to it, Bill."

He hung up, satisfied with the certainty that an important link in the chain had just been snapped into place.

52

He woke before dawn, far too excited about the day to go back to sleep. The CLOSED sign still hung on the door at the Loveless Café, although a few lights were on and he could see cooks and waitresses moving around inside.

Walking briskly, he faced the eastern sky and the road home.

The brisk pace did not let up throughout the morning. Could he be home by this time tomorrow? Was it possible? At times he found himself almost running along the highway.

This city, like every other city he had walked through, had its own character and flavor. Ordinarily, he would have wanted to explore, but today his one goal was to find the bus station and buy a ticket to Columbus, Ohio. From there, he would take the bus to Stevenson. He was hoping, though, that the famous Ryman Auditorium, housing the Grand Ole Opry, would be in the vicinity of the bus station. He would not stay for a show, but he wanted a peek at the renowned building.

He asked for directions and was delighted to find that the station was only a few blocks from the Ryman Auditorium. He would buy his ticket first, and then, if he had time, he would permit himself the luxury of sightseeing.

When he checked the bus schedules, he was dismayed to find that the quickest route home actually took him in a direction away from home. He would ride first to Indianapolis, Indiana, then change buses and go to Columbus. The bus to Indianapolis would not leave until 7 o'clock that evening. It was noon. He had time to explore the city.

He bought his ticket and walked back to Broadway. Just off Broadway, on 5th Street, he found the hallowed center of country music fame. He stood for a long time on the sidewalk, in awe of the building that had been constructed almost a century before as a tabernacle and then became the birthplace of country music. The arched windows and elaborate trim had been carefully preserved in this historic building. He had spent countless Saturday evenings hidden away in his tree house, listening to live shows from the Grand Ole Opry. Now he was actually standing in front of the building. He kept his eyes open, scanning the area around him, wondering if he might see some of his favorite stars.

There was another building he had heard of and wanted to see. This building, almost as old as the Ryman Auditorium, transported him even further from home. He walked west a few blocks and felt as though he had walked into another millennium. At the center of Nashville's Centennial Park stood and exact replica of the Parthenon, ancient Greece's temple to the goddess Athena. Although the classical architecture seemed an oddity surrounded by high-rise buildings and modern highways, the forty-six huge columns and intricate stone carvings of men and horses in battle were awe-inspiring.

From the Parthenon, Johnny made a wide circle to come back to the twentieth century and the United States Post Office, where a helpful clerk listened to his request and found two large boxes. Into one, Johnny packed his two walking sticks, the yellow and orange blanket, and Annie's notebook. As the clerk sealed that box, Johnny felt as though he were packing up and sending off parts of his own body. The U.S. Postal Service would deliver those things to his home. Into the second box went Wayne's equipment: the tent, the knife, the canteen, and the duffel bag. These belonged to Maureen, and he would return them.

Along with Wayne's gear went a letter Johnny had written the night before at the Loveless Motel.

Dear Maureen,

This letter is long overdue, I confess. But until now, I had no idea what to write or say to you.

I hope you will accept my apology for the abrupt and rude way in which I left your home. I am so sorry about the argument we had the night before and for leaving without even a thank-you for all your kindness. I was angry. I knew you were angry. And I just wanted to run away from it all.

However, now there are two things I must tell you and I hope that you will accept the first and rejoice at the second.

First, I finally understand why I reacted so strongly to your request to help you find your son. As you know, I grew up in a church and a culture that preaches and practices nonresistance. We believe that Christians cannot participate in the military or go to war. This is one of our strongest beliefs.

But you were right—I had never been forced to make life-or-death choices in the face of threats or possible harm at the hands of others. I knew all the right words to say, but I have never had to discern exactly what it means to live out the words. You challenged that, and I reacted defensively because I had no answer for you.

I will tell you that I have been tested in a very small way—and I failed. At a minor aggravation, I struck a man and caused blood to flow. And while I feel remorse that I can never ask this man's forgiveness, I did learn something from this. I know now that if I truly want to follow Jesus, I must deny that most basic and automatic reaction to defend and strike back. And I must do so because Jesus says that this is His way: Love your enemies and pray for them. Do good to those who hate you. The results of our obedience to our Lord are in His hands. If we suffer and even if we die, we suffer and die for His way.

I have learned—painfully—that this way is not my natural tendency, but I also have determined to follow Jesus, and so I believe this is the path I must take in all of life. I know that there are other Christians who believe just the opposite—that it is their Christian duty to defend our liberty. That decision is between each person and Christ. But I know that for me to pattern my life after Jesus' life, this is the way I must strive to live: loving my enemies, praying for them, and not striking back. I ask God's help in doing that.

The second thing I'm writing to tell you is that God is answering your prayers for help in finding your son. I cannot do anything about the situation myself, but I know a person who can possibly help you. Do you remember Bill McCollum, one of my visitors at the hospital? He will be calling you within the next week. If Doug is still alive, I believe Mr. McCollum is the one who can find him and bring him home.

I hope that the next time we talk, your son will have returned home and you will have forgiven me for my anger.

Johnny.

He had bent over the paper for the better part of two hours, considering every word. Now, as he watched the clerk seal up the box addressed to Maureen, he felt as though a healing balm had been spread over the raw wound that had festered ever since he had walked away from Odem.

53

Exuberance set in. He was free of everything that had burdened him, both material things and guilt and grief. He would soon board a bus, and the miles between Nashville and home would melt away quickly. The bus would leave at seven that evening. He had nothing to do now but enjoy the afternoon. Finally, he could simply wander the streets and enjoy Music City.

Back to Broadway he went, scanning displays in windows and listening to bits of music floating out to the sidewalk from cafes and bars. This was indeed Music City, in Dixieland, USA. The shops sold guitars and records, cowboy boots and hats, sequined jackets and fringed skirts.

In front of one store, a life-sized, moving model of Elvis Presley, outfitted in a glittering jacket and tight leather pants, gyrated to the music of "All Shook Up." Fascinated by mechanics that could mimic the movements of a living person, Johnny watched as the artificial Elvis went on to rock and sing his famous "Jailhouse Rock."

The manikin standing in a corner of the shop window behind Elvis never entered Johnny's consciousness, even though, unknown to him, it was already molding his future. The stylish model wore the latest style sweeping through Hollywood—Johnny BarnDoor denim pants.

He finally moved away from Elvis, thinking how happy he would be to get home. He had seen everything from a hippie commune in California to the glitz and glamor of Nashville, and his father had been right: Nothing out here in the world would satisfy him more than the farm in their own valley. He felt free and settled. Before he knew it, he was humming along with tunes drifting into the streets; he was grinning; he was going home.

When he heard a rapping on a window, he turned and peered into a small café. The first thing he noticed was a head of white curls, then Millie's round face and George's lanky frame. They were seated at a small table in the corner by the window, and Millie was motioning vigorously for him to come in and join them.

His smile broadened, and he pulled open the door and made his way to their corner.

"We almost didn't recognize you without that big lumpy bag you've been lugging around," George said, pumping Johnny's hand.

"And you were smiling like the cat that swallowed a canary," put in Millie. "You'll have to tell us what's up. I'll bet you just talked to your girl at home. Don't you think that might be what put that huge grin on his face, George?"

"Now, Millie, let him catch his breath before you start the cross-examination."

"Oh, George, you know you're just as curious as I am. So, John Miller, what have you been up to since we last saw you?" Millie was patting his arm, like a doting grandmother, and Johnny noticed that her small fingernails were painted a demure pink.

"Yes, ma'am, you are right. I have had a good day. That lumpy bag was attached to me for too long, and I just sent it back to its owner. I also sent a letter that I hope will mend a relationship and bring great joy, too."

"Sounds like a story there, John," said George solemnly.

"It is a rather complicated story. But I think what I am really smiling about is how God has been with me all along my journey, and He has worked things out that I never dreamed could happen. He's brought people into my life just when I needed them and for all kinds of purposes."

"Guardian angels," interjected Millie emphatically.

"You know, son, we have no plans for the rest of the day, other than to enjoy ourselves and our time in Nashville," said George. "And we would like nothing more than to sit here and listen to your long story. You really have not told us much about yourself. I'm afraid we've always done most of the talking."

"And we'd really like to hear all about you ... if you have the time and want to talk." Millie finished George's thought.

Johnny realized that he did have hours to sit with these two. He had nothing else to do the rest of the afternoon and evening. And these two were a delight. Where should he start?

"I don't have a girl back home. But I did have a wife ..."

54

George and Millie's company was so comfortable that Johnny forgot he had just met them briefly a few days before. He began his long story, and talked not only of events and places but of joys and sorrows, despair and triumph. He felt as though he were sitting and talking with family.

They must have felt a similar connection to Johnny, because Millie wept at the desolation of Johnny's loss when Annie died. Tears were still sliding down her cheeks as Johnny told of saying goodbye to his family and making his way across the country to begin his coast-to-coast bike ride. George listened to everything intently, and twice he reached out and silently rested an encouraging hand on Johnny's shoulder. When Johnny explained the water system he had set up at the commune, George's only words were, "Very smart." They laughed at the goat-milking story and shook their heads in amazement as Johnny introduced them to Wandering Willie, who had no home except the spot he slept on each night.

Millie beamed like the noonday sun shining on Johnny as he told of his experience at Big Bill's cross. And the twinkle in her eye as he recounted the story of Samuel and Audrey Cohraine did not go unnoticed; Johnny knew she was curious about Audrey, but he did not give her an opportunity to ask questions about that day at the ranch or Samuel's generous job offer.

George actually cheered when Johnny pulled River Man up the bank of the river. They listened, fascinated, to the strange conversation by the fire that night and wanted to know more about the carvings on the mesquite walking stick. By the time Johnny was leaving the Mountaintop Holiness Church, renewed and resolved, Millie was weeping again.

This was the first time since all the pages of his memory had been restored that Johnny had spoken of these experiences. The telling of his adventures seemed to heal some tears in his heart. It felt as though he were bringing together all of his stories to now end the book on his wanderings. Even the account of his agony in the hospital and his terrible plunge into the pit of drugs and alcohol seemed to cleanse his soul of some lingering toxin.

He did not tell them, though, about the revelations prompted by Annie's notebook or about the conversation at the gates of Heaven. Those stories were not yet ready to be spoken aloud. Not even to Mandy or John or Naomi.

***

"And so, I'm ready to be home. I have a ticket and will be leaving tonight, and I hope to be home in time for supper tomorrow." Johnny could hardly believe his own words. It seemed impossible that he was so close to finally walking up the road from Milford and turning into his own lane.

"What will you do?"

"I'll go back to farming. I'm a farmer; I discovered that on this journey. It's what I want to do and the life I want to live. That is … if Dad is still willing to sell me the farm. And if not," Johnny smiled, "then there will be something else. I guess that's what I've been smiling about all afternoon. Looking back, I can see how God was working even while I was doubtful and rebellious. And I'm learning that God's plans are much bigger and grander than anything I dream of. So I'm confident that there will be something for me, something that's right for me—even if it's not farming."

"And as soon as you're home, you'll call Audrey."

George and Johnny both looked at Millie in astonishment. Her round face was glowing with excitement. She was a woman on a mission. Johnny felt his own face beginning to flush.

"Mill! Let the boy—"

"George, John needs a wife. A handsome, healthy young man like this needs someone beside him to rebuild his life. He can't live out his life alone. I can't bear the thought of it, George."

The flush on Johnny's face was deepening to a very dark red. The other two did not notice, though, because George was gazing tenderly at his feisty wife. His eyes grew watery and his voice caught as he said, "I can't bear the thought of living without *you*."

Millie stretched her short frame to plant a kiss on her husband's wrinkled cheek. With her plump pink hand holding George's long, bony fingers, she turned back to Johnny.

"We have this argument about who's going first. Neither one of us wants to be here last, living on without the other, but neither one of us wants to go first and leave the other one to grieve alone." She grinned mischievously. "It is a dilemma we have not yet solved, so I guess neither one of us can go until we have it settled."

Then she released George's fingers and clasped Johnny's large hand with both of her tiny ones as she leaned over the table toward him and looked him in the eye. "Now listen, John. There is nothing better in this world than living in a happy marriage. Your Annie would want that; I know I can speak for her. You call Audrey, you hear me?"

Johnny finally found words to begin.

"Millie, that would never work. Look at me! I'm Amish. I'm going to stay Amish. Audrey is English."

"Fiddlesticks! What's all that got to do with anything? Do you love her?"

"Ah ... I ... I'm ..." This frank conversation about love and marriage had ambushed Johnny. Millie's persistence forced him to think about the question of Audrey and their friendship. How could he explain the way he had felt in her presence that day in California and the guilt that had come as a result of those feelings?

"John," Millie's voice had quieted a bit but it was firm. "You said she was at your bedside when you came out of the coma and she stayed for weeks, even though you didn't recognize her. Doesn't that tell you something? Maybe you don't know how you feel about her—or is it that you just don't want to admit how you feel?—but I'm pretty sure that I know how she feels about you, and I've never even met the girl."

Johnny cast a pleading look toward George, but Millie's husband just grinned and shrugged his shoulders as if to say, *I can't stop her.*

"And you have said yourself that God has placed people in your life for a reason. Think about all the 'coincidences' that led to you two meeting. Could it be that God brought Audrey into your life for a very special reason?"

Johnny shook his head.

"I don't know, Millie. I don't know. That's the dilemma *I* haven't figured out. We Amish live very differently than the rest of the world. Only a few English people have ever joined the Amish; and of those few, most of them eventually decide that our way of life is not for them. An English person would have to believe—be convinced without a doubt—that the way we live is the best way to live. It's very difficult to live with rules and dictates of a church if you don't believe in their ultimate purpose."

"If we visited you and your family, would we be welcome?" asked George.

"Oh, of course! You would be very welcome. We would even take you to church with us," grinned Johnny. "But for an English woman to marry an Amish man ..." he shook his head.

"I would say that's up to her, don't you think?" Millie patted his cheek. "You might be amazed at what a woman in love is willing to do, dearie."

Finally regaining his balance, Johnny smiled at her. "Yes, that would be up to her. But it's all very tangled, and all I can tell you is that right now I cannot see how such a relationship could possibly work ... I just don't know what to do."

That seemed to satisfy Millie. She dug in her big, flowered purse and pulled out a pencil and small scrap of paper.

"Well, I for one will need to know what is happening in the next chapters of your story. Here, write down your address. We'll keep in touch."

George raised his eyebrows at Johnny. "And she *will* be checking up on you!"

Johnny began writing, then paused and looked up at the two and said quietly,

"I will tell you that I am looking at my dream, as I look at you two. I wanted to grow old with a woman I dearly loved. I didn't lose only my wife. I lost my dream, too."

Millie's eyes filled with tears yet again. She reached over to squeeze his hand one more time.

"It might be, dear, that your dream is still out there in front of you."

55

The sleek, leaping dog on the side of the bus seemed like an old friend. Johnny felt as though he were closing a circle as he took the few steps up into the bus. His journey had begun in the same way, when he had boarded an identical bus and, for the first time in his life, had left Milford.

In the few hours of remaining daylight, Johnny watched the changing landscape between Nashville and Indianapolis. The mountains shrunk to hills; the hills flattened out to large farms. His imagination could see the fields of home. He had grown up on the Miller farm and had roamed every square foot of its fields and woods. The tree house he had built as a ten-year-old still stood sentinel on the hill behind the two houses; he had spent hours and hours up in that oak tree. Were the letters he had written to God still there? Was his proposal to Annie still standing on the shelf?

Although he knew that taking a bus from Nashville would shorten his journey by at least three weeks, his anticipation now chafed at the slow movement of time. The miles crept by, and he thought again how odd it was that he must go in a different direction than home in order to get home. And in Indianapolis, he would have a long wait for the next bus going to Columbus.

But descending the bus steps at the Indianapolis station gave him a small preview of homecoming. This place was familiar; he had been here before, on his trip westward. This was not home, but it was familiar and gave him a sense of comfort and welcome.

Even more comforting was recognizing people of his own faith. In the bus station, he met a group of eight Amish who were traveling from their homes in Pennsylvania to a wedding in another Amish settlement in Montana. They, too, had a long wait for their bus; and although it was midnight, conversing with likeminded people in his own Pennsylvania Dutch dialect kept Johnny awake and alert and brought him even closer to home. They had never met before, but the group opened bags and baskets and shared sandwiches and cookies and coffee with him. He relished the sense of community and belonging.

At three in the morning, the Pennsylvania Amish boarded their bus to go west. By then, Johnny was in need of a nap, but he was too afraid to fall asleep—he might miss his four o'clock bus. So he walked outside briefly for a few minutes of fresh air and was wide awake when he boarded for Columbus.

Welcome to Ohio, the lighted sign arching over the highway announced. In the darkness, Johnny could not stop grinning. He felt as though the entire state had thrown open its arms to welcome him back home.

The wait in Columbus for the bus to Stevenson was only an hour, and Johnny fought an almost uncontrollable urge to bolt from the station and run home. He knew he was still eighty miles away, yet he thought he could smell his own hay mow and hear the dried cornstalks rustling in the early morning wind. But wait he must.

In the faint light of dawn, three crosses on a small slope along the highway were outlined against the morning sky, causing him to reflect on the crosses that had appeared at crucial times in his journey, as though God were coming directly to him at just the right moments. At the foot of Big Bill's cross he had found assurance of his hope; in the chapel hospital, he saw that the cross brought healing; and River Man's carving of the cross into his mesquite stick would remind him for the rest of his days that the cross made new life possible for anyone. The cross, Johnny reflected, brought God's presence and power into every life.

He wondered what his new life would look like, once he was back on the farm. That is, *if* he was back on the farm. Dad had wanted him to take over the entire operation, and Johnny had been preparing to do that when Annie died. But then he had left and had made no promise to return. He had even talked of leaving the Amish church. Had Dad made other arrangements, thinking his son was gone forever? Might Dad have agreed to sell the farm or lease it to someone else? Had one of his brothers-in-law decided that they wanted the farm?

And then came the accusing voice, *Do you deserve the farm?*

He had brought great pain to his family when he left under such a cloud of doubt and rebellion. Now he wished he would have written to prepare them for his arrival. He had debated it, while writing his letter to Maureen. But he had decided to surprise them; he had imagined a joyous welcoming celebration.

But *would* they celebrate? Would they be happy to see him and have him back on the farm? How would they feel about his desire to return? Surely they had fallen into new routines that did not include him. He had turned his back on them and their way of life—could he ever belong to that life again? Johnny knew he had changed; he would never be the same person who had left. Yet he desired his family to be unchanged, to be the warm, loving, accepting family he had always known. But might they have changed, too? How would he now fit into the picture?

He did not deserve to be welcomed back, unconditionally accepted and brought back into the family. He had fallen short in so many ways. Was he the prodigal son who was so often the subject of his dad's sermons?

Half asleep, he saw himself sitting in church. Dad was preaching from Luke 15, the story of the father with two sons. Things are going well, the family is successful and wealthy—until the day the younger son demands his share of the inheritance. Johnny could hear his father's strong voice read the story from his German Bible.

"Ein Mensch hatte zwei Söhne."

A man had two sons.

"Und der jüngste unter ihnen sprach zu dem Vater: Gib mir, Vater, das Teil der Güter, das mir gehört. Und er teilte ihnen das Gut."

The younger one said to his father, "Father, give me my share of the estate." So he divided his property between them.

The younger son gathered all his wealth and left for another country, where he squandered everything by wild living. With his fortune gone, he was forced to work as a servant, feeding a man's pigs. Starving, penniless, and desperate, he even considered eating the pigs' food, until finally one day he determined to go home and beg his father to take him back, not as a son, but as a servant. He would not deserve to take a son's place, but even his father's hired help were better off than he was. So he trudged home.

Johnny's dreamlike state saw his father pause in his reading, raise his eyes to the people of his church, and then continue without looking at his Bible:

"Und er machte sich auf und kam zu seinem Vater. Da er aber noch ferne von dannen war, sah ihn sein Vater, und es jammerte ihn, life and fiel ihm um seinen Hals und küsste ihn."

So he got up and went to his father. But while he was still a long way off, his father saw him and was filled with compassion for him; he ran to his son, threw his arms around him and kissed him.

The son tried to deliver his practiced speech, asking only for a job as a hired hand. But the father ordered the servants to dress his son in the best robe and sandals, put a ring on his finger, and kill the calf they had been fattening. There would be a feast and much celebration!

"Den dieser mein Sohn war tot und ist wieder lebendig geworden; er war verloren und ist gefunden worden. Und sie fingen an fröhlich zu sein."

"For this son of mine was dead and is alive again; he was lost and is found." So they began to celebrate.

Johnny's mind wandered back and forth in that land between sleep and consciousness, hearing his father's voice read the well-known story and imagining his own homecoming. He was so ready to be home, but were they ready to have him?

Would they celebrate?

He did not deserve it.

56

His uneasy sleep brought dreams with scenes from childhood. In his dreams, he pushed a shiny new red bicycle up the sidewalk of Stevenson, his chest bursting with the satisfaction of accomplishment. He was only eleven, but he had built a business with his chickens and eggs and had paid for this beauty himself. The Greyhound bus roared up the street past him, exhaust fumes dropping like dew onto his hat and clothes, and he heard the air brakes as the bus pulled up in front of the county courthouse.

Johnny tensed slightly, as his body reacted to the braking and deceleration, and he awoke to find that he was not on the sidewalk but on the bus. And the bus had arrived in Stevenson—he was almost home.

Nervous energy poured through him. As he stepped down to the sidewalk, his first sight was the stately stone courthouse, solid and unchangeable in the morning sun. He recalled the buzz of activity as television reporters harassed the Amish assembled there to hear the verdict handed down to twelve Amish youths after a tragic death. Across the street stood Kauffman's Five and Dime where the red bike had been ordered so many years ago. Almost six months ago, on the day he pedaled away from the farm, he had stopped at the same store to purchase a razor to remove Amish from his visage; and across the street, the red and white pole still rotated in front of the barber shop where he had received his first English haircut.

He savored the comfort of the familiar views on Main Street. Nothing had changed, he reflected. At least, not in the scenes surrounding him. He turned toward the courthouse and descended the worn sandstone steps to the basement level. In the restroom, standing in front of the mirror, he stared at the reflection. He had shaved off his beard here and put on English clothes before beginning his journey, burdened with depression and confusion; when he had boarded the bus to leave town, his outward appearance had carried not one hint that he was Amish. Now, the same mirror showed him an Amish man with a bearded face resting in calm serenity. Main Street was unchanged, but this Johnny Miller was a different man than the one who had tried to rinse Amish down the drain.

He washed up now and spoke to the new man in the mirror.

"It's time to go home."

In more than two decades of life, Johnny had made the trip from Stevenson to home by many different modes—buggy, car, truck, bus, and bicycle. But this would be the first time he walked the fourteen miles from the county seat to home. Now so close to his destination, he admitted a reluctance to end his journey. He was ready to be home; he was eager to be home. But he needed the solitude and time afforded by walking these last miles.

He debated the merits and difficulties of two different routes to the Miller farm. He could stay on the busy state highway, the shortest route, and risk being seen by someone from Milford either coming into town on business or going home. He did not want word of his arrival to reach his family before he did. However, even though he had less chance of being seen on the back country roads, most of the homes he would pass would be either Amish or farmers who knew his family; any person who happened to see him on those roads would very likely recognize him. Johnny was well aware of the speed and efficiency of the community grapevine, so he took his chances on the main highway.

He had gone only three or four miles when his stomach reminded him that he should have eaten before he left Stevenson. He had had no breakfast or lunch, and he thought how foolish he'd been in his haste to begin the walk home—he had not even stopped for a drink of water. He recalled an old apple tree that had stood at the edge of a field for as long as he could remember. When it came into sight, he was happy to see red apples hanging from the branches and littering the ground.

Although he could not remember ever seeing anyone picking these apples, he still felt as though taking the fruit off the tree would be stealing, but scavenging the ground for one with only a few bruises would be acceptable.

Out of sight of those passing on the highway, he relaxed and rested while eating the apple. A Monarch butterfly winged its way above his head, and Johnny thought wryly that it was moving along as though it was on a mission. Perhaps it was. Perhaps it was one of the special fourth-generation butterflies, now leaving on the long flight to Mexico.

And now here I am, Annie, returning home from my pilgrimage, just as that butterfly embarks on his own long journey to fulfill his special purpose in the cycle of Monarch life.

As he continued walking, cars or trucks sometimes passed and acknowledged Johnny with a raised hand. Each time, he thought perhaps he had been recognized. But as he returned the greeting, he saw that he did not know any of the drivers or passengers; the friendly salute between two people who met was simply a common thing in this community. Yes, it *was* good to be home.

By early afternoon he was on the streets of Milford, passing stores and businesses he had known all his life. He had considered leaving the highway and cutting through fields to bypass the little town—suppose Dad was at the bank or the feed mill? But the familiar scenes evoked the memory of the morning he had left home, pedaling through the darkened and deserted streets, long before most of the town was awake; and he knew that walking through the town, greeting all the well-known sights and sounds, was a necessary thing to close the circle of his journey.

At the Milford School, some of the younger children were on the playground. Bats cracked against softballs, the chains of the swings squeaked, and the teeter-totter boards groaned just as they had when he was a boy on that same playground. Everywhere children shouted and squealed and chattered. Nostalgia took Johnny back to the days when he played ball on that diamond or ran races on the grass. He had been desolate when his time at the school was over and his friends went on to high school but he stayed home and began to work on the farm.

Now, looking back at that time, Johnny had no regrets. His life was good—it would be good—and he no longer felt as though he had been cheated of *something* because he was not permitted to go to high school.

He remained alert and watchful as he walked through Milford. Most people there knew him, and he did not want to attract attention. Then, as he was leaving the small town, he felt a greater tension rise in his chest. He knew what the next landmark would be; and though he cherished every memory he had of his lovely Annie, the sight of the little Amish school where she had taught and they had first met—on just such a September day as this— would surely bring a pang of loneliness and sorrow.

***

Simon's subconscious detected what he knew milliseconds before he knew what he knew.

The new year of school had just started, and the boy's mind

could not stay indoors with his body. With a window view out over the valley, he sat daydreaming. The new teacher was busy with the first graders, and Simon should have been working on his arithmetic problems. Instead, he was thinking about the tree house and wondering if his uncle would care that he had become something of a squatter there. Whenever he could sneak off from his chores, he'd hide away in the tree house, reading, daydreaming, or listening to the little transistor radio.

He was sure his uncle would have no objection. But if Simon ever got the chance, he would officially ask his uncle if he might claim the deer stand as his own sanctuary.

Far down the road, a lonely figure walked along at a brisk pace. This was nothing unusual in their community. People walked as often as they drove their buggies or rode their bikes. But this figure paused every now and then, looking around in all directions as though he were lost or in serious contemplation. Then he would start off again, with a stride that indicated he was on urgent business. Could it be one of those hoboes Simon had heard about? Or maybe an escaped prisoner, running from the law, and looking for a hay loft where he could hide out, or perhaps …

"It's Uncle Johnny!" yelled Simon, startling everyone in the quiet schoolroom.

Without so much as a glance at the teacher or even a thought of asking permission, the boy jumped up from his desk and raced outside. The whole valley had been waiting for this news. Word had reached them that Uncle Johnny could be arriving any day now, and the valley lived in expectation of their wandering child, neighbor, and friend returning home.

And he, Simon, was the first to see him!

Without so much as a wave or a yell toward the walker, Simon yanked his bicycle from a tangle of handlebars and spokes and pedaled furiously towards his grandparents' home.

57

On his way to the barnyard, John Miller walked slowly across the gravel driveway. He glanced toward the road running eastward to Milford. This had become an unconscious habit as he went about his daily work—looking down that road many times a day. He was certain that someday he would look up and there *he* would be. Johnny would be coming home.

Now, though, what he saw was a young boy on a bicycle, his legs pumping furiously as he came careening down the road toward the farm. The boy caught sight of John and shouted a string of unintelligible and passionate words.

As the figure approached, John saw it was his grandson Simon. Dread crept in. What had gone wrong now? *Is it one more hardship, Lord?*

"Grandpa! Get Grandma! Get Naomi! It's Uncle Johnny! He's coming! He's home!" Simon shouted. He barreled up into the driveway and skidded to a stop in front of his grandfather so quickly that the bike fell and the boy almost lost his balance and went tumbling over with it.

"It's him," he gasped. "It really is! I know his walk."

"Run, Simon! Tell Grandma! She's in the kitchen."

John rushed out to the road. From far off, the father recognized his son.

"It really is you," he whispered. His eyes filled with tears and he broke into a run.

***

Johnny saw the familiar figure come down the driveway and begin to run toward him. His legs, strong and fully healed, quickened their gait and carried him swiftly to meet his father.

They came together on the road that John had watched for months. Johnny felt his father's strong arms around his shoulders and heard the words, "I love you, son. Welcome home."

Johnny could not speak for a moment; then he asked jokingly, "Know where a fella could get a job around here?"

His father pulled back. Tears slid down his face and disappeared into the salt-and-pepper beard. "There is no job here for you, son. But there is a life for you here."

One arm swept wide, taking in the expanse of the fertile valley with fields ready for harvest. The other arm remained around Johnny's shoulder.

"Look around you, son. It's yours; it is all yours."

Johnny's throat was too tight to force out words, and then he saw that it was useless to try to speak because Naomi came flying down the road toward him and into his arms. Just a few seconds behind her was Mandy.

Tears and laughter and the general commotion of everyone talking at once welcomed him home. Simon somehow managed to wiggle his way back to the center of the hubbub, grinning from ear to ear. Naomi was talking in that "mile-a-minute" way he had always teased her about, Mandy kept wiping tears from her cheeks, and John's hand never left his son's shoulder.

"Grandpa, should I go and tell everyone?" asked Simon, eager to be off spreading such an important message.

"Ring the bell!" John commanded. The brass bell that hung on the side of the barn was rung only to tell the entire valley of important news at the Miller farm. Naomi had sobbed as she rang it the day Annie died, and she had prayed as she rang it the day they received the news of Johnny's accident. The clanging called to neighbors and friends, asking for help and support. Today, it would call everyone to celebrate.

"Simmy, you go ring it," said Naomi.

"Really?" Simon was wide-eyed with excitement and new importance. "I can do that?"

"Yes, go ring the bell, Simon. Let everyone know we have good news," said John, and the boy scampered off, assured of his new stature in the family: He was old enough to ring the bell.

Throughout the valley, the bell tolled news. In fields and shops and kitchens and gardens, folks momentarily froze as they recognized the source of the tolling. Everyone knew Johnny Miller was out there somewhere, wandering. Did this bell ring for life or for death?

In less than an hour, everyone who heard the bell knew: Its call announced a celebration of new beginnings at the Miller farm.

In less than two hours, several long tables were set up on the lawn and folks were streaming down the country roads carrying baskets and towel-wrapped dishes. The shared bounty covered the tables; one more table was brought out—and still more neighbors arrived, every group carrying more offerings of comfort food.

Savoring the joy of belonging, Johnny sat on a lawn chair under a tree, enjoying the impromptu feast that was more sumptuous than the most carefully planned banquet. Family and neighbors were everywhere, on blankets and chairs and church benches. The wandering son did not miss the fact that he had been given his father's favorite chair. A dozen conversations went on around him while he ate. He knew he was expected to be engaged in every dialogue; but for the most part, he heard no details, aware of only the harmony of glad celebration and joyful welcome in the ebb and flow of voices.

Surely this was as close to Heaven as he could get in this earthly life.

And with that thought, he understood why his father always wept when he sang the old hymn "Amazing Grace." His father knew what it was to be lost and then found, to be blind and then to see. His father, too, must have been a wanderer who had come home to love and undeserved welcome. He remembered all those times he had heard his father read, with great feeling, *"For this son of mine was dead and is alive again; he was lost and is found." So they began to celebrate.*

Johnny blinked rapidly. From this day forward, he, too, would likely be brought to tears by amazing grace.

Dangling Conversations

Through the haze of happy contemplation, some snippets of conversation did reach the ears of the wanderer. Young Simon was at his elbow, asking something about the tree house and painted bottles. Neighbors wanted to know how hot it was in Texas and had he seen cotton fields down south? His best friend, Paul, came over repeatedly and clapped him on the shoulder without a word.

Trying to catch her son in a quiet moment, Mandy stopped by his chair and asked in a low voice, "Johnny, do you want to move back to your old room?" He was taken aback by the suggestion; he had never even considered that. She gave him no time to answer, however. "And who is Sydney?" she asked. "We've had letters and checks from him. Why is he sending you money?"

Naomi, overhearing her mother's question, reached inside her apron and pulled out an envelope. With an impish grin, she dangled the white rectangle in front of her brother. He caught sight of the word *Malibu* in the return address and felt a thrill run through him. His sister's face was flushed with the excitement of the afternoon.

"This just came today. And I have a stack of them up in my room. We need to talk about this."

For once, the little sister had caught her brother off guard.

"You mean … *now?*"

Johnny's story continues in

WANDER NO MORE

(Now available)

71349208R00155

Made in the USA
Middletown, DE
22 April 2018